Just as I was beginning to seriously wonder where he was, I heard Joe's voice, a low murmur, coming from the living room . . . and then I heard a woman's voice answering him.

I stood frozen, certain I had to be imagining things. But then I heard her again, this time ending whatever she said with a light laugh, and I was frozen no more. My feet carried me double-time into the living room, and what I saw left me dumbfounded.

Joe was standing by the window, stark naked. His head was thrown back, hands out, palms up.

There was something about his pose that was incredibly erotic—he looked like some dark, pagan fertility god, gilded by the moonlight that slanted through the blinds. A living statue paying tribute to the night sky, leanly muscled, nude, and completely unashamed.

Most important, and perhaps most puzzling, he was alone.

By Terri Garey

SILENT NIGHT, HAUNTED NIGHT
YOU'RE THE ONE THAT I HAUNT
A MATCH MADE IN HELL
DEAD GIRLS ARE EASY

TERRI GAREY

SILENT NIGHT, HAUNTED NIGHT

AVON

An Imprint of HarperCollinsPublishers

This is a work of fiction. Names, characters, places, and incidents are products of the author's imagination or are used fictitiously and are not to be construed as real. Any resemblance to actual events, locales, organizations, or persons, living or dead, is entirely coincidental.

AVON BOOKS
An Imprint of HarperCollins*Publishers*
10 East 53rd Street
New York, New York 10022-5299

First Avon Books paperback printing: November 2009

Avon Trademark Reg. U.S. Pat. Off. and in Other Countries, Marca Registrada, Hecho en U.S.A.
HarperCollins® is a registered trademark of HarperCollins Publishers.

Printed in the U.S.A.

10 9 8 7 6 5 4 3 2 1

This one is for Anna and Keith.
May they live happily ever after.

ACKNOWLEDGMENTS

I'd like to thank all those people who helped bring the character of Nicki Styx to life: the wonderful women of Rotrosen (Meg, Annelise, and Christina), my talented editor Erika, Tom Egner for his fabulous covers, Esi and Amanda for being so incredibly easy to work with, and everyone in the marketing department at Avon Books who helped me share Nicki's books with the world.

But most of all, I'd like to thank my readers. There's no greater compliment to a storyteller than being told you've made someone laugh, made someone sigh, or caused someone to leave a light on while they sleep. Your enjoyment of my stories is what makes writing them worthwhile. I hope you enjoy this one.

Ebenezer Scrooge isn't the only person who's ever had to deal with ghosts at Christmas.

You remember the tale; crabby old man, three spirits coming to visit on Christmas Eve—the ghosts of Christmas Past, Present, and Future—all there to show him the error of his ways and to give him a second chance at life before it was too late.

Unlike Scrooge, my second chance at life came much earlier. My name is Nicki Styx, and I'm only twenty-nine. A faulty heart valve nearly did me in last year. In fact, it *did* do me in; I've been to the other side and back again—and I mean that quite literally. Bright light, tunnel, and lifetime instructions to "do unto others as I'd have done unto me" before waking up in the hospital, sore and forever changed. I was very lucky, although getting kicked out of the afterlife definitely came with some strings attached; the restless dead, the ones who weren't so lucky, keep popping up with unfinished business, expecting me to finish it for them.

Which I do, if I can.

Even if it gets me in trouble, which it frequently does.

This year, however, the holidays seem to have brought nothing *but* trouble: three unpleasant spirits out to teach me a lesson for interfering in the "natural order of things." Three ghouls, three harpies, three sisters in crime . . . better known as the Three Fates.

The worst of the three is a succubus, a beautiful woman who can seduce any man alive by invading his dreams.

I know 'tis the season to be jolly, but this year, Santa's "ho, ho, ho" is all too real, and worse—she's out to steal my boyfriend.

CHAPTER 1

A little girl's laughter woke me in the middle of the night. High-pitched, giggly, and quickly shushed.

"Quiet, Kate. You'll wake them." A woman's whisper, delivered in a scolding tone. "I like watching young lovers sleep."

"Too late," came another feminine voice, at normal volume. "Her eyes are open."

My eyes *were* open, but I seriously doubted what they were seeing. Floating in the air directly above my bed, peering down at me as if I were a bug under a microscope, were three faces: a little girl, a beautiful dark-haired woman, and an old lady. Just faces, no bodies attached. I wasn't dreaming, though I'd been asleep a moment ago—I could feel the mattress beneath me, see the gleam of my digital clock from the corner of my eye. Terrified, I tried to scream, to leap from the bed, but I was frozen in place, completely unable to move. To my right lay my boyfriend, Joe, warm and solid, and snoring very faintly.

"He's quite handsome, isn't he?" the brunette said to the others. "This will be no hardship."

In my mind, my hand clawed at Joe's sleeping figure, and my throat filled with shrieks. In reality, I just lay there like a block of wood, my heart beating a mile a minute, as I stared wild-eyed at the trio of disembodied spirits who'd obviously decided to pay me a visit in the middle of the night. My panicked gaze passed briefly over the clock—it read 3:00 a.m. on the dot, in big blue numbers that were hard to miss.

"You're such a slut, Selene," said the old woman, shaking her head. Her gray hair was scraggly, lank, framing a face seamed with wrinkles.

"And?" asked Selene, idly. Her hair was gorgeous; thick and wavy enough for a shampoo commercial. Even in the middle of being terrified out of my mind, her face reminded me of an old painting—one of the classics I could never remember. "What do you think he sees in her, I wonder?" Selene cocked her head, examining me closely. "She's nothing special."

The little girl giggled again, but I found nothing funny about being paralyzed, analyzed, and, quite literally, scared stiff.

"I knew I should've done this by myself," said the old woman, shooting the others an annoyed glance. "You two have no sense of decorum."

"Quiet, you old hag," said the little girl, shocking me even further (if that were possible). "Why should you be the only one to have any fun? Choke this one, smother that one . . . I mean, really, Mary. Do you think we don't know what you do to them when you're alone?"

"Give her a mirror and she's even worse." The woman named Selene joined the girl in a chuckle, while the old woman pursed her lips and glared at them both. "Bloody Mary, indeed."

"What's the harm?" Mary answered defensively. "I don't kill them." She tilted her head, gray hair straggling across one withered cheek as she stared down at me, considering. "Usually."

"Never mind," said Selene. "We got what we came for." She eyed me speculatively from her perch in midair. "Shall we make her forget, or let her remember?"

"Oh, let her remember," said the little girl, carelessly. Shoulder-length brown hair with bangs, tucked behind her ears, Kewpie doll lips. "She brought it on herself, and what can she do about it? She'll just think it was a dream, anyway."

Unbelievably, as she spoke, the fog of sleep drifted up to claim me. Unable to fight it even if I wanted to, I slid into it with relief, glad the nightmare— if that's what it was—was over.

It *had* been a dream, hadn't it?

I couldn't stop thinking about it the next day, replaying it over and over in my mind as my best bud Evan and I worked on the Christmas window display at Handbags and Gladrags. The store was a mutual dream come true, conceived back in our teens, brought to fruition in our midtwenties, and now the coolest vintage fashion store in Little Five Points, Georgia.

"Earth to Nicki," Evan said, none too patiently. "I've been chattering away for five minutes about ideas on what to get Butch for Christmas, and you've been no help at all."

Giving him a teasing grin, I said, "Why don't you just put a big red bow on your—"

"Tut, tut, tut." He raised a finger, interrupting me. "Santa doesn't bring presents to naughty girls, you know. Particularly sparkly presents that fit on one finger."

I shook my head. "You've really got it in your head that Joe is going to propose to me this Christmas, don't you? Just because your boyfriend gave you a ring doesn't mean mine will do the same."

Evan sighed happily, admiring his platinum band for the umpteenth time since Butch had given it to him, months before. "I'm a hopeless romantic," he said, "and you and Dr. Gorgeous have been dating well over a year now. It's your second Christmas together. It's time."

"Who says I want to get married?" The very idea made me nervous. There was no question that Joe and I were in love, but marriage was a scary thought. When I did get married, I wanted my marriage to be like my parents', but how many people achieved that level of happiness and commitment?

"Of course you want to get married," he said complacently. "June wedding, you in Vera Wang, me in Armani. Pink tulips in the bouquet, to match the streaks in your hair." He shot me a warning glance. "Don't you dare switch to blue or purple streaks in the meantime, either. I want a pink tulip for my boutonnière."

I just shook my head and went back to work. Arguing with Evan while he was envisioning my imaginary walk down the aisle was a waste of time. He'd been planning my wedding since I was fifteen, and it was always changing, depending on his favorite designer du jour.

"Hand me that box of ornaments, would you?" We were going for a true vintage Christmas look for the window display, lighting up an old aluminum Christmas tree with a color wheel. We'd framed the entire window with a bunch of old Christmas cards we'd gotten in a box lot at auction. Box lots were always a gamble, but one person's junk could easily be another man's treasure, and you could find tons of treasures by buying boxes of stuff that nobody had taken the time to sift through.

The silver tree stood in one corner of the window, the color wheel tinting it from silver to green, to red, to blue. I was draping it in handmade ornaments dripping with glitter, obviously made by somebody's kids: Popsicle sticks and pipe cleaners and empty spools of thread all put together to form sloppy but cute stars, angels, and Santas. Every time I pulled one out of the box I couldn't help but envision someone else's long-ago Christmas, and the happy memories that must've led to their making.

That unknown family probably never expected their kitschy heirlooms to end up in a store window display, but hey, such was the commercialism of Christmas. Besides, I liked to think they'd be happy that their family treasures were still giving enjoyment to somebody, even if the somebody was just me.

"What the heck is this?" Evan held up a very twisted little brown lump with a single red pom-pom, which I took from him.

"It's a reindeer," I said, grinning. "Rudolph, in fact." I uncurled the pipe cleaner legs and antlers and showed it to him. "Very cute."

He gave it, and me, a doubtful look. "I can buy dozens of cheap ornaments at Family Dollar, you know, and they'd be all shiny and new. You sure you want to go this route?"

"Absolutely," I said, reaching to find a place on the Christmas tree to hang the reindeer. "It's going to look fabulous. I'm going to spray the whole tree with fake snow when I'm done."

"An aluminum Christmas tree and fake snow. How special," Evan murmured, turning back to the boxes.

"Hey, this look was considered extremely modern back in the early sixties," I returned. "Anything 'space age' was very hot in those days."

His criticism didn't bother me. I knew the display was going to look cool, and I suspected his mild pique was only because he hadn't thought of it himself.

"Why don't you go get Lucy ready?" I knew he'd

rather dress our Lucille Ball mannequin than dig through boxes, anyway. All the mannequins at Handbags and Gladrags were modeled after classic movie stars from the fifties and sixties, and we kept them posed and dressed accordingly. "The Santa suit is hanging in the office, and don't forget the hat and the ice skates." The Santa suit was a real find—plush red velvet with a flouncy skirt trimmed with white fur, made for a shapely female instead of a chubby guy—some glamour girl had probably worn it to a ritzy Christmas party back in the day.

"You sure you want to go with Lucy?" he asked doubtfully. "Red hair, red suit . . ."

"She's perfect," I said cheerfully. "We'll pose her flat on her butt like she slipped and fell on the ice."

He cheered up at that image, like I'd known he would, and stepped down from the window to begin Lucy's transformation.

Which left me alone again to wonder about last night's dream, and whether I needed to be worried about it. Maybe three women's faces hanging over my bed and discussing me like I wasn't there was just some weird hallucination my overtired brain had cooked up.

It had just seemed so *real*. I could see them in my mind's eye: the ugly old woman, the beautiful younger one, and the cute little girl. I could even remember their names: Mary, Selene, and Kate. Most of the strangers who appeared in my dreams didn't *have* names, so where had I come up with those?

The shop bell rang as the front door opened, but my back was to it and my mind on other things.

"Excuse me," someone said, "but do I know you?"

I turned, and my heart nearly stopped. The woman in front of me had dark, wavy hair and a face that belonged on the cover of a magazine; she was beautiful, absolutely beautiful, and I recognized her instantly.

She was one of the women from my weird dream—the gorgeous one called Selene.

"Oh," she said, smiling at me with ruby red lips, "I guess not. You remind me of someone, that's all."

"I . . ." I was staring, but I couldn't help myself. "You look familiar, too," I managed to say.

Was it possible?

"Do I?" She cocked her head playfully. "Maybe we *have* met before."

"Maybe we have." I was getting my equilibrium back. "My name's Nicki," I said, determined to find out hers.

"Selene," she answered easily, still smiling.

I swallowed, hard.

What was I supposed to say now? *Oh, you're the woman who was floating above my bed last night— nice to meet you in person.*

It obviously hadn't been a dream, after all, and there was no other way around it—here was another spirit with unfinished business, one who evidently enjoyed freaking people out in the middle of the night. "What do you want?" I asked abruptly.

She frowned a little at my tone. "I just came in to look around," she said. "I love vintage."

I was in no mood for games, more certain by the second that she was playing one. "Sure you do," I said sourly. "Vintage clothing comes in real handy during those late night visits with the talking heads."

The look she gave me was distinctly puzzled. "Is that a band or something?"

I wasn't buying it. "You and your friends, three a.m.? Ring any bells?"

"I'm sorry," she said, turning away, "but you've obviously mistaken me for someone else."

I eyed her narrowly, wondering what was going on, but she'd plainly decided that our conversation was over. She'd turned her back, and was browsing through the jeans rack. Size six section, I noticed; she'd obviously had a body that could stop traffic when she was alive, and I was disliking her more with every moment that passed.

"Nicki, we need some ones," Evan said, from behind the counter. He had no idea what was going on. "Do you have change for a twenty?"

"No," I said shortly, not bothering to look.

"I might," said Selene, turning her megawatt smile on Evan.

"That'd be great," Evan said cheerfully, and I nearly jumped out of my skin. If Evan could see her, hear her, then that meant she was . . .

"Let me check my wallet," she said, moving past me toward Evan. I got a whiff of her perfume—expensive, exotic. "I'm pretty sure I got a bunch of ones in change at the grocery store the other day, and I hate carrying small bills."

Alive. She was alive, not a spirit; she couldn't possibly have been floating above my bed.

What the hell was going on?

"Oh my god, is that a Furla?" Evan's eyes, big as saucers, locked on Selene's red leather handbag. She'd laid it on the counter while she dug around for her wallet.

"It is," she said, laughing. "I got it in Milan last year; a gift from my last boyfriend."

"You must've been a very good girl to get a gift like that," he answered, practically drooling. (Over the bag, of course.)

"Of course, darling." Her casual use of the word "darling" to a total stranger set my teeth on edge, and I'd expected it to do the same to Evan, but he didn't seem to mind. "Better than 'good', if you know what I mean."

They laughed together, and the sound made me want to grit my teeth.

"Too bad his brain didn't match his body." Selene sighed, tossing her hair over a shoulder. "I might've kept him around longer. Male models can be so self-absorbed, don't you think?"

"You're preaching to the choir, sweetheart," Evan said, though I couldn't remember him dating any male models. "It's hard to be in a relationship with someone who's more in love with their own reflection than they are with you."

Oh, please.

"Yes, the next man I date is going to be smart as well as sexy," she said, pulling a wad of ones out of her wallet. "Kindhearted, good-natured, gorgeous . . ." Here she paused, offering Evan the bills. ". . . and well-endowed."

They burst out laughing again, and I couldn't take any more. I walked up to the counter and came around to Evan's side. "Good luck finding Mr. Perfect," I said, reaching into the cash register and handing her a twenty. "And thanks for coming in."

It would've been obvious to anyone that I was trying to hustle her on her way—it was certainly obvious to Evan, who gave me a look.

"Oh," she said, turning her sunny smile in my direction without missing a beat. "I think I already have." She tucked the twenty into her wallet. "Last night, in fact." Slipping the wallet into her bag, she picked it up and slung it over her shoulder. The bright red leather was almost the same shade as her lipstick. "I'll have him under my spell in no time."

With a waggle of her fingers to Evan, she turned and headed for the door, dark hair cascading over her shoulders and down her back. "Ta-ta, darling. I'll be back when I have more time to shop."

"Bye," Evan said, waving like a schoolgirl.

"Stop that," I snapped, the moment she stepped onto the sidewalk.

He turned to me, frowning. "What's your problem? It's not like you to be rude to customers."

"I didn't like her," I said flatly. "And you're not allowed to like her, either."

His eyebrows rose. "I thought she was nice!"

I curled my lip. "Yeah, I forgot how much you love to play with Barbie dolls."

"Now *that* was just uncalled for," he said, slamming the cash register drawer shut.

Realizing that I was about to pick a fight with

Evan for no reason, I backed off, but not very graciously. "I can't help it. There's something not right about her." I was hesitant to tell him what the real problem was, because, quite frankly, it sounded pretty bizarre.

Either I'd seen her in a nightmare, which sounded completely stupid to say out loud, or she was a spirit, in which case Evan shouldn't have been able to see or hear her. Neither of those scenarios made sense. If she was alive, how could she have been in my nightmare, and if she'd been in my nightmare, then how could she be alive?

Evan leaned against the counter, a wry twist to his mouth. "Let's see . . . what is it you might not like about her?" He lifted up a hand, counting on his fingers, "Perfect hair, perfect face, perfect body . . ."

"Exactly." I didn't care if I was interrupting him or not. "She's too perfect. I can't stand that in a person."

"Uh-huh." He turned away, walking toward the back room. "Jealousy does not become you, darling."

I raised my voice, aiming it at his retreating back. "I'm not jealous, and don't call me 'darling.'"

Wisely, he didn't respond.

It wasn't jealousy that had my hackles raised;

Selene's appearance in my store left me feeling threatened, and I didn't like that feeling.

I wasn't buying her Little Miss Innocent routine. We *had* met before, and she knew it as well as I did, or my name wasn't Nicki Styx.

The buzzer at the back door rang, and a moment later I heard Evan's voice raised in greeting. Then I heard a voice that completely brightened my day. "Ho, ho, ho! Merry Christmas!"

It was Joe, carrying something bulky under his arm as he walked down the hall in my direction. I was surprised to see him since his shift in the E.R. wasn't over until early evening.

"Hey, gorgeous," he said with a grin. "I come bearing gifts."

The rich scent of cinnamon hit my nose as he held up what he was carrying—two big mesh bags full of pine cones, obviously steeped in cinnamon oil.

"What—"

He cut me off by swooping in for a kiss, green eyes twinkling. "One of the nurses was selling these as a holiday fund-raiser for her kid's school, and I thought they'd make the store smell great. 'Tis the season, you know."

Delighted, I took a deep breath. "Mmmm . . ." I went on tiptoes to steal my own kiss. "How sweet!"

"I've got a bunch more in the car," he said, obviously pleased with himself. "My leather seats are going to smell like these for weeks."

Laughing, I took the bags and stood there, arms full of pine cones, looking up at him. His dark hair was mussed by the wind, the tip of his nose just a teeny bit pink. He radiated good health, good looks, and a good heart, and I felt my own heart swell with love in response.

"Other girls get flowers, but I get cinnamon pine cones," I said smugly. "Am I lucky, or what?"

He slipped his arms around my waist and pulled me closer, nestling himself between the two bags of pine cones I now held in my arms. I leaned into him, enjoying the feel of his solid warmth against my thighs and belly.

"We're both lucky," he said, smiling down into my eyes. "I can't imagine life without you anymore—I can barely remember life before you." And then he kissed me, cold lips firm against mine.

Then he pulled back. "Let me get the rest of these in. I've only got an hour. Dr. Aldridge called in with the flu, and it's a full moon—we've got our hands full today. Can Evan watch the shop while you grab a bite to eat with me?"

"Go ahead," Evan said, coming up behind him. "Maybe food will sweeten her disposition. She's being quite the pain today."

"I am not," I answered indignantly, but my attempt to defend myself was aborted as Joe's attention was caught by something outside the front window.

"Call 911," he said, and dashed for the door.

A small crowd had gathered, bunched around Joe's broad back as he knelt over someone lying on the sidewalk. I held the store cell phone in my hand, trying to describe to the dispatcher what was going on. "Somebody collapsed on the sidewalk in front of 8219 Euclid Avenue," I told her. "There's a doctor on the scene. Other than that, I don't know what's going on."

A woman near the back of the crowd murmured to the woman standing next to her, "Is she dead? She looks dead."

"I don't know." Her friend was shaking her head, both of them craning their necks and staring.

I couldn't see much of anything except a plump pair of legs, encased in black pants, and a pair of white tennis shoes. A couple of shopping bags lay on the sidewalk near the person's feet.

"Is the victim breathing?" asked the dispatcher, in my ear.

"I have no idea."

"He looks like he knows what he's doing," said the first woman, to her companion. She was obviously talking about Joe, who was oblivious to the crowd.

He was leaning over the woman, stiff-armed as he pressed rhythmically on her chest.

"Step back, Alma," said an older man on the woman's other side. "Give the man some room."

They shifted, and I could clearly see the figure of an elderly woman lying spread-eagle on the sidewalk. I heard someone crying, and saw a little girl with her face buried against another woman's leg. "There now, dear," the woman murmured, stroking the girl's head as she watched the scene on the sidewalk. "Calm down. It will be okay."

"Grandma," the girl choked, shooting the figure on the ground an agonized glance.

"Shhh," murmured the woman who held her against her leg.

"Nicki!" Joe raised his head long enough to look around, and saw me at the edge of the crowd. "Come help me!"

"I've got to go," I told the dispatcher. "Please hurry." I hung up and stuck the phone in the pocket of my jeans, wishing I'd thought to grab a jacket before rushing out of the store. The temperature had definitely dropped since morning, and I was freezing. I worked my way in between a couple of people to get closer to Joe.

"Get on the other side," he said, never ceasing

his rhythmic pumping of the lady's chest. His green eyes were intent on mine, face grim. "Ever done mouth-to-mouth?"

Under different circumstances that question might've been funny, but now was obviously not the time for humor. "No," I answered, terrified at the very thought.

"I'll walk you through it," he said tersely.

I dropped to my knees beside the lady, feeling the chill of the sidewalk through my jeans. Then I looked at her face, and time stood still.

"Tilt her head back," Joe said, unaware of my shock.

When I didn't react, he repeated himself, more urgently this time. "Put your hand under her neck and tilt her head back."

"I—" I couldn't do it.

The woman on the ground was far too familiar. Her gray hair was in a sedate bun this time, not straggling around her cheeks, and she was wearing a black velour jogging suit like any modern-day grandmother might wear out Christmas shopping.

Except modern-day grandmothers didn't float above beds in the middle of the night, cackling about occasionally killing people while they slept.

"Nicki." Joe's voice was sharp, eyes sharper still.

I looked into those green depths—unable to speak, unable to explain—and shook my head, numbly.

"I'll do it," said a man's voice, from the crowd. "I took a course once, years ago."

"Oh, Arthur," a woman breathed, "are you sure you want to get involved?"

The man didn't answer, merely lowering himself to his knees beside me and nudging me aside.

I was still staring at Joe, and what I saw in his face made my stomach clench. Disbelief, disappointment . . . then he looked away, and I could breathe again.

"Here," he said to the man who'd offered to help. "You take over the chest compressions while I clear her airway."

I rolled back onto the balls of my feet and stood up, making way for the guy to reach the old lady's chest. He put his palms where Joe's had been and starting pumping, keeping the same rhythm Joe had.

Joe slipped a hand under the back of the woman's neck and lifted, so her head tilted back and her mouth fell partly open. With his other hand, he pinched her nose shut and leaned in to put his mouth on hers.

I had a really bad feeling about this. "Joe, don't—"

He ignored me, blowing into the old lady's

mouth once, pulling back slightly, then again. Letting go of her nose and turning his head so his ear was near her mouth, he listened to see if she was breathing on her own.

"Oh my," murmured one of the women in the crowd, obviously spellbound. The little girl was still crying, her sobs beginning to sound like hiccups.

"Keep it going," Joe said to the man pressing the old lady's chest. A second later, he blew into her mouth again, twice.

This time, when he let her nose go, her entire body spasmed as she coughed a weak little cough. A collective gasp and excited murmurings came from the crowd around me.

"Don't stop," Joe said sharply to the man doing the chest compressions. "Not until I tell you."

"This is that woman's lucky day," I overheard a man say to someone on the sidewalk. "If this guy hadn't been here, she'd be a dead duck."

I took a step back, mentally as well as physically. The man's companion pushed forward, and I found myself looking at Joe over his shoulder. That teeny bit of distance gave me a new perspective somehow, and I suddenly saw Joe as these strangers must see him: dark hair, broad shoulders, strong hands . . . the sexy, playful lover I was used to was gone, and in his place was a man who didn't hesitate to do what needed to be done to save a person's life. A competent, capable, self-assured guy who just happened to be majorly handsome.

The wail of sirens filtered into my consciousness, breaking my odd sense of separateness from the scene. The old lady on the sidewalk coughed again, moving a little, and Joe gestured to the man to stop his compressions. As the ambulance pulled to the curb, people scattered to make way for the paramedics.

Joe was on the other side of the woman, while I stood with the group of bystanders. He spoke to the two EMTs, who immediately started oxygen on the old lady.

"Grandma!" The little girl who'd been clinging to a woman's leg broke free and darted toward the woman on the ground.

"Whoa there, now," Joe said, catching her by the arm before she could get in the way. "Your grandma's going to the hospital where she can be looked after. You stay back here with me." And before I knew it, he'd scooped her up into his arms. She was wearing a red wool hat and a bulky coat—I couldn't see her face, but her hair was brown beneath the hat, shoulder-length.

"Kate?" Another woman's voice was raised

above the din, sounding frantic. "Mother? What's happened?"

And there was Selene, at Joe's elbow, looking worried and upset, and utterly, impossibly gorgeous. She was weighted down with shopping bags, which she dropped to the sidewalk in apparent shock. "Mother!"

"Grandma got sick," sobbed the girl, from Joe's arms. "She fell down."

"Oh, my poor baby," Selene said. She reached for her, but Kate buried her face in Joe's shoulder, clinging to his neck.

I wasn't buying it. An overwhelming sense of foreboding came over me; it just didn't seem real. It didn't seem genuine. I wanted to scream, *It's an act! It's all an act!* but I didn't dare. As far as the world was concerned, someone's life had just been saved, and it wouldn't do to ruin the moment.

Staring at Joe, Selene, and Kate, clustered together on the sidewalk like some perverted version of a family I wasn't a part of, I somehow knew *my* life was the one at risk. There was menace here—I could feel it.

Once the paramedics got the old lady onto a stretcher and loaded her into the back of the ambulance, I moved to stand beside Joe. He was still holding Kate, but she wasn't looking at me, and neither was Selene. They were both focused on their so-called grandma.

I touched his arm.

He glanced down sharply, as if surprised to see me there.

"Joe, I—"

"I'd like to shake your hand, young man." The guy who'd helped with the CPR had come up, flanked by the two women who'd kept up a running commentary with each other while today's drama played out on the sidewalk. "You're quite the hero."

Joe finally put the little girl down to shake hands, and I breathed a sigh of relief. I didn't like him touching her, just as I hadn't liked him putting his mouth on the old lady's mouth. Something was rotten in Denmark—or in this case, Little Five—and he just didn't know it yet.

"Oh, yes," fluttered the man's wife, a chubby woman with gray hair, "that was so impressive! Are you a doctor?"

"Yes," Joe said.

"I knew it," the man said to his wife. "Didn't I tell you, Alma?"

"How incredibly lucky," breathed the other lady. "What are the odds of you being here when that poor woman collapsed like that? It's a miracle, I tell you, a Christmas miracle!"

It sure was.

"Oh, I'm so grateful to you, Doctor." Selene, who'd been listening, reached out and grabbed Joe by the arm. She had Kate on her hip now. "I don't know what I would've done if—" She teared up, ruby red lips trembling. "Mother had just stepped out with Kate while I was at the cash register. I had no idea she was ill! I would never have dragged her out Christmas shopping if I'd known . . ." She broke down entirely, covering her face with her free hand as she sobbed. Kate started wailing again, too, in sympathy. The two women bystanders looked at each other and made sympathetic noises.

"It wasn't your fault," Joe said soothingly. "She's in good hands now. You can follow the ambulance to the hospital and meet her there when she arrives."

"Oh." Selene made a charmingly valiant effort to cease her crocodile tears. "You're right. You're absolutely right. I should get to the hospital." Her fake effort failed, unsurprisingly, as a new spate of tears spilled down her perfect alabaster cheeks. She held out a slender manicured hand, staring at it as if it belonged to someone else. "I'm shaking so hard I'm not sure I can drive."

Oh no, you don't—

"I'll give the two of you a ride." Joe made his offer before I could stop him. "I have to get back to the hospital anyway."

I was beginning to feel invisible. "Joe."

He turned to me, a slight frown on his face. I had the feeling I hadn't been forgiven for not leaping into action with mouth-to-mouth when he'd asked me to. "I'm sorry about lunch, Nicki. I'll call you later."

"I need to talk to you." I kept my voice low, but urgent.

"I want Grandma!" Kate began to cry again, and Selene comforted her.

"There now, darling, don't cry. This nice man is going to take us to Grandma, don't you worry."

Joe had already turned away, and I knew that for the time being at least, I was outmanned, outgunned, and outmaneuvered.

Grimly, I set my lips and said nothing. *This* battle might be lost, but the war was far from over.

CHAPTER 2

I waited a couple of hours before going down to the hospital. It was tough to wait, but I knew Selene would have to let go of Joe's arm long enough for him to do what he needed to do once they got there, and I'd have a much better chance of convincing him she was up to something if she wasn't around.

I filled the minutes as best I could by staying busy, and thinking hard.

"Did you see how Joe leapt into action?" Evan had watched the scene from the store's front window, and now, unfortunately, seemed to want to talk about nothing else. "He sprinted across that street like an action hero. Reminded me of Hugh Jackman."

"Joe's cuter than Hugh Jackman," I said, and meant it. "But yes, he was awesome."

As far as Evan and the rest of the world were concerned, Joe had saved the life of some old lady who'd apparently had a heart attack on the sidewalk. I was the only one who knew there'd been some type of supernatural setup involved, but I said nothing about it to Evan. There was no need to get him worked up about Selene and her friends until I knew what was going on.

Besides, Joe *was* a hero. He'd seen a need and jumped to fill it, heedless of the consequences. My feelings for him had deepened since we'd first met, but today it really hit me: Joe had qualities a lot of men didn't. His quiet self-confidence, his "take charge" attitude, combined with that dark hair, those intense green eyes that saw straight into your soul . . .

Forget Hugh Jackman; I had a *real* man in my life.

Evan went on, in full gush mode. "Those broad shoulders, that cute butt!"

"Stop drooling over my boyfriend," I told him flatly. "*I'm* the only one who gets to drool over my boyfriend."

"I was talking about Hugh Jackman."

"Yeah, right."

Silence greeted that remark, and a moment later

I heard the distinctive flip of a magazine page being turned. I went back to sweeping the last of the glitter and snowflakes from our window dressing from the carpet, and back to my own thoughts.

Broom in hand, I looked out the window at the store across the street. It was an organic market now, no longer the site of Divinyls Music.

Could Sammy be behind this?

Sammy Divine was a sexy, lying devil who'd raised all kinds of hell in my life, then disappeared from it. To be entirely accurate, Sammy wasn't just *a* devil . . . he was *the* Devil. A blond fallen angel with a lust for the flesh, he was hotter than Hell, and lived there, too. I hadn't seen him in at least eight months, and had begun to hope he might be gone for good.

Had he sent these three to start trouble? Why had they shown themselves to me last night, and then behaved like strangers today?

Let her remember, the little girl had said. *She brought it on herself, and what can she do about it?*

Brought *what* on myself?

I made it until two o'clock before I skipped out to see Joe. "I've got some errands to run, Evan. Would you mind if I left a little early?"

"Not at all." By now, he was up to his ears in shoeboxes, packing up what was left of our summer stock so we could fill the shelves with boots and flats. "You've been no fun at all today."

"I know." I sighed, not bothering to deny it. "I'll be better tomorrow." *I hoped.*

"Go on." He waved a sandal in my direction. "Go do some Christmas shopping or something. Macy's has cashmere sweaters on sale, but don't forget, beige makes me look washed out."

"Very subtle," I teased. "I was thinking pink for you this year."

"Amethyst," he returned, without missing a beat. "Or emerald. Jewel-tone colors are in."

"Got it," I answered dryly, on my way out the door.

I texted Joe as soon as I got in my car, offering to bring him a sandwich since he'd missed lunch, and had to be starving.

WILL BRING FOOD AND HOT COFFEE 2 UR OFFICE IN 30 MINS LUV U

That would give him time to break away and meet me, I hoped. If not, I'd wait in his office until he did show up.

Forty-five minutes later my strategy was rewarded when Joe walked in, looking harried but pleased. He smiled as he leaned in for a kiss. "Hey, thanks," he said. "You're an angel."

My heart lifted and fluttered at the sight of him, as usual. I was happy to sense no lingering disappointment on his part about my lack of help out there on the sidewalk.

I'd been a little worried about that. Heroes preferred to be around other heroes, didn't they?

Joe picked up his coffee, removed the lid, and sighed happily at the steam rising from the surface. "Still hot," he said, taking a sip, and then took a seat behind his desk. "My girlfriend is a bona fide angel."

"Barbecue chicken from Nellie Belle's," I said, handing him his sandwich, "with a side order of baked beans."

He made an appreciative noise, and wolfed the sandwich while I watched, glad just to be there, with him.

"You're not eating?" he asked, a few bites later.

"I had something earlier," I lied, not the least bit hungry.

I waited until he'd almost finished the sandwich, then jumped in with both feet. "How's Mary?"

"She's stable," Joe answered. "Her rhythms are normal, blood pressure elevated, of course, but . . ." He paused, barbecue-glazed eyes gone suddenly sharp. "How did you know her name was Mary?"

I sighed, glad he'd caught it. "Because I had a very weird encounter with her last night, along with her so-called daughter, Selene, and her so-called granddaughter, Kate."

His eyebrows went up. "An encounter," he repeated, obviously needing more to go on.

"They're not what they seem, Joe. They came to me last night, floating above the bed while we were sleeping."

He stared at me, blank-faced, while he processed that. I'd wanted to catch him off guard a little, just to make sure he took me seriously.

He cleared his throat, once. "You think they're ghosts?"

"Not ghosts."

And here is where it got difficult, because I didn't understand it myself.

"They're something else; I don't know what. They were just floating there, watching us sleep, talking to each other. It's hard to explain—it was very weird—and then I fell back asleep."

"You fell back asleep." His voice went flat.

"I wasn't dreaming," I protested, unfortunately making it sound like I'd been doing just that. "They were real, they were carrying on a conversation— I just couldn't do anything about it."

"You could've woken me up," he said mildly.

"I was paralyzed." I sounded defensive, and I hated that. "I couldn't move."

Wiping barbecue sauce from his fingers suddenly became very important to Joe, and I realized that I'd somehow blown it.

"You're telling me that you dreamed about Selene and her family"—a shiver of alarm went down my spine at his casual use of Selene's name—"and because of that, you think they're supernatural beings?"

"I—"

"I can assure you that Mary Mathews is quite human," Joe said. "I've been running tests on her for the last two hours. Her granddaughter Kate seems to be your typical preteen girl. A little sheltered, maybe, but otherwise normal."

"Selene is the one I'm worried about. She said she found you handsome."

He raised both eyebrows at me, and asked quite calmly, "She did, did she?"

As if he didn't know how any woman in her right mind would love to run a hand through his dark hair, trace that sensitive lower lip with a finger . . .

I wanted to smack him.

"And when did she say this?"

"When she was floating over the bed." *Why is it I was feeling more like an idiot every time I said that?*

"Okay," Joe said calmly, "and yet she was standing next to you today, right there on the sidewalk, as human as you or I."

"She came in the store earlier today, too." Might as well tell him everything. "She walked right up and introduced herself, said I looked familiar." I was now even more convinced that had been Selene's opening shot across the bow.

"You talked to her *before* her mother collapsed?" Finally he looked surprised.

Her mother.

"Oh yes," I said sourly. "She was very talkative. She told Evan and me both that she was looking for a new boyfriend."

Joe burst out laughing. "Is that what all this is about?"

I didn't find any humor in the situation, so I just gave him a look.

"You think she's going to set her sights on me." He was still smiling as he said it, which made it hard to get mad at him—he obviously *liked* the idea I might be jealous, the big goof. "You think she's so attractive that I—being the weak-minded male I am—will fall instantly under the influence of her big blue eyes, and dump you like yesterday's news."

He'd noticed the color of her eyes.

"No! Well—" *What's the use of denying it?* "Yes, I

am. She's hot, she's on the lookout for a new boy-friend, and she's *already* set her sights on you." I looked at the wall, beginning to lose my temper.

He leaned back in his chair, chuckling. "Nicki . . ."

"Don't Nicki me," I returned shortly. "I'm telling you, that woman is up to no good, and she's not human. I don't care what you say."

I couldn't believe he was taking what I said so lightly—I'd told him some pretty wild truths in the past, and he'd believed me every time. Why didn't he believe me this time?

He was quiet for a moment, then he stood up, coming around the desk. When he offered a hand to pull me up from my chair, I took it reluctantly, fuming a little. I wasn't sure how to make my point without sounding like a jealous shrew.

Joe, however, had a solution, leaning in until his forehead was against mine. "How about this," he murmured, cuddling me closer than a doctor probably should. "If you say you dreamed about them, I believe you dreamed about them. You probably have some of the same traits as your Grandma Bijou." My grandmother was a sensitive who lived in Savannah, who often knew things before they happened.

Almost against my will, a teeny bit of tension eased from my body. "You think so?" It was a hope I couldn't help but cling to, dammit. It would all be so much easier if I'd just had a weird dream about some people I hadn't met yet—with my family history, it even made a strange kind of sense.

"I think it's entirely possible," he murmured. "Just because you dreamed about them doesn't mean your dream will come true."

I didn't answer.

"It sounds like quite a nightmare."

"It was," I admitted.

"So you're afraid of them because you saw them in the context of a nightmare," he said, with a logic that was hard to deny, "but they haven't actually done anything to you, have they?"

I hesitated, feeling his heart beat steadily beneath my palm. "No."

"You've been living like this for over a year now, Nicki"—by "like this" I took it he meant "seeing spirits"—"and we both know some sort of psychic gift runs in your family."

"The 'knack,'" I admitted resentfully, nose against his chest. "That's what Grandma Bijou calls it." I still hadn't quite come to terms that my biological mother had made her living as a psychic, or that my grandmother could often read a person's mind, even when you didn't want her to.

"I think it's entirely possible that it has something to do with that," he said, slipping a hand under my chin and raising my face to his.

I smoothed the shoulders of his white lab coat with my palms, feeling better already. Looping my arms around his neck, I looked full into his eyes. *Green, warm, smiling.*

"So you promise that if Selene Mathews makes a move on you, you'll tell me about it?" I was comforted, but my instincts still told me the brunette was trouble.

"I will, I promise," he said, bending his head to brush my lips with his. He tasted of barbecue sauce and pure, unadulterated male. I savored both.

There was a knock at Joe's office door, and a nurse stuck her head in. She checked briefly at the sight of Joe and me in each other's arms, but otherwise didn't miss a beat. "Dr. Bascombe? There's a problem in the lab, and Dr. Jenkins is waiting to consult with you over the hematoma patient."

"Be right there." Joe eased back, and I could tell his brain had already shifted into doctor mode. The nurse gave me a quick glance, then took off.

"Duty calls," he said to me.

"Will I see you later?"

"I'm planning on it. How about I pick up Chinese takeout and bring it to your place around eight-thirty?"

"Sounds great."

A quick kiss, and he was out the door.

I trailed him out into the hallway, watching his broad back as he strode away, lab coat flapping. He turned a corner and the hospital swallowed him up like a big, busy labyrinth.

I turned in the opposite direction, heading for the door that led to the parking lot. Was it possible I was making too big a deal out of some weird dream? I made myself a mental note to Google the meaning of dreams when I got home. If I'd inherited Grandma Bijou's gift along with the knack, it might help to know what I was dealing with.

"I hope I don't start reading people's minds," I muttered to myself. "Seeing dead people is enough to deal with."

A couple of minutes later I realized that somewhere along the line I'd taken a wrong turn, because I found myself facing a set of double doors I'd never seen before. Knowing I couldn't be that far off my bearings, I went through them anyway, and found myself in a waiting room, empty but for a little blond-haired girl watching television, and a black nurse who sat talking on a phone behind a sliding glass window. She glanced up at me briefly, then went back to her conversation.

"Hi," the girl said to me, cheerfully. She was young, no more than six, with a sprinkle of freckles across her nose.

"Hi," I said with a smile, and turned to go, realizing I'd have to backtrack to find the door to the parking lot. Hospitals could become such a maze.

"Are you here to see someone?" The child was obviously precocious, and no doubt bored. Something made me glance at her again, and the way she brightened when I did made me pause, hand on the door.

"No," I said. "I'm just lost."

She shook her head, grinning. "No, you're not."

It occurred to me to wonder why an adorable kid like this would be sitting here all alone, so eager to talk to strangers. I looked toward the nurse, who was still on the phone, and for the first time noticed the sign next to the window.

PEDIATRIC ICU
ALL VISITORS MUST SIGN IN

Then I looked at the little girl again, and was shocked to see that she was wearing a blue and white hospital gown, when I could've sworn she'd just been wearing jeans and a Hello Kitty T-shirt.

My heart sank. This was no ordinary little girl. This was a *dead* little girl.

"Don't be scared," the girl said quickly. She shot the nurse a look. "That's the worst part, when people are scared."

I didn't know what to say.

"I'm not here to scare people," she went on. "I'm only here to help."

Blue eyes, blond hair, and freckles. A wiry-looking girl child who'd no doubt been a tomboy—her skin was tanned beneath the freckles and she looked healthy, vibrant, full of life.

Except she wasn't.

"Who—" I licked my lips, speaking softly. "Who are you trying to help?"

"The babies," she said earnestly. "They need someone to help them cross over. They're too little to do it by themselves."

My knees became wobbly. I groped for the arm of the nearest chair and sat down, never taking my eyes from the sweet little angel in the blue and white hospital gown.

"That's very nice of you," I said, wanting to cry.

"You could do it, too," she said, nodding with certainty. "You couldn't see me otherwise. The only ones who ever see me are the babies." She smiled, as if the thought gave her great pleasure. "They see me all the time."

"What's your name?" I wasn't sure what I needed to do here, but names seemed a logical place to start.

"Dani," she said, confirming my tomboy suspicions.

"Dani what?"

She shook her head. "I don't remember. It doesn't matter."

"What about your parents?"

Still smiling, she shook her head again. "I don't know." She seemed completely unconcerned.

"Don't you want them to know you're okay, so you can"—I made an ushering motion with my hands—"cross over yourself?"

She giggled, a tinkly sound that it seemed for a moment even the nurse behind the glass heard, because she looked up from her phone long enough to give me a glance. "They know I'm okay," she answered, as if to think otherwise was ridiculous.

I was struck by how mature she seemed, even if she *was* swinging her legs like any normal child of six. "They said it was okay to go, and that I'll see them again when it's time."

A lump rose in my throat. I could picture the scene all too clearly. A sudden illness, perhaps? An accident? Either way, a nightmare no parent should ever have to go through.

"Anyway, it isn't time yet," Dani said cheerfully, "so I get to stay with the babies until it is."

Then I understood.

Dani's life might have been short, but for now, she was in baby-doll heaven, and even I could see the benefit of that situation all the way around.

I was no deep thinker, but I couldn't help but wonder if that's how angels were made—a new purpose for a soul too bright to be extinguished.

"I have to go now," she said, and jumped up from her chair, blond hair bouncing. She tossed me a quick wave. "Bye."

I blinked, and she was gone. I looked toward the nurse, who'd finally hung up her phone and was rising, her attention on something going on in the area behind the glass.

Instinctively I knew what was happening, and pushed through the double doors into the outer corridor with a heavy heart.

Which immediately lightened when I thought of Dani, who'd be there to hold out a hand to any innocent soul who needed her.

Who was I to question the ways of the universe?

Taking a deep breath, I started walking, resuming my search for the door that led to the parking lot, relieved I hadn't been asked to do the universe any favors today.

A couple of minutes later, I finally found my way back to the original main corridor, and breathed a sigh of relief, knowing I'd soon be away from all this echoing linoleum and in the front seat of my own car.

I briefly considered going back to the store and

helping Evan close up, but I really just wanted to go home and let my nerves settle.

It had already been quite a day—ending it with an angel didn't seem like such a bad idea.

A woman's heartbroken wail interrupted my thoughts. "I didn't mean it," she shrieked, somewhere down a hallway. "It was a mistake!"

My heart sank at the pain in her voice. Someone was going through a bad time, that was for sure.

"No!" she cried, louder now. "No! I didn't mean it!"

Uncomfortable eavesdropping on someone else's drama, I walked faster.

"Please—" The wailing got louder, and a woman stumbled into the corridor. She looked around wildly, and seeing me, rushed in my direction. "Help me! Please!"

I flinched as she reached out to grab my arm, but there was no need. Her hands went through me like a breath of wind, leaving goose bumps in their wake. "No!" she screamed again, horrified. She stared at her hands as though they belonged to someone else. "Why can't anyone see me? Why can't anyone hear me? Please, help!"

Oh, shit.

It was happening again.

Up close, I could see she was young, mid-thirties maybe. Slightly chubby, light brown hair that could use a shampoo. She was wearing a pink bathrobe and looked disheveled, distraught, and obviously—at least to me—very much dead.

I hesitated, tempted, for the first time since I'd started seeing spirits, to pretend I didn't see her. I didn't have to answer her, didn't even have to look at her if I didn't want to. She'd give up and go away eventually. I could act the way normal people did, and just keep walking, ignoring her cries for help, her obvious panic.

Except . . .

I couldn't do it, particularly after my visit to the pediatric ward. If a child of six could do the right thing, so could I. "Try and calm down," I murmured, looking straight at her. I hoped no one would hear me and think I was talking to myself. "I see you."

The woman stared at me blankly, like someone in the grip of a horrible nightmare, intent, yet unseeing . . . and then her mind skipped somewhere else.

"Josh." Her face screwed itself into knot of pain. "What will happen to my son?" she wailed.

And that's when my heart truly sank, a familiar flutter caused by more than just a wimpy mitral valve.

"Josh, oh God, Joshua . . . he's only fourteen."

Sobbing now, shaking fingers pressed to her mouth.

Poor woman.

"I'm so sorry," I murmured, meaning it from the bottom of my heart.

"What have I done?" she choked, burying her face in her hands. I was silent, not knowing the answer to her question, giving her a little time to absorb the situation. I was worried someone was going to walk down the corridor any moment and find me talking to myself, but no one came.

"Am I . . ." She looked at me through her fingers, barely able to speak through her tears. "Am I . . . ?"

I don't think either of us could manage the word "dead."

"Yes," I said, as gently as I could.

The look of horror in her eyes would stick with me for a long time.

Before she got all panicky again, I added, "I'm really sorry this happened to you. I know what it feels like." *Well, not exactly, because I didn't have kids when I died, but close enough.* "Maybe I can help."

"How?" she choked through her sobs, "How can you help me?"

"There's a Light," I said, knowing the only thing that could comfort her. "There's a Light, and you'll see it if you just look. Your son will be with you there one day. It will be all right." Hard to explain how I was so sure of that, but I was confident it was true. "If . . ." I hesitated, wimp that I was. ". . . if you want me to tell him anything for you, I can get him a message." I wasn't sure how, but I was sure I could figure it out—a nice sympathy card with a note, maybe.

Thoughts of sympathy cards dissolved, however, as a coiling, shifting mass of black shadows began oozing its way into the hallway, directly behind the woman.

Dumbstruck, I couldn't believe my eyes.

Spirits were one thing, but this . . . this was something entirely different. I stepped back, ready to bolt.

Blackness. Fluid shadows, alive in their relentless, greedy spread; boiling and bubbling as they made themselves into something deeper, something *bigger*.

Cold. It was cold.

And suddenly, I knew beyond a doubt what I was staring at.

The Dark. The total opposite of the Light, the very antithesis of the incredible brilliance and warmth that could draw lost souls like a lodestone. The Dark was manifesting, right in front of me, and it was cold.

The look on my face made the woman turn.

She gave a low moan and grabbed for my hand. Her fingers slipped through mine like the tickle of spiderwebs. "It's come for me, hasn't it?" she whispered, terrified.

The black mass of shadowy evil expanded to fill the corridor in front of us, shifting and boiling to a height of eight to ten feet.

"I knew it was a sin . . . I knew it and I did it anyway. I thought it was a way to fix things, but I've made it so much worse." She was staring into the Dark, babbling in fear, more to herself than me.

I'd never been so scared in my life. There was an actual horror-flick-made-real moment going on, right before my eyes.

"Don't look at it," I said, trying hard not to look at it myself, and failing. It was horrible, hypnotic in its horribleness, and somehow *alive*. No longer advancing, it became darker and darker until its blackness was absolute, a tunnel of inky depths I couldn't begin to fathom. It was as if it had its own consciousness, and worse, it was *waiting*.

"I tried, really I did." The woman started talking, choking back sobs. She seemed mesmerized by the Dark, compelled to speak her confession, I suppose, with no one to hear it but me. "It was fine the first few years, after David and I got married. But when Josh became a teenager, everything changed." Her eyes were haunted, and desperately sad. "Father Donovan said suicide was a sin, but there was no other way out! Josh kept getting into trouble, and I didn't have the patience or the energy for it. The counselor said I needed to take my medicine and 'rise to the occasion,' but I couldn't. David was disappointed in me."

I was having a hard time following her since I didn't know these people, but it didn't matter. Her gaze was inward, despite—or perhaps *because* of—the cold blackness that boiled in front of her eyes. She looked at me, and my heart clenched at her pain.

"I was a terrible mother, a terrible wife. Josh hated his stepdad, and I . . . I just hated myself." Her voice trailed away as she looked again toward the Darkness. "I took the coward's way out, and now I have to pay the price."

My knees were shaking. I was petrified of the twisting, roiling mass, but I refused to accept that suicide—as awful as it was, especially to those who are left behind—was a valid reason to condemn someone to Hell.

For surely this was the gateway to Hell. No flames, no screams of the dead and dying, just cold nothingness waiting to absorb desperate, guilty souls and smother them into oblivion.

While the Dark waited, moving no closer, my

mind was racing. I couldn't help but think of Crystal Cowart, who'd killed herself, too, although she'd let anorexia do the work. I was convinced, in the end, that poor Crystal had gone into the Light despite her bad choices, and somehow that made me think that this woman could, too.

"You don't have to go," I blurted. "You made a mistake, but that doesn't mean you have to suffer for it forever."

She stared fixedly into the Dark.

"Hey." I snapped my fingers, trying to get her attention. "Look at me. I'm trying to help you."

She tore her eyes from the blackness with an effort. "I deserve it." Her face was tight with fear.

"No, you don't." I took heart from the fact that the Dark was moving no closer. "You don't have to go." I held my breath, but nothing reached out to grab her (or me, thank God), no lightning or thunder, or scaly-armed demons from Hell. Just that constant, steady, inexorable sense of waiting . . .

"What can I do?" she whispered hopelessly.

I glanced one final time at the inky evil that loomed over us both. It completely blocked one end of the corridor, but the way behind me was clear. "Run," I said grimly, eager to take my own advice. "Now!"

CHAPTER 3

She bolted, and I was right behind her.

One second we were both running down the corridor, and the next second I was by myself. Alone. With a big, black cloud of evil at my back.

I didn't know where she'd gone, and quite frankly, I didn't care.

I reached the door that led to the parking lot and wrenched it open, not daring to look behind me. Outside, I darted around an old couple shuffling toward the parking lot. Ignoring their curious looks, I just ran, wanting to put as much distance between me and what I'd seen as possible.

It wasn't until I reached my car that I risked a backward glance, fumbling with my keys with shaking hands. Nothing. Once inside the car, I locked the door and sat there, trembling, wondering what the hell kind of trouble I'd gotten myself into this time.

Why hadn't I stayed out of it? I could've just kept my mouth shut and kept walking and . . . *crap.*

I buckled my seat belt and turned the ignition key. A series of wimpy sounding clicks made my heart sink. "No, no, no . . ." I tried again, and only got one or two clicks this time. Letting my head fall to the steering wheel, I thought about my options.

Go back inside. *Out of the question.*

Call Joe. *Busy. Very busy.*

Call Evan. *Manning the store alone.*

Call a tow truck. *Would require going back inside to find a telephone number. See option #1.*

I needed a minute. Sitting up, I kept an eye out in the direction of the hospital, but there was no sign of pursuit, no sign of the woman in a pink bathrobe. My heart was racing, which was not good for the wimpy valve that had gotten me into this mess to begin with. My hands were shaking. I waited until I had both heart and hands somewhat under control and then, with a sigh, dug in my purse for my cell phone and called Evan at the store.

"Handbags and Gladrags." He sounded distracted.

I'd made up my mind to be calm. I'd long ago learned that it wasn't always a good idea to tell him every scary thing that happened to me, at least not right away. He spooked so easily, poor thing. "Evan, my car won't start."

"Oh no! Where are you?"

"In the hospital parking garage. Can you come get me?"

"I've got a Buckhead mom and three teenage girls in here, Nick—two of them are in the dressing room." Buckhead was Atlanta's most upscale neighborhood, and a sharp store owner like Evan could spot a "Buckhead mom" a mile away. He lowered his voice so the customers couldn't hear. "I'm pretty sure we're about to sell the Bonwit Teller."

The Bonwit Teller was a gorgeous Parisian "flapper" style dress from the 1920s—very hard to come by, and very expensive. I'd priced it over eight hundred dollars, figuring the beadwork alone would eventually sell it. It was jet black, sassy, and in all honesty, I would've loved to keep it for myself, but the store's bottom line came first.

"These girls need new jeans, new jackets, and a new way of looking at fashion, and I'm *just* the man to give it to them!" He was speaking low into the phone, but I could hear the genuine enthusiasm in his voice. Nothing made the man happier than decking someone out in fashionable vintage, which is why he was so good at it.

"Okay," I said, reluctantly conceding. "Can you call me back when they're gone?"

"It may be a while . . . can't you call a tow truck, Nick?"

I could picture him, blond head bobbing as he kept an eye on the dressing rooms.

"Can you look me up a number?" I asked hopefully.

"I'll be right there," Evan sang out to someone, and I knew my shot at immediate help was over. "Nicki, I've got to go. Even if I came to get you, we'd still have to call a tow truck. Just go back inside and look in the phone book, okay?"

I couldn't blame him. I wasn't even mad, just . . . scared.

"Okay," I said. "I'll be in soon."

"Good," he answered, with relief. "I haven't had a potty break in over an hour." And then he hung up.

"Get a grip, Styx," I muttered to myself. "It didn't hurt you. It can't hurt you."

Liar.

"You're not dead, you idiot. It came for her."

Great . . . not only was I talking to myself, I was arguing with myself.

"It didn't follow you. It wasn't there for you."

What if I'd made it mad? What if it was still there, in the corridor, waiting?

I shuddered, feeling cold again at the very thought.

It took me a good five minutes, but I finally got my nerve up to get out of the car. There was a steady stream of visitors coming and going through the parking lot, which made me feel somewhat safe, though I had no idea why.

Human beings would be of no use against the thing I'd seen.

Walking slowly, I made my way back to the door I'd come out of, encouraged to see a nurse and an old man go in and out ahead of me. If there was something there, it wasn't bothering them, so maybe it wouldn't bother me.

When I reached the door, I almost turned back, but I didn't. Taking a deep breath, I opened it and went in.

The corridor was empty. To the left was the door that led to the E.R. waiting room, and far down at the other end of the hall was the door that led to the main hospital—nothing in between.

Breathing a sigh of relief, I turned to the left and went into the waiting room, knowing there would be a phone book in there.

The place was full, as usual. Columbia Memorial was always busy. A woman with a whiny two-year-old sat closest to the pay phone. I gave her a little smile as I picked up the book and started riffling through it, but she didn't smile back. She looked tired and wan, a wad of tissues in one hand and a sippy cup in the other. I'm sure having to take care of a kid when you weren't feeling well wasn't very fun.

Ten seconds later I was dialing the number for Tony's Towing Service. Doing my best to ignore the increasing loud screeches from the toddler near my feet, I gave them directions on where to find me.

I was putting my phone back in my purse when the main door to the Emergency Room whooshed open, and a teenage boy ran in, followed by a plump, older woman. She looked worried and he looked agitated.

The boy was wearing all black, down to his tennis shoes. His hair was black, too, so dark a shade I knew it was dyed. He had at least one eyebrow piercing and looked far too thin for his age—a baby goth if I'd ever seen one. He rushed up to the nurses' station and rapped loudly on the glass, which was closed. "Hey!" he shouted, uncaring that a room full of strangers was watching, "Hey! I need to see my mom!"

The woman with him said nothing, merely looking worried as she came up to stand behind him.

The glass opened, and a nurse spoke. "Can I help you?"

"I need to see my mom," the boy repeated loudly. "My stepdad called and said she was here." He couldn't hold still, peering past the nurse as if his mom were behind the counter or something.

"Angie Rayburn." The woman stepped out from behind the boy, finally speaking up. She had a fairly pronounced Hispanic accent. "Her name is Angie Rayburn."

By then I knew who the boy was looking for.

The nurse gave a telling glance toward someone else behind the glass, another nurse probably, then turned back to the boy. "You'll need to have a seat, son. Someone will be right out."

"No!" he shouted. "I'm *not* going to have a seat. Where's my mom? Take me to her right now."

The Hispanic woman touched the boy's arm tentatively. "Josh," she murmured, but he shook her off. Given her accent, I doubted they were related; she could be the housekeeper, the next-door neighbor.

"I want to see my mother right now!" he shouted at the nurse, completely uncaring of the attention he was drawing to himself.

The nurse, a black woman who easily outweighed him by at least sixty pounds, stood up, looking him in the eye.

"Son," she said quietly, "I know you're upset, and I know you're worried about your mama, but you need to take yourself a seat until the doctor can speak with you."

The boy was breathing hard, and opened his mouth to argue.

"Don't make me call security, now." Her voice was firm, but kind. "Sit yourself down. It won't be long."

Maybe it was the kindness in her voice that did it.

Joshua slapped his hands down on the counter, hard, but did as she said, throwing himself into the nearest available seat. The woman with him could've been invisible as far as he was concerned, though I noticed the continued worried looks she gave him as she found a seat next to him.

I felt sick to my stomach at the news this poor kid was about to get.

Without a word, I turned and left, not needing—or wanting—to see or hear any more.

"Dead battery." The guy from Tony's Towing was fat and balding, with grease stains under his fingernails. His breath smelled like cigarettes, and he wore an old jacket that probably hadn't been cleaned since he bought it back in the eighties. "I can probably jump it. That'll get you to an auto parts store where you can buy a new one."

"What good will that do me?" I'd been waiting for almost a half hour for the guy to get there, torn between nerves and boredom as I paced the parking lot. "I don't know anything about car batteries. Will they put it in for me?"

The guy gave me a look. "Ain't you got a boyfriend that can do it for ya? Pretty girl like you?"

"My boyfriend needs his hands for other things."

He sniggered, obviously thinking I was making some kind of dirty joke.

I didn't bother to enlighten him. "Can't *you* do it?"

"I don't carry batteries with me in the truck," he said, like I was an idiot. "I can jump it, or I can tow it. Your choice. If I was you, I'd take the jump and drive it to an auto parts store." He looked me up and down, real quick-like. "I'm not supposed to do this, but I could slide a new battery in for you—you could pay me under the table. We could work out a deal."

"No, thanks." I could just imagine what *that* deal might entail. "Go ahead and jump it. Just get it started. I'll take it from there." No way was I gonna do any "sliding" with this guy, literally or figuratively.

Tow Truck Driver Guy shrugged, heading for his truck. "Suit yourself."

I waited while he dragged out a pair of jumper cables, taking his sweet time about it. All the while I tried not to think about Angie Rayburn, her family, or the big black mass of evil I'd seen in the corridor.

Ten minutes and ninety dollars later I finally pulled out of the hospital parking lot. Tow Truck Driver Guy said to go straight to the auto parts store without turning off the ignition, but I drove instead to Ernie's Engine Repair.

Ernie's was a podunk little station on the edge of Little Five, a throwback to the sixties, the days when family-run stations were common. My dad had always taken our cars there, and I couldn't help but think of him as I pulled in. He'd made a big deal about bringing me to Ernie's when I was a teenager, showing me how to check my own oil and put air in the tires. I'd continued to come here as an adult to get my gas, even though they only had one pump.

Don't ever buy that old "running out of gas" routine, Dad would say. *Oldest horny teenage boy trick in the book.* I smiled, remembering how I'd cringed at that one. *Anytime you're in a bind on the road, you call me, you hear? I'll come get you, wherever you are.*

I'd have given anything to be able to call him to come get me today. My dad knew his way around cars, though it hadn't saved him in the end. He and my mom had died in a car accident on a rainy night nine years earlier.

I made a mental note to take flowers to their grave; I hadn't been out to the cemetery in a while.

Just to be on the safe side about the battery, I left the engine running while I got out and went inside.

Ernie himself was behind the counter. Well into his eighties, he left the repair work to his son and grandson now while he manned the air-conditioned office, which mainly meant he read the newspaper and watched the tiny little TV that was always tuned to CNN news.

"Hoo-ee," he said, when I came in. The corners of his mahogany-colored eyes were seamed with wrinkles, and his smile was missing a tooth on the lower right side. He looked as old as Methuselah and twice as feisty. "If it ain't a purty little pink-haired angel, come to pay me a visit. How you doin', chile?"

I was pretty sure Ernie had forgotten my name, but that was cool; he'd been around a long time, and seen plenty of pink-haired girls in his day.

"I'm not doing too good today, Mr. Phelps," I answered, giving him a smile in return. While my dad had called him Ernie, to me he'd always been Mr. Phelps. "My battery died. Can you get me a new one?"

The old man leaned back in his chair and bellowed his grandson's name with more volume than you'd expect from a skinny, withered old coot. "Leland! Get yourself on up here, boy!"

Lee stuck his head in the door that led to the garage. "What is it, Granddaddy? I got plenty to do—" He saw me and stopped, a slow grin replacing a look of annoyance. "Hey, Nicki."

Lee and I had sort of known each other since we were kids, but he was at least five years older than me, so I couldn't say I knew him well. His caramel-tinted skin was a lot lighter than Ernie's, and his toffee-colored eyes had a slight slant, both compliments of his mom, who, though I didn't know her name, was obviously of Asian descent.

"Hey, Lee," I returned.

"What are you doin' in here?" He wore his hair close-cropped, and had a lean, lanky build. Smiling, he came all the way into the office, wiping his hands on an oily rag. "Granddaddy givin' you a hard time?"

"What you mean 'givin' her a hard time,' boy?" Ernie bristled, but I knew it was just for show. He and Lee were tight. "You the one wantin' to give her a 'hard time,' and don't think I don't know it!"

"Granddaddy," Lee tried to shush him, but Ernie wasn't to be shushed.

"This pretty little thing knows what I'm talkin' about, don't ya?" He gave me a wink and a snaggle-toothed grin, obviously enjoying his grandson's discomfort.

"Lee's never given me a hard time," I said, with a straight face. "He's always been very nice to me."

"Nice!" Ernie leaned back, disappointed that I wasn't going to play naughty. "Sometime he can be *too* nice." The look he gave Lee was laden with hidden meaning, but I didn't have time to decipher it.

"I've got a dead battery," I told Lee. "Had to call a tow truck to jump it."

"Sorry to hear that." Lee was studiously ignoring his grandfather. "You should've called here. I would've jumped it for you at no charge."

"Oh, he'd a jumped it all right," Ernie muttered to himself, turning back to his CNN.

I could've kicked myself, because the thought of calling Ernie's hadn't even occurred to me. I could've saved ninety bucks and avoided a serious case of the icks. But, in my own defense, I was pretty panicky at the time, having just seen—

"Thanks." I interrupted my own thoughts, not wanting to go where they were taking me. "I didn't think of that, but I sure will next time. It's out front; I left the engine running."

"I'll need the key." He smiled at me again, almond-shaped eyes becoming more pronounced. "I'll have it ready for you tonight, before we close."

I breathed a sigh of relief, glad to have this particular problem taken care of.

"You need a ride somewhere?"

I hesitated, but only for a second. "Yes, actually. I'd like to go home."

Needed to go home. It had been quite a day.

A grin split his face. "Give me a minute to move your car into one of the bays and wash my hands." He was already moving toward the door. "I'll be right back."

"Don't you go breakin' his heart, now," Ernie said idly, as soon as his grandson left. He was talking to me, but kept his eyes on the TV. "He talk a good game, but he too soft when it come to women."

I laughed a little. "Lee's virtue is safe with me, Mr. Phelps. I've got a boyfriend."

"All ya'll got a boyfriend," the old man said, with a negligent wave of a hand. He wasn't being rude, and I took no offense. At his age, he had the right to say whatever he wanted. Besides, I'd been raised not to argue with the elderly. On CNN, the talking heads had moved on to news coverage of a tropical storm over Cuba, and I watched the footage with interest, thinking how awful it must be to have no electricity for days on end.

"Your friend don't look too healthy," Ernie went on, in a complete change of subject.

"Excuse me?"

"Your friend." Ernie was still watching TV, not even turned in my direction. "The woman you drove up with. The one wearing the bathrobe, lookin' all pale and peaked. She in the ladies' room?"

A chill ran down my spine.

He gave me an over-the-shoulder glance. "She got the flu? 'Cause I don't need no flu." He looked back at CNN. "At eighty-six, I damn sure don't need no flu."

"No," I said faintly, "she doesn't have the flu." And then I turned and walked outside, not knowing what else to say.

Was it possible?

I hadn't seen Angie Rayburn since I left the hospital, but she fit Ernie's description; pale, unkempt, wearing a bathrobe. Had she hitched a ride with me? If she did, why hadn't she shown herself? Even more pressing, where was she now?

I looked nervously around the parking lot. My car had been moved into a bay, and there was no one at the gas pump. The restroom was on the side of the building, so I walked over and tapped on the door.

No answer.

I tried the knob and found it unlocked. "Hello?" I opened the door and stuck my head in—it was empty, and in dire need of some air freshener. "Anybody here?"

No response.

I shut it and walked away.

Was Mr. Phelps just a confused old man, thinking about someone else, or was I being followed? *When you're old, the veil is thinner*, my Grandma Bijou would say.

And she'd probably be right, as she was in most things having to do with spirits. Living in a haunted house for over forty years had left her pretty in tune with the veil.

I shook my head. I was just being paranoid. After the day I'd had, nobody could blame me for being paranoid.

All I knew was that I didn't want this particular problem. Angie Rayburn came with some very scary strings attached.

That cold, oozing mass of blackness . . .

I rubbed my arms briskly to keep warm, wishing Lee would hurry up. Selfishly, I hoped I never saw her again.

CHAPTER 4

"So it didn't work out," Lee was saying. "I needed stability in my life, not drama, and Chanel was all about the drama." He turned left, his old Lincoln Town Car gliding down my street like a big old-fashioned yacht, complete with hood ornament. "I see the kids every other weekend, though—we worked it out. Daryl's into Little League, and Kayla is my little prima ballerina." He smiled, glancing at me as he drove. "I go to all Daryl's games, and Kayla's recitals. It's all good."

Lee's car was immaculate, a great example of how a classic car should be treated. He said he'd had it since high school. The interior gleamed with leather polish, and the silvery-blue paint job looked elegant, not overdone.

"It's great you guys can get along for the kids," I said, and meant it. "How's your mom and dad?" I was just making conversation, still distracted by the thought of Angie Rayburn. What if she was sitting in the backseat of the Lincoln right now, with neither of us able to see her?

"They're good. Granddaddy's good, though he's starting to get a little spacey."

"Spacey?" *Like hallucinations, maybe?* I was ashamed to find myself hopeful at the thought.

He waved a hand. "Oh, you know, like he's not there all the time. Sometimes he don't hardly make sense, and sometimes he's sharp as a tack. He's just gettin' old, that's all."

"Sorry to hear it," I told Lee.

"Part of life," he said comfortably. "What about you?" I noticed a quick check of my ring finger. "Are you seeing anybody?"

Lee was a good-looking guy, by anyone's standards. Mocha latte skin, high cheekbones, strong hands. If he'd made his play before I met Joe, I would've definitely taken him up on it, no strings attached. As it was now, I was so knotted up in strings that I'd never be untangled, and I liked it that way.

"I am. His name's Joe." I smiled at the thought of him. I was flattered by Lee's interest, but I wanted to be clear. "Over a year now. I'm crazy about him."

Lee shook his head, still smiling. "He's a lucky guy."

"Thanks."

"So there's no chance that you and I . . ." He hesitated, and I jumped in.

"No, darn it." I opted for honesty, with a side of teasing. "We missed that window. While I was off sowing my wild oats, you were settling down, making babies." I kept my voice light, teasing. "Now I'm in a relationship, and you've got some wild oats to sow, boy! I mean, you were what, in high school, when you got married? You need to go out there and have some fun!"

He laughed, recognizing the truth as well as the irony in my statements. "Always thought you was cute, though," he said, giving me honesty in return.

"Thanks." I was glad we'd laid it all out on the table. Lee was a nice guy, and didn't want any awkwardness between us. "And thanks for the ride." We were nearing my house. "It's the white one with the porch, right here."

"This where you live?" He craned his neck to get a good look. "Nice neighborhood."

"Thanks." I got out, leaning in before I shut the door. "You'll call me when the car's ready?"

"I'll call you," he said, "probably be after six, though."

"That's fine," I said, shutting the door and backing away with a wave.

"Nicki." Lee leaned way in over the seat so we could see each other clearly. "He's a lucky guy."

I laughed, flattered, yet agreeing completely.

"Thanks," I said, with a final wave good-bye. "I'll remind him of that."

Depression is a medical illness that affects both the mind and the body, and is one of the most common health conditions in the world. It affects approximately 12 million people each year, and can strike anyone, anytime, though it typically arises in the late twenties, and affects twice as many women as men.

Symptoms range from mild to severe, from depressed mood and irritability to morbid thoughts of death. It is estimated that 15 percent of those suffering from major depressive disorder eventually resort to suicide.

An interesting turn of phrase, "resort to suicide," as if death truly were the only way out. Poor Angie—it wasn't her fault she'd been overwhelmed—this condition could've happened to anybody.

Which was a pretty scary thought in itself.

I pushed myself away from the computer and got up, needing a break. Joe wouldn't be here until eight-thirty, and I was hungry, having missed lunch because of all the drama over Selene and Mary Mathews—an incident that already seemed distant, as if it had happened days ago instead of just a few hours.

Luckily for me, the house stayed quiet. If Angie's spirit had followed me, she hadn't shown herself, so there was nothing I could do. I refused to worry myself into a frenzy over it, not when I could eat instead. Not much in the fridge except yogurt and apples—anyone could tell Joe was spending more time here. I helped myself to a yogurt, smiling at the thought.

Then I wandered my quiet house while I ate, pausing to notice more evidence of Joe. His favorite navy blue sweater, tossed over a chair. The latest issue of *Scientific Review* on the bedside table. The shaving stuff in the spare bathroom. His toothbrush in the cup next to mine.

Evan was right. Joe and I had been together quite a while now. We were good together, and I didn't want that to end.

Or change.

But what if he did *ask me to marry him?*

The phone rang just after six, as promised.

"Hello."

"Nicki? This is Lee, at the garage."

"Hey, Lee. Is the car ready?"

Silence for a moment, then, "So you didn't pick it up?"

"What? I've been waiting for you to call me."

Lee heaved a sigh. "I was hoping maybe Granddaddy called you, and that you'd already picked it up."

Confusion set in.

"I'm really sorry to tell you this, but your car is gone, Nicki. Someone must've stolen it from the lot."

"Gone?" I thought maybe I'd misheard him. "My car's gone?"

"I picked up a battery after I dropped you off," Lee said. "Came back to the shop, put it in, moved it to a space out front. Had a couple of customers to take care of—Granddaddy went home, said he wasn't feeling good—and next thing I know, I look out the window, and your car's gone. I'm really sorry, Nicki. As soon as I hang up with you I'll call the police and report it stolen."

"Shit," I said, unable to say anything else. *Shit, shit, shit.* I *loved* that car—fire engine red, sporty, good gas mileage. And my CDs . . . I groaned, hating to think of all the great music I'd lost. I'd have to rebuild my entire collection.

"I'm so sorry, Nicki." Lee obviously felt terrible. "We've never had anything happen like this before."

That was no consolation. "Are you sure it's not there?" I asked hopefully, even though I knew the answer wouldn't be the one I hoped for. The parking lot at Ernie's wasn't all that big, and it's not like a red Honda would be hard to find.

"I'm sure. I went out and walked all around the building before I called you. It's gone."

I wanted to yell, to hit, to break something, but I shut my eyes and took a deep breath instead. "Do I need to come down there and talk to the police?"

"I don't think so," Lee said. "I'll give them your information, and they'll probably just call you. I'm afraid the Atlanta police don't get too excited about stolen cars. Happens every day."

Not to me, it doesn't.

"Okay." I sighed, in defeat. "But get the officer's name for me, will you? I want to be able to call if I need to. I don't want to just sit around and wait for them to call me."

"I will," he said promptly. "I'll call you back with it. You've got insurance, right?" He sounded a little worried at the thought I might not.

"Of course I do."

"I'd call 'em right away." Lee said. "They'll need a copy of the police report, but most policies have a rental car agreement—comes in handy at a time like this."

"I'll do that." *Why weren't you this helpful when it came to keeping an eye on my car?*

"I feel really bad," he said. "I'm sorry," he repeated. "I'll be in touch."

I hung up, staring glumly at the floor.

"Okay, universe," I said, out loud. "You win today. You've kicked my butt. I give up."

CHAPTER 5

The evening got better.

After I'd talked with the police and dealt with the insurance people, I finally got to spend time with Joe, and that made all the difference.

"I'll drop you at the rental car place in the morning," he was saying. It was just after nine, and we were eating Chinese takeout over the wooden chest I used as a coffee table, him sitting cross-legged on the floor while I lounged on the couch. Half-empty bottle of wine, candles flickering, Sting on the CD player. *Yeah, definitely better.*

"You drive a rental for a week or so," he said, "get a check from your insurance company to cover the value of your car, then we get to pick out a new one."

I looked at him archly while I speared a few more noodles from the carton. "*We* get to pick out a new one?" I was perfectly willing to car shop with him, but this was going to be *my* car. I liked small and sporty with a nice-sized trunk, big enough for spur-of-the-moment garage sales, sleek enough to look good on the road.

"*You* get to pick out a new one," he conceded. "But I get to go with you, which means I have input in your decision." He smiled in triumph, reaching for the soy sauce. "Simple logic. *Ipso facto.* We'll look at BMWs first."

"I'm not impressed with your Latin *or* your logic," I teased, "and I can't afford a BMW. You can go with me to look at Hondas, but only to keep the sales guys away until I'm ready to test drive one. You can be my muscle," I teased. "Like my guardian or something."

Joe flicked a snow pea at me, but I ducked.

"You *need* a guardian," he said, to get me back, jabbing a chopstick at me as emphasis. Luckily, he was smiling as he said it. "Here I am, running all over Atlanta on a regular basis to help you with your problems, and yet when *I* need help, you're totally useless." He popped a bit of rice into his mouth, grinning to take the sting from his words as he chewed and swallowed. "Cute, but useless."

Inwardly I cringed. It was his first mention of the way I'd frozen when he'd asked for help with Mary Mathews's CPR.

"I'm sorry about that. I guess I was a little freaked when I saw her lying on the sidewalk, particularly after what happened the night before."

"Oh yes," he said, with a teasing glint in his eye, "your horrible nightmare where a beautiful woman found me attractive."

I arched an eyebrow at him, only willing to be teased so far.

He took the hint and left it alone. After a moment, I asked, "How is she? Any change?"

He shook his head. "She's stable, vitals look good. The cardio boys have her now, so she's in good hands. With any luck there'll be no lasting damage to the heart muscle."

"Good." I meant it. The sooner Mary Mathews recovered and left our lives, the better, as far as I was concerned—mainly because she'd be taking Selene with her.

I hadn't told Joe about the rest of my day yet, saving my encounter with Angie Rayburn for after we'd eaten and enjoyed a glass of wine, but it was time. "Not all your cases have such a happy ending, do they?"

He didn't answer immediately, but I knew what he was thinking—he didn't like to let death win. "No, they don't." He usually spared me the ugly details when it happened, but there had been times when he'd come home subdued, and I'd known it was because someone died on his shift.

"Like the woman at the hospital this morning, the one who committed suicide."

He looked up from his food, green eyes sharp.

"I saw her in the hallway. Her name was Angie Rayburn."

"You saw her?" He abandoned his chopsticks, leaving them in the carton.

"It was in the corridor, right after she died." I remembered the look of panic on Angie's face when she'd come bursting around the corner, begging for help. "She felt terrible about what she'd done. She starting talking . . . babbling, really, about her son and her husband. She was pretty panicky."

"How sad," he said quietly. Joe had a very caring nature—it was one of the things that made him such a good doctor. "Depression during the holidays is more common than people think." He paused, then asked me directly, "Did you help her pass?"

What a nice, simple word: "pass." As if you could pass from this life into the next as easily as leaving a room. For some, the Light gleamed, then blossomed into brilliance, and it really *was* that easy. A step, and then peace.

Unless the Dark slunk in from the shadows, and pulled you into its smothering blackness, miring you down until you were sucked into an altogether different existence.

I shuddered involuntarily, not wanting to remember.

"I don't know if she passed or not," I answered honestly. "I offered to give her family a message for her, though." *Which I hope I didn't come to regret.* I'd gotten myself into some sticky situations trying to help the dearly departed, as Joe was fully aware, having been in most of them with me.

"And?" He was clearly anxious to hear the end of the story. "What did she ask you to do?"

"She didn't ask me to do anything." I shrugged, trying to act nonchalant and probably failing miserably. "We didn't get a chance to talk very long, because something . . ." and this is where I hesitated, ". . . something *else* showed up."

His eyes narrowed. "Something else?"

"I don't know how to describe it," I said, abandoning my carton of lemon chicken. "It was black and cold, like a cloud of oily smoke, floating in the air, filling the corridor." Trying to keep my voice from trembling, I told him all of it. "It came for her—the woman who killed herself. I'm pretty sure it was the Dark."

His expression didn't change.

"The Dark," I tried to explain. "The opposite of the Light. It came for her."

Joe looked at me, speechless, I'm sure, for one of the few times in his life. Sting was singing about fields of gold, while I was talking about things that would make any sane person think I was crazy. I had a surreal instant of déjà vu, surprised at how normal everything seemed.

"Did she go into it?"

I wasn't sure how I felt about this next part. "No." Part of me was proud of myself for keeping her out of the Dark, but that didn't necessarily mean she'd gone into the Light. A *big* part of me was worried I'd stuck my nose where it didn't belong. I mean, what if Angie Rayburn showed up again—would the Dark be with her?

"Why not?" he asked, very quietly.

"I told her to run."

Joe closed his eyes, briefly. "You told her to run."

"Yes, and she did. So did I."

He shook his head, once again at a loss for words.

"And that's it," I finished, a little nervously.

"I haven't seen her since." *Although Ernie Phelps might've.* No need to mention that, though—totally unsubstantiated, and not worth worrying Joe over. "That's all there was to it."

He made an exasperated noise, leaning back against the ottoman behind him. Putting both hands in his hair, he kept them there while he stared up at the ceiling for a moment.

"That's it?"

I could almost see him making mental calculations: *How much trouble has she gotten herself into this time?*

I nodded, wishing I didn't have to tell my boyfriend things like this. Other girls just worried about their boyfriends finding out how much they spent on a pair of shoes, or whether they'd hooked up with someone else over the weekend. I had to worry about my boyfriend dumping me because I saw dead people.

"Okay, then," he said with a sigh. Lowering his arms, he reached forward to pick up his chopsticks. "Let's hope you don't."

And that was it. And that was also when I knew that those girls with the too-expensive shoes and the weekend hookups weren't nearly as lucky as I was.

"You know what?" I slid off the couch and onto my knees, coming over to him on the floor. I took his chopsticks away and laid them down very carefully before climbing onto his lap, straddling his thighs and trapping them between my own. Winding my arms around his neck, I brought my face to his, smiling into his eyes. "You're the best boyfriend ever."

He grinned and slipped his hands down to grab my butt firmly with both hands. Giving both cheeks a squeeze, he maneuvered me into a slightly better position. "I am, aren't I?"

I laughed, enjoying his cockiness.

He nuzzled his face into my neck and kissed me just where I liked to be kissed. His warm breath touched my ear as he murmured, "I think we're a pretty good pair." He kissed me again, nipping the lobe of my ear.

My nipples sprang to life, and I felt him begin to harden beneath me. Rubbing myself against him shamelessly as I offered my neck for more attention, I agreed completely.

And while the candles flickered, the food cooled, and Sting sang about love, we made some of our own, right there on the living room floor.

Sometime later we got up and went into the bedroom, and made some more.

The clock by my bed read 3:00 a.m. I wasn't sure what woke me; the room was dark and the house was quiet. I stretched out a hand for Joe, but the bed beside me was empty.

I lay there drowsily, half-listening, expecting to hear a toilet flush or Joe's footsteps in the hall on his way back to bed, but there was nothing. The harder I listened, the more awake I became. Finally I tossed back the covers and got up.

The hallway was dark except for a faint spill of light from the nightlight I kept in the bathroom. There were no lights in the living room or kitchen, either. Just as I was beginning to seriously wonder where he was, I heard Joe's voice, a low murmur, coming from the living room. He must've gotten paged while I was sleeping, and gone in the other room to return the call.

And least that's what I thought, until I heard a woman's voice, answering him.

I stood frozen, certain I had to be imagining things. But then I heard her again, this time ending whatever she said with a light laugh, and I was frozen no more. My feet carried me double-time into the living room, and what I saw left me dumbfounded.

Joe was standing by the window, stark naked. His head was thrown back, hands out, palms up. He was rock-hard, an erection jutting from his hips.

There was something about his pose that was

incredibly erotic—he looked like some dark, pagan fertility god, gilded by the moonlight that slanted through the blinds. A living statue paying tribute to the night sky; leanly muscled, nude, and completely unashamed.

Most importantly, and perhaps most puzzling, he was alone.

There was no woman, though a moment ago, I'd been certain I'd heard her laugh.

"Joe?"

He didn't answer me. Didn't even move, so I went closer. "Joe? What are you doing?"

It wasn't until I touched him on the arm that he reacted, jerking as if I'd stung him. He swung his head toward me, staring with wild eyes as he pulled away.

"Joe, what is it?" I took another step toward him, touching him on the shoulder this time. "Are you okay? What are you doing in here?" The wildness left his eyes as he took a deep, shuddering breath, and it dawned on me that he might've actually been *asleep*.

"Where is she?" he mumbled, sounding befuddled. "What've you done with her?"

Her?

"Joe," I said sharply, "wake up." I leaned over and switched on the lamp by the couch.

We both flinched at the onslaught of light, even

though I was prepared for it and he wasn't. A quick squint around the room showed it was definitely empty but for Joe and me.

And yet I could've sworn I heard a woman.

"What the . . ." He'd raised a hand to shield his eyes. "What's going on?"

"That's what I'd like to know." I looked pointedly at his erection, which was still rock-hard.

He squinted down at himself, obviously confused. "What time is it?" He glanced around. "Why are we in the living room?"

I wasn't sure why I was mad, but I kinda was. "You tell me."

He looked baffled, then a little sheepish, as he looked down at his now dwindling hardness. "I was dreaming."

"Must've been some dream." I crossed both arms over my middle.

He looked at me blankly for a second, and then, to my surprise, he started to chuckle. "Wow. I haven't sleepwalked since I was a kid."

"That's all you've got to say? Aren't you going to tell me about your dream?"

With a grin, he said, "Nope, no point. People can't be held responsible for what they dream."

I had to agree. In dreams, little green men from Mars could come and paint your kitchen bright purple, using two-headed cows to do it. No one was to blame for what their brain cooked up while they were sleeping.

Exasperated, I gave in. "Okay, okay. But what happened to your clothes?"

"I believe I went to sleep naked." His grin was infectious, daring me to remember why that had been the case. He shook his head, bemused. "No more Chinese food for a while."

"You going to blame the Chinese food for *that*, too?" I teased, pointing at his groin.

"What can I say?" He grinned at me, unashamed. His green eyes glinted as he led me back toward the bedroom. "I could give you all kinds of scientific reasons why men get erections in their sleep, but the truth is, it really was quite a dream."

CHAPTER 6

"I don't care how many times you try those on, they're still going to make your butt look big."

"But they're my size," I argued, twisting in the mirror to see the truth of Evan's statement for myself. "Original Chess King bell-bottoms. The woman I bought them from said she wore them to Woodstock."

"She should've left them there." He eyed me critically in the dressing room mirror, giving a dismissive shake of the head. "The rainbows on the back pockets make your ass look huge. Either that or it was all those extra helpings of mashed potatoes at Thanksgiving."

"Hey!" I hadn't eaten *that* many mashed potatoes.

He turned away with a teasing little smirk, twitching the curtain closed. "Magically delicious they are *not*. Put them back on the rack and hope someone else will buy them."

Frustrated, I stuck my tongue out in his direction, knowing he couldn't see.

"Don't shoot the messenger," he sang out, knowing me all too well. "It's definitely the pockets."

With a sigh, I took them off. Evan's fashion sense was rarely wrong. We disagreed, occasionally, but when he played the "big butt" card I knew better than to argue.

So I slipped back into the black tights and plaid miniskirt I'd been wearing. I was plenty warm enough, particularly with a lightweight black turtleneck and a fleece vest. Once I pulled on my black leather boots, I was resigned to giving up the bell-bottoms. My mental motto of "Look like a million bucks, feel like a million bucks" would never work with them now. With a final peek in the mirror to fluff the pink in my hair, I came out of the dressing room to find Evan flipping through the takeout menus we kept beneath the counter.

"How about sushi for lunch?" he asked absently.

"Ugh."

"Burgers?"

I put the jeans neatly back on the hanger. "Again?"

"Pizza."

I shrugged, not very hungry after all that talk about my butt.

"You're a big help."

"A grilled chicken salad would be good," I said. "Any type of salad, actually."

Evan sighed. "Boring."

"I know you are, but what am I?" I deadpanned, using one of Pee-wee Herman's favorite phrases.

"You've been watching old movies again, I see," he said, giving me a look. "Don't you and Dr. Tall, Dark, and Handsome have better things to do in the evenings?"

I smiled at him archly, remembering exactly what we'd done last night—several times—but not about to share the details. *Warm skin beneath my hands, warm lips against my . . .*

"Never mind," he said hastily. "No offense, but picturing you naked will spoil my lunch. I'm going to call Butch and see if he can bring us something from that new deli over on Highland."

"Sounds good," I answered absently. "Grilled chicken salad for me. I'm going to walk down to the dry cleaner and pick up the sweaters I dropped off last week." One of the nice things about being in a business district like Little Five was that everything you needed was within walking distance. "Maybe I'll even stop by the bookstore on the way to the dry cleaner, do a little Christmas shopping."

He gave me a sideways glance. "I need to do a little Christmas shopping, too."

I knew a hint when I heard one. "Okay, you closed by yourself last night, so when I come back you can leave early. I'll close up tonight."

It was only fair, and it made him happy.

"I'll be back in an hour, tops."

"Don't hurry," he said, with a wave. "If I'm leaving early, you can take a long lunch break. Walk around the block a few times and work off those mashed potatoes."

I gave him the evil eye, but he just laughed.

The air outside was perfect; crisp without being too cold, filled with the scent of wood smoke from somebody's fireplace. Crystal Blue Persuasion had traded their regular New Age music for instrumental Christmas carols today, and the notes of "Angels We Have Heard on High" spilled out onto the sidewalk through the open doors of their shop, mingling with the tinkle of wind chimes. I hadn't been in there in a while, so I ducked inside, thinking a set of wind chimes might make a nice gift for Grandma Bijou. I could just picture her on the big front porch of her house in Savannah, listening to them while she rocked in one of the old wicker rockers.

The smell of incense overcame the scent of wood smoke, and I breathed in deep while I browsed, letting the peaceful atmosphere work its magic. Ten minutes later I was enjoying a beautifully illustrated J.R.R. Tolkien calendar when I felt the presence of someone by my side.

I glanced over to see a young girl, about eight, staring at me. Shoulder-length brown hair with bangs, tucked behind her ears, Kewpie doll lips.

I barely had time to be surprised, because right then I heard a familiar laugh, warm and seductive, which instantly got my attention.

Craning my neck around the calendar display, I saw the person I least wanted to see: Selene, flirting with the guy behind the register.

"She's much better today," Selene was saying. "Thanks for asking." She smiled at him with those ruby red lips, and the guy's eyes glazed over—I mean, you could practically *see* the drool begin.

And no wonder, because she was beautiful. Movie-star beautiful. Flawless.

"Last night, after we left the hospital, my daughter realized she'd lost her blanket. It's pink and white—she last remembers having it here, just before my mother collapsed. Has anyone seen it?"

Eager to be of service, the drooler checked under the counter. "No pink and white blanket in the lost and found, but I'm due for a break—maybe I can help you look for it."

That was about all I could take without puking, but I had nowhere to go. Besides, the little girl was still staring at me. It was creepy, actually, how she was staring at me . . .

"Hello," I murmured, giving her my best fake smile.

She didn't answer.

"Oh no," said Selene to the clerk. "Katie Bug has had that blanket since she was a baby, and it would be such a comfort to her right now. She's been practically hysterical without it."

Katie Bug didn't look hysterical. She looked calm and thoughtful, the expression in her eyes far older than her years.

Let her remember, the little girl had said, floating over my bed. *She brought it on herself, and what can she do about it? She'll just think it was a dream, anyway.*

Abruptly, Kate giggled, as though she'd read my mind.

I broke out in goose bumps. "Damn," I breathed, feeling strongly that whatever ill wind had brought these people into my life was not a fluke. I was back to square one, thinking the weird dream had *not* been a dream, and that their appearance in my store and my neighborhood was no coincidence.

"You said a bad word," Kate said loudly. Spitefully, she added, "Mommy, this lady said a bad word."

So much for slinking away when Selene's back was turned.

"Oh, Nicki, it's you." If I was supposed to be flattered that she'd remembered my name, I wasn't. "We didn't perhaps leave it in *your* store, did we?"

She was smiling in a friendly way, yet the hair went up on the back of my neck.

"No," I answered, evenly enough. "I haven't seen it."

She strolled toward me, tossing her hair back as she shifted her purse on her shoulder. She was wearing red heels today, with black slacks and a camel-colored coat. "Are you sure? Maybe that nice man behind the register has seen it."

I shook my head. "You didn't bring your daughter into my store. You were alone when you came in." I didn't want her in my store again, ever.

"Mother is so much better today," she offered. She stopped to idly pick up a candle, admired it, then put it back on the shelf. "I'm so relieved."

She didn't look relieved—she looked bored. I

hated to be so paranoid, but I suddenly got the feeling that the whole "lost blanket" routine was just an act, and that she'd come to this store because she knew I'd be in it.

"Wasn't it incredibly fortunate that there was a doctor on hand to save her life?" Selene asked mildly, with a smile. "Joe is quite a man."

The little girl giggled again, as the casual use of Joe's name set my teeth on edge. To anyone else in the store, we might appear to be having a polite conversation, but to me, it felt like blades had just been drawn.

"Yes, he is," I agreed, shooting Kate a wary glance. Looking Selene in the eye, I added, "I'm a very lucky woman."

My mind was screaming, *Back off, bitch*.

"Have you two been dating long?" The question was innocent, but I was certain her motives were anything but.

"Over a year." I shoved the calendar back into the rack.

Blue eyes shot to my left hand, then widened in feigned surprise. "What, no ring? You're not engaged?" She came to within two feet of me, the scent of her perfume invading my space.

I quite literally *felt* the challenge she was issuing.

"Not yet," I said coldly, "but that's hardly any business of yours."

She shrugged. "Just making conversation. If I had a man like Joe, I'd make sure he didn't get away."

"Maybe you should go find one, then"—I stepped past her, heading for the door—"because Joe is already taken."

Her cell phone rang. "Oh, wait just a minute, Nicki, please," she said, raising a finger to hold me while she took the call.

Annoyingly, I found myself waiting as she said, "Hello? This is Selene Mathews." She drew Kate closer, an arm around the little girl's shoulder, as she listened to the person on the other end of the line. "Oh no." Perfectly arched brows drew together in perfectly arched distress. "Yes. Yes, we'll be right there." She shut her phone with a click, then said to me, "I'm sorry, I have to go. Mother's taken a turn for the worse."

"Oh—"

But she was already gone, dashing out the door with Katie Bug in tow, a jumble of dark hair and mother/daughterly concern.

The perfect damsel in distress.

Both the guy at the register and some guy browsing the book section nearly broke their necks watching her go.

Was I overreacting? Did my dislike of Selene stem from *who* she was, or from who I *thought* she was? Was she just a hot mess with a sick mother and a bratty kid, on the prowl for a new boyfriend? Or was the predatory gleam in her eye, hidden so well behind that perfect veneer, indicative of a bigger problem?

Either way, I didn't like her.

The scent of the incense I'd enjoyed earlier suddenly became very cloying. I'd lost any interest in shopping, so I left Crystal Blue Persuasion and headed out to run my errands, hoping, quite spitefully, that Selene Mathews would twist an ankle in her mad dash toward the hospital.

"It's not because she's perfect," I murmured to myself, in my own defense, on the way to the dry cleaner. "It's because she's not what she seems, and I don't trust her."

"Mary Mathews didn't make it," Joe said, as we lay naked in each other's arms later that night. "She died this afternoon."

The warm glow I'd been basking in quickly dissolved.

"I'm sorry to hear that." Shocked, actually—I'd pretty much convinced myself that the Mathews women were up to some supernatural mischief, but if that were the case, then how could Mary be dead? You had to be alive to die, which meant Joe had been right all along. "I know you did all you could to save her."

I tried to muster some pity for Selene. It was hard to lose a mother, as no one knew better than I. But somewhere, in the back of my mind, I couldn't help but think: *No mother to visit at the hospital, no more contact with Joe.*

A terrible thought, but I couldn't help it.

"The heart attack brought on a stroke. It was quick. There was nothing we could do." He sighed, stretching beneath my hand. "It's a shame, really. She seemed to be improving. It was tough to have to break the news to the family."

I lifted my head from his chest. "*You* broke the news?"

"My shift, my patient." He was staring at the ceiling, obviously remembering. "I feel so bad for them. Poor Selene . . . single mother, struggling to get by—"

The back of my neck began to tingle.

"—that cute little girl with no father figure in her life—"

My head began to feel light.

"—the grandmother watched Kate after school while Selene worked. Who's going to watch her now?"

"Um . . . day care?" I couldn't believe what I was hearing. Joe treated a lot of people, but he seldom pondered their personal lives—in his profession, there simply wasn't time, and yet here he was, on a first-name basis with the ones I liked the least.

He frowned. "Day care? That seems a bit cold, doesn't it?"

I pushed myself farther up on his chest. "I'm not being cold, I'm being practical." And I was beginning to get practically pissed, though I tried to contain it. "It's what working mothers do, all over America. I'm sure they'll be fine."

He gave me a look. "Is that what you plan to do with your kids?"

My kids? "I don't know," I answered honestly, shocked to my core at how I'd wished he'd said "our kids" instead of "my kids." I stuck with honesty, though. "If I ever do have kids, I do plan to continue working at the store, so . . . maybe."

He didn't say anything.

After a moment, I asked, "What's wrong with day care?"

With a shrug, he answered. "Nothing. It's great for socialization, and can definitely stimulate early learning. I have no problem with it. My sister's kids are in day care, and they're doing fine; bright, happy, well-adjusted. It just seems like in this situation, it's going to be hard enough for that poor little girl to get over the death of her grandmother; throwing her into a totally new environment at the same time seems cruel. I'm surprised you don't have more sympathy for her."

"I have sympathy," I protested, "plenty of sympathy. But believe me, her mother is the type who always lands on her feet. They'll be fine."

An exasperated noise escaped him. "This isn't about Selene, Nicki. The woman's mother just died—it's no time to be jealous."

The way he said her name, as if she were a friend, blew the lid on my temper. I pushed myself off him a little harder than necessary and sat up in the bed.

"I'm not jealous," I said hotly. "But I *am* beginning to wonder why you keep bringing her up."

"I don't keep bringing her up," he said irritably.

"Then why are we talking about her now?"

Joe pulled himself up on an elbow. "Excuse me for telling you something about my day." He was getting angry, too; it was unlike him to use sarcasm.

"Tell me something else," I shot back. "Tell me who was the sickest person to come into the E.R. today, or how the lab screwed up, or something, anything that doesn't have to do with Selene Mathews."

Unsmiling, Joe just looked at me, and for a moment, just a moment, I felt like I'd been judged, and found wanting.

Abruptly he swung his legs over the side of the bed and got up. "I'm going to take a shower," he said. "I'm beat."

He'd been to the gym before he came over, yet he'd been far from tired when he got here. He'd tumbled me into bed and made love to me within five minutes of walking in the door.

Not that I was complaining.

Not about that, anyway.

"That's it?" I sat back on my heels, heedless of my nakedness. "You're just going to walk away and take a shower? We're not going to talk about this?"

"You're obviously being irrational," he said, showing me his all-too-beautiful bare back and bottom as he walked away. "There's nothing to talk about."

I'd just been dissed, make no mistake.

Yet another reason to dislike Selene Mathews.

Knowing it'd be better for both our sakes to let Joe take his shower than to push the issue, I threw myself back down on the bed and dragged on some covers, listening as the rush of water began in the bathroom down the hall. Fuming, I took comfort in the supreme self-control I was exercising by not getting up to flush the toilet while he was showering. In my house, that meant a total lack of water pressure until it filled back up again.

I must've dozed, because the next thing I knew, Joe was leaning over me, fully dressed, smelling of soap and clean male.

"Shhh . . ." he murmured, kissing a bare shoulder. "Go back to sleep. I'm going home to catch up on some paperwork before I hit the sack."

"You're not staying?" Groggy, no longer angry, and hoping he wasn't, either.

"I'll talk to you tomorrow," he said, kissing me again. "Go back to sleep."

I decided to be content with that, and lay there quietly as he gathered up his wallet and keys, then let himself out.

I lay there, awake, for a long time.

Somewhere in the wee hours of the morning, I woke to the sound of someone crying. It was a quiet type of crying, the kind you did in the bathroom stall when you didn't want anyone to hear you.

I moved, sat up in the bed, and the sound stopped.

Afraid, frozen, I listened for it to come again.

It did, in the form of a muffled sob.

"Is someone there?" I scrabbled a hand toward the bedside lamp. Light bloomed, but my room was empty except for a long-neglected treadmill in one corner.

A whimper this time, sounding as if it came from my closet. Goose bumps rose on my arms, and the room suddenly seemed very cold. I wished fiercely for Joe, and for a moment was angry he wasn't there.

But that wouldn't do me any good, now or later. I was going to have to handle it.

"I know you're there," I said boldly, to whatever was in my house. "I can hear you."

There was no answer. I sat there, debating the wisdom of opening the closet door. What I wouldn't give for my dad to be sleeping just down the hall, like he did when I was little. One screech and he'd be there; he'd throw open that door, check for closet monsters, and take a look under the bed for me, too. Then he'd kiss me on the forehead, tuck me back in, and I'd sleep like a baby the rest of the night, knowing that closet monsters were no match for good old Dad.

But Dad wasn't here, and I was going to have to save myself.

More whimpers were coming from the closet.

"Who is it?" I asked loudly, feeling hysteria rising in the back of my throat like vomit. "Who's there?"

"Shh . . ." I heard a woman whisper. "Please be quiet. I can't let it find me."

I was breathing hard, trying not to panic, when

I suddenly realized I could see my own breath. The room was freezing.

"Turn out the light," the woman whispered. "I won't bother you, I promise."

No way was I turning out the light.

"Go away," I said loudly, pulling the covers up to my ears. "Leave me alone." *Which one of the three was it this time? Selene, Kate, or Mary?*

No answer, but I could hear her crying, quietly, trying to muffle her sobs. "I shouldn't have done it," she whimpered. "I can't believe I did it. So selfish, I was so incredibly selfish."

A wave of sadness hit me, and I knew who it was.

"Angie?" A hitch in her sobs told me I was right. "Angie Rayburn?"

"Be quiet," she hissed, sounding on the verge of hysteria herself. "Don't say my name! It will find me!"

Oh boy. She hadn't gone into the Light. She was still here, hiding from the Dark.

In my closet.

"Listen to me," I whispered, looking around the room as I spoke. If any black, smoky goo starting creeping in anywhere, I was going to run like hell and let Angie take her chances this time. "You need to look for the Light. It's really bright and peaceful, and once you see it you'll be okay."

"I can't," she whispered back. "I can't go yet. Josh and David . . . they need me!"

Should've thought of that before you— I didn't say it, though, didn't even let myself finish the thought. It was too mean.

"No offense, but if you want to hang around, you should go haunt your own house, not mine."

"I'm afraid for them," she said urgently. "What if it follows me there?"

"You can't stay here!" I was starting to get panicky. Being a beacon to the dead was one thing, being a beacon to the Dark that *wanted* the dead was something else. "Go hide somewhere else!"

Silence for a moment. "I understand," she finally said, in a very small voice. "I wouldn't want to be around me, either."

Aw, man.

"It's nothing personal," I said uncomfortably.

She didn't answer.

"If you'd just look for the Light, this would all go away."

Still no answer.

"Angie?"

I sat there for a full minute, listening, but I didn't hear anything further. Finally I gathered my nerve and threw back the covers. The hardwood floors felt like ice beneath my bare feet as I padded to the closet. "Angie?" The door opened with a familiar creak, one that I was getting rid of tomorrow with a spritz of oil.

There was no one there.

With a sigh, I went to my dresser and pulled out a thick pair of socks, then pulled the comforter off my bed and headed for the living room.

I might as well turn on the TV. Sleep was going to be hard to come by tonight.

CHAPTER 7

The rental car I was driving was a pale blue PT Cruiser. Its retro look had vaguely appealed to me before I drove it, but a day later I wasn't too impressed—it was just an oddly shaped station wagon.

I missed my car.

Admittedly down in the dumps, I drove slowly through my morning errands; a spin through the drive-through lane for a cup of hot coffee, a stop by the bank, a trip to the pharmacy to refill my birth control pills.

After a not-so-restful night, I tried to look on the bright side: Angie Rayburn was gone, and the Dark hadn't shown up in pursuit of her, so maybe I was good. Maybe she'd stay away, dissipate on her own, and I'd be home free. Joe hadn't left angry, and Selene should now be out of our lives for good. Which left us with nothing to fight about. It hadn't been that bad, really; a minor flare-up that thankfully hadn't gotten out of hand.

By the time I'd finished my errands and my coffee, I was feeling more cheerful. At a red light, I called Joe's cell and left a message on his voice mail. "Hey baby. I love you and I hope you're having a good day. Call me when you get a chance." I hung up, figuring less was more after last night's tension. The ball was in his court now, and Joe had good hands. I knew he'd call me when he could.

I even tried to be positive about the clunky Cruiser. It was a van next to my Honda, but the extra room in the back would come in handy this weekend. The Buckhead Women's Auxiliary was holding their annual Christmas bazaar on Sunday afternoon, and Butch, Evan, and I were going to make an afternoon of it.

A quick phone check with Evan at the store revealed all was quiet, so I decided to run one more errand.

I drove to Bethlehem Baptist Cemetery to visit my mom and dad.

Bethlehem Baptist Church was exactly what it sounded like—a humble little white clapboard in the middle of nowhere, nowhere being the outskirts of Marietta. This was the Georgia foothills, and there were still pockets of the old South everywhere you looked. At some point when I was a kid, I'd developed a macabre fascination with tombstone rubbings, which my parents had indulged by taking me to the local cemeteries. Somehow, we'd found Bethlehem Baptist. It was isolated and peaceful, as most of the graves were from the Civil War era. When my dad found out that there were still a few empty grave sites, he'd bought two of them, one for him and one for Mom.

"Not for you, Nicki." He'd smiled as it he said it, as if banning me from their burial site was like banning me from their bedroom. "You'll be buried next to the love of your life one day, some-where else. Come visit us sometime."

Mom said it was the most romantic thing anyone had ever done for her.

Smiling as I wiped away a tear, I parked the Cruiser under the shade of a large oak, and got out. I was ashamed to admit that I came here less often since I'd starting seeing dead people. I'd been carrying around a niggling fear that going near a graveyard—any graveyard—just wasn't a good idea for a girl in my position.

But I was glad I hadn't let fear rule me, for there were no lost or unhappy spirits under these oaks.

Time had worked its magic here in the quiet woods, granting peace to those who lay beneath these headstones.

The air was crisp, dead leaves crunching under my feet. The only sound was my own footsteps and a birdcall, high in the mostly bare limbs of the trees. I wound my way past the oldest headstones, feeling comfortable enough to rest my hand on one whenever I needed to. In the nine years I'd been coming here, the stones had begun to feel like old friends.

When I got to Mom's stone I patted it in greeting, then did the same to Dad's, lingering in between them as I would've done in life. "Hi, Mom and Dad. I guess you're wondering where I've been."

I always talked with them as though they were there, because, well . . . they were. "Christmas is coming up, and I really miss you guys." The bird trilled again, joyously. "You'll never believe it, but Evan's engaged. Butch is a great guy—you would've liked him. The store's doing well, and I'm still seeing Joe, the guy I told you about last year."

For the next few minutes, I caught them up in bits and spurts, relishing the quiet and grateful to the bird who kept me company. "I think he's the one, Mom," I whispered, near the end. "I wish you two could've met him."

And then I cried, just a little, before rising and

brushing dead leaves from my jeans. I patted the stones in farewell, then headed for the Cruiser.

Halfway there, my cell phone rang, spoiling the quiet with a reminder of reality. I sighed, but kept walking as I dug it out of my purse. The caller ID said STORE.

"Hey, Evan. What's up?"

"Nicki?" He sounded frantic. "Are you *sure* nothing followed you home from the hospital the other day?"

My heart sank. "What happened?"

"Butch stopped in to bring me lunch again. He went in the bathroom to wash his hands, and saw the creepy-looking ghost of an old woman in the bathroom mirror."

Give her a mirror and she's even worse, Selene had said about Mary, as they floated over my bed.

"Say *what*?" I didn't want to believe it.

"He's completely freaked out, Nicki. I'm afraid he's going to faint or something."

The idea of Evan's boyfriend Butch fainting would've been funny if not for the circumstances. Butch was well over six feet, heavily muscled, and bald as an egg. He made his living as a bouncer, even though he was a total pussycat.

"Sit him down and tell him to put his head between his knees." I'd heard that somewhere. "I'll be right there."

"Hurry, Nick," he said, and hung up.

I broke into a little trot, even though I had no idea what I was supposed to do when I got there.

"Evan's overreacting, as usual," Butch said, but he looked a little pale, and he was clutching his mug of hot tea with both hands. He was sitting in the chair behind the counter, the one we called the catbird seat. "It was probably just a weird reflection or something."

"I'm not overreacting," Evan contradicted, his voice a little too high. "You're underreacting. What the hell is going on, Nicki?"

I stowed my purse beneath the counter and took a deep breath. It would do no one any good to get defensive. "I don't know, Evan. I wasn't here, remember?" I put a hand on Butch's brawny shoulder and rubbed it soothingly. "You okay?"

"I'm fine," he insisted, shooting Evan a worried glance. "I just thought I saw something, that's all."

"You came running out of that bathroom like a bat out of hell, Butch Bernaducci," Evan retorted. "Your eyes were as big as saucers. I've never seen you look like that—never."

Butch shrugged, obviously having decided to downplay the incident. "I spook easily. What can I say?" He took a sip of tea.

Evan's lips compressed into a thin line. "Don't

you play the 'big, bad bouncer' card with me," he said. "I know you, and you were scared to death!"

"Why don't you just tell me what happened," I said, knowing full well how touchy Evan could be when he was worried.

Before answering me, Butch leaned back in the chair, doing his best to relax his body language. He reached out and took Evan's hand, pulling him closer to the chair. "It's okay, babe," he murmured. "Calm down."

Evan sighed, letting his shoulders slump. "More tea?" he asked him, in a much softer tone.

Butch shook his head, then looked at me. "Seriously. It was nothing. I was washing my hands at the sink, looked up, and thought I saw an old woman, standing behind me. I whipped around, but there was nobody there."

"An old woman?" I asked him faintly, feeling more and more doomed.

"I imagined it," Butch said stubbornly, squeezing Evan's hand. "I didn't get home until almost four this morning, I haven't had a lot of sleep."

Evan looked at me mutely, obviously not buying it. Unfortunately, my buddy knew all too well that I was a dead-chick magnet, and it was entirely possible that what Butch had seen was all too real.

"I'll go check the bathroom," I said bravely, though I felt anything but brave.

"I'll go with you," Butch said, and I could've hugged him. I knew his concern was mainly to allay Evan's fears, but I'd take whatever support I could get.

He stood up, handed Evan his mug of tea, and together we walked down the hall that led to the bathroom. Evan stayed behind, watching us nervously. The bathroom door was wide open, and the light was on—Butch had obviously left in a hurry. Screwing up my nerve, I walked in and looked around, then looked in the mirror. Aside from me and Butch, who was standing in the doorway behind me, there was no one reflected in it.

"See?" he said loudly, for Evan's benefit. "The lights are on but nobody's home. I just need some sleep."

I turned around, looking Butch in the eye. Evan couldn't see me as I mouthed the words, "Thank you." I knew full well what he was doing. If Evan got it into his head that the store bathroom was haunted, it could be the end of Handbags and Gladrags. I couldn't keep it going without my best bud. At best, he'd insist on moving the store to another location, but we'd just recently renewed our three-year lease.

"There's nothing here, Evan." I stuck my head out the door so he could see me. "The bathroom's empty."

"I don't care if it's empty or not," he retorted. "Talk to it. Tell it to leave."

I really wished he'd stop saying "it." With a resigned sigh, I straightened up and turned around to face the mirror again. "If there's anyone here, could you please leave us alone? You're scaring my friend."

"*Friends*." Evan called out from down the hall. "It scared Butch, too."

I couldn't help myself. "Stop saying 'it,' Evan, and be quiet. On the off chance there *is* someone here, you could provoke them."

"Hmph," I heard him mutter. "It doesn't seem to mind provoking *me*."

"Okay, enough of this," Butch said, behind me. "For the last time, I'm sure it was nothing. I'm just tired."

I turned around, flipped out the light, and stepped out of the bathroom. "Why don't you take Evan home and get some sleep, Butch?"

He glanced at Evan, then back at me. "Maybe we should stay."

I smiled at him, knowing he was worried about leaving me here alone. Big as he was, he couldn't do a thing to protect me, but it was sweet that he was willing to try.

"Go home, Butch. I'll be okay."

* * *

The store was very quiet after they left.

I'd been there alone many times in the past and I planned on being alone there many times in the future, so I refused to let the quiet bother me. I could've turned on some music—I usually did, particularly when I was there by myself—but not today.

Instead I locked the front door, flipping the CLOSED sign toward the sidewalk. I was going to find out what was going on, and I was going to deal with it. I'd fought for my life before—my friends, my house, my store, my relationship with Joe—and I'd won.

I had to believe that I'd win this time, too.

I stood at the front door for a moment, looking through the glass onto the streets I walked every day, listening to the faint yet familiar sound of traffic on Moreland. This was my world, and I had to sharpen my wits to save it, so I'd start with what I knew.

Three spirits had visited me the other night in my room. They'd shown up the next day, very much alive, right here in Little Five Points.

Selene seemed determined to needle me from the start, flaunting herself in my store, teasing with Evan, and finding a way to get Joe's undivided attention.

And what was up with that, anyway? Faking a

heart attack was a masterful stroke, but why have Mary fake her own death, too? Seems like Selene would get more face time with Joe if her so-called mother was alive but lingering.

Maybe the three of them thought it would be more fun for Mary to haunt my store than to lie in a hospital bed all day.

"Great," I muttered, wishing the thought hadn't occurred to me. It was just twisted enough to make sense.

I was so screwed.

Closing my eyes briefly, I swallowed hard and got a grip. Right now, right this second, I had a more immediate problem; was my store being haunted?

Heart pounding, I walked down the hallway to stand in the bathroom doorway.

I took a deep breath and flipped on the light.

"Mary?" Who else could it be? "I know you're here."

No answer.

"I remember the other night, you know, and I recognized Selene when she came in here earlier."

Nothing.

My intent was to be bold, to show no fear, but I had an ulterior motive, too—maybe Mary could be reasoned with. Old people usually liked me.

"I know what's going on," I lied.

Silence.

"Talk to me, Mary. Let's work this out."

The mirror showed a dark-haired girl with a hopeful look on her face, and I almost felt sorry for her in one of those "oh no she's about to be murdered" movie kind of ways. She was me, of course, and I didn't look nearly as brave as I was pretending to be. Staring at myself in the mirror, a memory surfaced; a slumber party when I was twelve, when my girlfriends and I dared each other to go into a darkened bathroom and play "Bloody Mary."

A total freak-out game, perfect for inspiring squeals of terror among pajama-clad teenage girls. All alone in the dark, you'd light a candle, face the mirror, and say, "Bloody Mary" three times. Legend had it that anyone who dared say it the third time would go insane.

Say it.

The instant those words came to my brain, the bathroom lights went out. I screamed, I couldn't help it, and leapt back through the doorway into the hall.

It would've been so easy to grab my purse and get the hell out of Dodge right then and there, but the sudden fright made me furious. I was no longer a pajama-clad teenage girl, and I wasn't going to act like one.

"Okay," I said, admittedly jittery. I started pacing the hallway to regain my calm. "Whatever." I took a deep breath and raised my voice a little, not particularly eager to get near the bathroom just yet. "I don't know why the three of you decided to start trouble with me, but whatever your problem is, you've picked the wrong girl to mess with." I was proud that my voice wasn't shaking, because my knees sure were. "I'm not easily spooked."

Hah.

A loud thump immediately made a liar out of me—I must've jumped a foot. The noise had come from the office, down the hall to the right. I forced myself to take the few steps to that doorway and looked in—the magazine Evan had been reading earlier was lying on the floor in front of the desk. I bent over to pick it up, and heard a scraping noise, which seemed to be coming from the front of the store. Tossing the magazine onto the desk, I headed that way, only to let loose another shriek of fright at the woman standing by the cash register.

She hadn't been there a couple of seconds ago. She showed no reaction, just stood there, unmoving. And then I realized why—it was one of the store mannequins. Elizabeth Taylor, dressed in a glittery holiday cocktail dress I'd put on her just yesterday. She'd been moved from her place in Better Dresses.

I had goose bumps on my arms, and my feet felt like lead, but I made them move. I walked slowly toward her, not knowing what to expect. Nothing happened, though; her blank-eyed violet gaze was fixed on the wall, as always, her pose as wooden as ever.

"Very funny," I said loudly, to whoever'd done it, and was rewarded (if you can call it that), with an old woman's cackle. "I heard you," I called out, refusing to be cowed. This was an obvious attempt to scare the bejeebers out of me, but I wasn't ready to hide under the bed just yet. "I know it's you, Mary."

No answering cackle this time, which I wasn't sure was good or bad.

Silence. She evidently liked to play hide-and-seek.

Grimly, I took the mannequin around the waist and dragged her back to where she'd been standing. I'd never feel the same about Elizabeth Taylor again—Evan could dress her from now on.

"Ouch!" I felt a pinch, but there was no one there when I spun around.

Rubbing my arm and setting my chin, I went back down the hall to the office, determined to do some research and find out what the hell was going on. This was all too weird, and I was just as capable of using Google as anyone was.

"This is my office," I said as I sat down at my desk, "and my store. You're not running me off. I'm ignoring you now," and got down to business.

Fifteen minutes later, having determinedly ignored tapping noises in the ceiling and scratching sounds from the file cabinet, I hit pay dirt. A Web page about ghosts and hauntings led to an article about visitations vs. nightmares:

> The "mare" in "nightmare" does not come from a female horse, but from the word "mara," an Anglo-Saxon and Old Norse term for a demon that sat on sleepers' chests, giving them bad dreams. Those suffering from vivid dreams while experiencing sleep paralysis are often said to be victims of "Old Hag Syndrome."

I groaned aloud, unable to help myself.

Quiet, you old hag, the little girl had said. *Why should you be the only one to have any fun? Choke this one, smother that one . . . I mean, really, Mary. Do you think we don't know what you do to them when you're alone?*

Mara. Mary.

I took a deep breath, staving off panic.

Okay, so were all three of them some kind of dream smothering monsters? Selene seemed to prefer the more direct, human-to-human method of torment, and I knew nothing at all about Kate's methods.

Yet.

The three of them were an unholy triad of different ages and different styles, it seemed. I sighed, and went back to reading. Clicking along, a snippet of information regarding the "Triple Goddess" caught my eye.

"Mother, maiden, crone," I read, and my heart beat faster.

> *The three main aspects of femininity embodied as one. This concept was embraced by a variety of ancient cultures, and continues to be a central idea in neo-pagan theology. The notion of a female triad is directly related to the three phases of the moon (new, full, and waning) as well as the basic theory of reincarnation.*

A footnote filled with links directed me to see "Brigid," "the Moirae," "the Fortunae," and "the Norns," which I did, reading for quite some time.

Holy crap on a cracker.

They were real, they were ancient, and judging by the mischief they'd already stirred up, they were going to be a major pain in the ass.

CHAPTER 8

A psychic disturbance of this magnitude required backup. As much as I loved Joe, I didn't feel like we were on the same wavelength in this situation. Bringing up Selene again would only start trouble, and besides, I had a much better resource.

My sister, Kelly, and her boyfriend, Spider, were a fountain of information when it came to the paranormal. They lived in Savannah, where Spider made his living as a haunted tour guide. Kelly lived with our Grandma Bijou in a stately old mansion called the Blue Dahlia, rumored (and rightly so) to be haunted.

She and Spider were obviously made for each other, and Kelly couldn't be happier in that drafty old house full of creaky floors and hidden secrets. We were twins, though neither of us had even known the other existed until just last year, when fate finally brought us together. We hadn't known about our grandmother, either, though she'd known about us. Grandma Bijou was quite the character; a "sensitive" who lived a double life as Leonard Ledbetter, an elderly man who ran a florist shop, and as Bijou Boudreaux, aging Southern belle extraordinaire, stalwart denizen of Savannah society. Her daughter Peaches had been our birth mother, and made her living as a psychic, as the "knack" for communicating with the dead seemed to run in our family. It had been at Bijou's urging that Peaches had given us up for adoption, and nobody's fault but the adoption agency's that we'd been separated. Peaches was gone now, killed in the car accident that brought Kelly and me together, and we were at peace with the decisions Bijou and Peaches had made; they'd only wanted to give us a shot at normal lives, far away from the world of spirits.

Hah. Best-laid plans oft go awry, as they say.

Kelly answered on the third ring. "Hey, Nicki."

"Hey. I've got a problem." No need to mince words with your sister. "Three female spirits are after me, and I don't know what to do. Have you ever heard of the Moirae?"

"Are you kidding me?" She obviously had. "The Three Fates? Tell me what happened."

I told her, as best I could, about the dream that hadn't been a dream.

"I couldn't move or speak or—"

"Sleep paralysis." She sounded like a college student offering the correct answer to a quiz question.

"Old Hag Syndrome," I said, just a teeny bit proud of myself for knowing that before Kelly did. "Except I wasn't asleep, and I've since seen them all in the flesh. They showed up in Little Five the next day. They're out to cause trouble, Kel—" I glanced toward the hallway. "They're already causing trouble."

Quiet now, she listened.

"There's three of them; a dark-haired woman, a young girl, and an old woman."

"Mother, maiden, crone," she murmured, confirming the direction of my Internet searches. "It's a common representation of the Fates; all three phases of womanhood."

"The brunette is hardly the motherly type," I said sourly, "but she's pretending to be. The girl is pretending to be her daughter, and the old woman is pretending to be the grandmother."

"I don't understand," Kelly said. "Why?"

"I don't know. She faked a heart attack . . ."

"Who faked a heart attack?"

"The old one."

"Why?"

Having Kelly ask me aloud the same questions I was asking myself actually made them easier to sort through.

"To get Joe involved, I guess."

There was a silence. I knew Kelly was thinking hard, and took comfort in that. Even if I screwed up and ended up dead, I'd discovered it was invaluable having a sister who understood my very strange life, and had my back.

"What time did all this happen?" she asked quietly.

In my mind, I immediately saw the blue numbers on my clock radio. "Three a.m.," I said without hesitation. "Exactly."

"The witching hour," she murmured, almost to herself.

"Say what?" I didn't like the sound of that.

"Three a.m. is known as the witching hour," she repeated. "The time when evil spirits are the strongest. It's supposedly the inversion of the time when Christ died on the cross, which is said to be three p.m."

"How do you know this stuff?"

"Paranormal forum boards, mostly, but you can Google it. People who work in hospitals claim that more people die at three a.m. than any other time of day."

Great.

"Did the old woman say anything to you?"

"She didn't say anything." Another mental roadblock loomed. "She died."

"She died? But you just said the heart attack was faked." Her confusion was clear.

"I don't completely understand what's going on, Kelly—that's why I called you."

"Does Joe know what's going on?"

I sighed. "Yes and no. I told him about the dream, but he's convinced that Mary was human because of all the medical stuff—the CAT scans, X-rays, blood work. He doesn't know anything about Butch seeing the old woman's ghost in the store's bathroom mirror."

The noise she made could only be described as strangled. "The old woman's ghost in the bathroom mirror?"

"Let me finish," I said, and did. "So Mary, the old lady, has supposedly died, and now it seems that she's hanging out here in the store. She spooked Butch pretty badly."

"Have *you* seen her?"

"No." *Thankfully.* "But she moved the Elizabeth Taylor mannequin, played with the lights, and has generally been trying to annoy the hell out of me while I looked up all this stuff on the Internet."

A loud bang made me jump, followed by what sounded like clapping. "I'm still ignoring you," I said loudly, not amused.

"If she died at the hospital, then how can she be one of the Moirae?" Kelly was thinking out loud. "Could an entity become human for the time it took to die?"

Good question, but not one that concerned me at the moment. "Does it matter?"

"No, not really. Definitely supernatural, regardless." I couldn't miss the teeny note of envy in her voice. Kelly could see and hear the dead, too—male spirits, while I saw only female ones—but she hadn't seen one in a long time, despite being fascinated with them, and having a boyfriend who considered himself a paranormal investigator. As far as I knew, she and Spider spent a lot of time *looking* for ghosts, without actually finding them. Apparently the spirits of Savannah didn't seem to show themselves very often, or, as I'd begun to suspect, once you actively started looking for them, you lost their attention.

Making myself a mental note to take up ghost hunting as soon as I got a life, I answered Kelly with, "None of that matters. I need you to help me get rid of her."

"Hmm." That noise meant she was getting down to business. I heard a rustling, then, "I'm going to put the phone down while I use the computer. Be right back." Then nothing but the click of keys.

I stared at the Elvis Costello poster on the wall opposite my desk, waiting patiently. *You and me, Elvis—the angels wanna wear my red shoes.*

Meaning, every time you got happy, the universe wanted a piece of it.

My patience was finally rewarded when Kelly came back to the phone and said, "There's not much here—old legends and stories, mostly, but I did find an old English charm to ward off the Night Mare, also known as the Old Hag."

"Let's try it," I said, willing to try anything. My last experience with charms had been surprisingly effective. Of course, that had involved turning some Wicca widdershins, but in the end, it had worked.

"Repeat after me," she said, and I did.

St. George, St. George, our ladies' knight,
He walked by day, so did he by night.
Until such time as he her found
He her beat, and he her bound,
Until her troth she to him plight,
She would not come to him that night.

"Okay then," I said, feeling incredibly stupid. "I'm sure that fixed everything."

Surprisingly, the store stayed quiet while we talked a little longer. We finally hung up with promises to be careful and to call each other as we learned more, and I felt a bit better. I'd stood up for myself, and the sky hadn't fallen. Maybe I could keep it patched up there with duct tape while I figured out what was going on.

I closed up the shop just after five, then headed home; I wanted to be there before it got dark. After making myself a sandwich for dinner and washing it down with a glass of merlot, I tried calling Joe again, but got his voice mail, so I left him another message, hoping he was just busy, not avoiding me.

Five minutes later the phone rang, and I smiled to see it was him, returning my call.

"Hey baby."

"Hey," he said, sounding distracted. "Is everything okay? I'm kind of busy."

Taken aback by his abruptness, I kept it lighthearted. "Everything's okay. I just hadn't talked to you all day, that's all."

"It's crazy down here today, Nicki. We're shorthanded. I probably won't see daylight until tomorrow afternoon."

Tamping down a surge of disappointment, I

said, "That's too bad. I was hoping you could come over later."

"Not tonight, babe, I'm sorry."

Silence.

Normally I understood completely when his schedule got crazy, but this time, I had to admit, it bothered me. Maybe it was because of last night's tension, but I felt like I needed to be near Joe to make sure we were good. Besides, I was pretty nervous being here all alone tonight; last night I'd had a ghost in my closet, and today I'd had an old hag in my store.

Who knew what would show up next?

Despite my disappointment, all I said was, "Okay. I guess I'll see you whenever."

He picked up on the obvious. "Hey, listen . . . I didn't mean to . . ." Trailing off, he tried another tack. "How was your day today?"

"It was fine," I lied, not in the mood to share. Since the bad part of my day revolved around a topic that seemed to be a sore point between us, I didn't see the point. "Everything's fine. You go back to work and call me when you're able."

Another brief silence, broken by the ding of an elevator and the murmur of voices—a hospital never sleeps. "Okay, I will. Love you, babe."

"Love you, too."

For just a moment, I stared at the phone in my

hand, thinking. He'd initially seemed distant, and I'd gotten my feelings hurt. It was as simple as that.

"You're overreacting, Styx," I told myself. "Get a grip."

Determined to behave normally, I did some laundry and watched a little TV while I put out some Christmas decorations, including the snowman collection I'd been working on since I was twelve. Every year my mom and I would pick out a new one, and my favorite was the last snowman we'd bought together, hand-painted porcelain from a craft fair.

Mom always loved craft fairs.

I found myself avoiding the mirror when I went in to wash my face and brush my teeth, and I seriously considered leaving the lights on while I slept. The dark didn't seem to be my friend these days. In the end, I couldn't bring myself to do any more than settle myself on the couch with a blanket, a pillow, and an old black-and-white Christmas movie on TV, knowing I'd fall asleep eventually.

Jimmy Stewart was busy having a wonderful life, but mine wasn't going so hot at the moment.

CHAPTER 9

A long pointy nose, coal black eyes, and a leering grin . . . those were the first things I saw when I opened my eyes the next morning.

I struck out blindly. The snowman on the coffee table went flying across the room, bounced off a chair, and hit the floor with a loud crack.

"Dammit!" I'd already slid halfway off the couch and couldn't stop myself as I hit the floor, landing hard on a hip and an elbow, the comforter tangled around my lower half. I lay there, feeling stupid and dazed. A snowman . . . I'd been freaked out by a porcelain snowman. "Way to go, Styx," I muttered.

Talking to myself didn't help, except to wake me

up a little. What I really needed was coffee and a shower, so after a second or two, I got up to get them both, wincing at the pain in my hip.

I checked on poor Frosty first. His top hat was chipped and his broom was broken—a day that started like this was bound to be bad news.

Strangely enough, when the phone rang at eight-thirty, it was good news.

"Ms. Styx? This is Detective Irwin, Fayetteville Sheriff's Department. I'm calling to let you know your car has been found." Fayetteville was about thirty minutes south of Atlanta. "No damage that we can see, and we got the kid who was driving it."

"It was stolen by a kid?"

"Teenage boy, fourteen. I assume you'll be pressing charges?"

The "bad news" feeling came back. "Um . . . what's his name?"

A rustle of papers, then the detective said. "Joshua Rayburn. A runaway from Atlanta. His dad reported him missing yesterday morning."

Great. Angie Rayburn's kid had stolen my car. What were the odds of that?

I had a sudden flashback to the time I'd died, and how I'd known, if only for a little while, that everything in the universe was connected, an infinite spiderweb of chances and possibilities.

A zig here, a zag there, but you still ended up in the same place. No point in worrying over coincidences, flukes, or twists of fate; life was what it was, and it was how you dealt with it that mattered.

With a sigh, I gave in. I'd obviously been dragged into Angie Rayburn's life—and death—for a reason, and whatever it was, avoiding it wouldn't help. "Would it be possible for me to talk to him?"

"That's up to his father, ma'am. If I were you, I wouldn't waste my time—this kid's obviously heading down a bad road."

You're not me. "I know the family. Josh just lost his mother; he's going through a tough time." I don't know why I cared what he thought about Josh Rayburn—I didn't even know the kid—but it seemed important not to lump him in with a bunch of juvenile delinquents.

His mom couldn't stick up for him anymore, but I could.

"Sounds like you've already made up your mind not to press charges," he said shortly. "We'll cut him loose, but take my number, just in case, and you'll have to come down to the station to claim your car. It's up to you, but you'd probably be doing the kid a favor by teaching him a lesson now, while he's got a chance at learning it. I've seen too many kids end up in jail because they got off with a hand slap instead of being held accountable for their actions."

"I'm sure you have, Officer." Sadly, I knew what the detective was saying was true, but I didn't think pressing charges was the way to help Josh.

Helping Josh was bound to be a lot more complicated, and I wasn't quite sure how to go about it. Somehow, I figured the universe would show me the way.

Getting to the Fayetteville Sheriff's Department to pick up my car meant I would need a ride. I couldn't drive the rental car, because then I'd have no way to get it back to Atlanta. I couldn't call Joe, because he'd be either working or sleeping, and either way couldn't help.

I called Evan.

"You're in luck," he said, sounding much more chipper this morning than he had the day before. "Butch spent the night. He can drop you on his way home."

Butch lived in Peachtree City, which was in the same general area as Fayetteville.

I was almost afraid to ask, but I did anyway. "Are you going to be okay at the store by yourself while I'm gone?"

"I'll be fine," he said, without any hesitation. "If you can be there alone, I can be there alone."

An unexpected lump rose in my throat. I wasn't used to Evan being brave, but I'd take as much bravery as I could get these days.

"Listen to you," I teased, to get past the lump. "I'll have to start calling you Rambo."

"Right," he retorted, "like I'd be caught dead wearing camo pants."

A half hour later, Butch pulled into the driveway and honked his horn. I grabbed my purse, locked up, and slid into his front seat. There wasn't a lot of conversation beyond the initial pleasantries—I was tired and Butch was subdued. We stopped for lattes before hitting the road, which helped. Still, everything was fine until we got near Fayetteville, and Butch brought up what happened at the store the day before.

"I have to ask you something," he said.

Conversations that started out with "I have to ask you something" were rarely good, but I just smiled bravely and said, "Ask away."

"It was real, what I saw yesterday, wasn't it?"

"I honestly don't know, Butch. I wasn't there."

He shot me a "shame on you" glance. "C'mon, spooky chick. Even if you saw what I saw, you weren't about to admit it in front of Evan. But since Evan's not here . . ."

I sighed, not willing to BS my best friend's boyfriend, particularly when he could smell BS a mile away. "I didn't see anything, I swear, but there's some stuff going on I can't really explain."

Didn't want to, either.

Butch wasn't going to let it go. "Like what?"

I wasn't sure I wanted to tell him about the moving mannequin or the rapping noises at the store, and trying to explain about the triple Trio of Trouble was just out of the question. How much could I really expect somebody *normal* to believe?

"There are things out there other than ghosts, Butch, and I think . . ." How to put this? ". . . I think some of them are out to cause me as much trouble as they possibly can."

He was quiet at that, frowning.

"There's the Fayetteville exit," I pointed out, and we pulled off the highway, following the map to the sheriff's office I'd printed off the Internet.

"Do I need to be worried about Evan?" he asked, after making the final turn onto Johnson Avenue.

I wished I had a definitive answer for him, but I didn't. "No more so than usual, I guess."

He didn't seem to like that answer.

We pulled into the parking lot of the sheriff's office, and Butch slid his car into a visitor's spot. He put it in park, then shifted on the seat to give me his full attention. "You really *didn't* see what I saw, did you?"

The serious look on his face was making me nervous. "No. Why?"

"I didn't tell Evan, but that old woman in the mirror . . ." He looked away, swallowed. "She had blood all over her face."

I felt a chill. Bloody Mary, indeed.

Their bag of dirty tricks just got deeper and deeper.

"No wonder you were freaked out," I said faintly, unsure of what else to say. "Why didn't you just grab Evan and get the hell out of there?"

"I probably should have." He scrubbed a hand over his bald head, a sure sign he was thinking hard, then took a deep breath. "But if I had"—he looked at me steadily—"he'd probably never go back. He loves that store, and he loves you, and I don't want to come between him and what he loves."

My throat tightened, and I found myself wanting to cry. What a great guy Butchie was. Evan was lucky to have him.

"I also don't want him running scared, jumping at shadows the rest of his life. If there's one thing I've learned as a bouncer, it's that you can never let a bully get the upper hand."

"A bully?" That was an interesting way of looking at such a scary experience.

"Absolutely," Butch said, nodding. "That old lady obviously wanted to scare the crap out of me—and she succeeded—because she knew there was nothing I could do about it. I mean, even if she was real, what was I going to do, hit an old woman?"

I smiled a little at that. Even though he was a bouncer, Butch was a lover, not a fighter.

"Evan and I have talked about this before," he said. "You know . . . the whole 'my best friend sees ghosts and what can I do about it' thing. The way I look at it, he has two choices. He can break things off with you"—he raised a hand before I could protest—"or he can toughen up a little, and face these things head-on, just like you do."

"So that's why he was so brave today," I said. "He even gave me a lecture a couple of days ago— said I needed to learn how to say no to the spirits more often. Told me I needed to toughen up."

Butchie smiled. "That's my boy," he said. His smile faded. "But I have to tell you, Nicki . . . if I start to feel like he's in any real danger, I'm going to change my mind and start pushing for option number one. You got me?"

I had two choices myself: I could get pissed at Butch for threatening to pull Evan away, or I could respect the man for trying to protect my best friend.

Even if it was from me.

"I understand." Forcing myself to move, I unhooked my seat belt and opened the car door, ready to get out. "I love him, too, you know."

"I know." He reached out and grabbed my hand before I got out. "I wish I . . . I wish *we* could do more to help you, Nicki. It must be tough to have to deal with shit like this all the time."

I met his eyes, big, brown, and full of sympathy, then leaned in and kissed his cheek. "You've already helped me more than you know, Butch."

And he had, reminding me that love and loyalty were more important than fear, and that bullies came in all shapes and sizes: young, old, and—unfortunately for me—brunette, sexy, and disgustingly gorgeous.

CHAPTER 10

The inside of the Fayetteville Sheriff's Department was pretty much what I expected it to be: gray walls covered with antidrug and anticrime posters, uncomfortable-looking chairs, nondescript carpet. The officer behind the desk took my name and asked me to have a seat in the empty lobby. It took a while, but eventually the paperwork was processed, my ID confirmed, and the car key I'd left at Ernie's garage handed over with instructions on where to find my car in the department's rear parking lot.

"You were lucky," the grizzled old cop behind the counter said. "Most of the time we don't get 'em back, and if we do, they're usually trashed;

broken windows, broken steering column, that kind of stuff. Yours looks to be in pretty good shape."

I breathed a sigh of relief. "Where did you find it?"

He gave the paperwork a cursory glance. "Report says it was in the Wal-Mart parking lot, over on Pavillion. Kid who stole it was asleep in the backseat. Store security said it had been there overnight, and when they saw the kid, they alerted us."

"Is he still here?"

"The kid?" The cop nodded. "His dad showed up just before you did. Should be out any minute."

Right on cue, an elevator dinged, and out stepped a red-faced, sullen Joshua Rayburn and a middle-aged man with a receding hairline and dark circles under his eyes. The tension between the two was palpable.

"We'll talk about it when we get home, Josh," the older guy was saying, as they stepped from the elevator.

"No, we won't," Josh shot back. "You'll be too busy."

"Maybe if you helped around the house more," the man, who was obviously Angie's husband, David Rayburn, returned, with an edge in his voice, "I'd have more time for you."

"Hah," Josh said sarcastically, heedless of the officer and me overhearing every word, "like I wanna spend more time with *you*."

David was striding toward the door, a few steps ahead of Josh, so the boy didn't see the wince of pain his sarcasm caused.

"Excuse me," the cop behind the counter called out to the Rayburns, startling me. "This lady is here to pick up her stolen car. I think you owe her an apology, son."

Both David and Josh paused, turning in my direction.

The officer gestured at Josh to come over. "It's the least you can do," he said sternly. "If she wanted to press charges, you'd be in juvie right now."

I'd had no idea this was going to happen. The crusty cop was obviously old school, and out to teach Josh Rayburn whatever lesson he could, even if it was just a lesson in good manners.

The boy flushed, looking angry and uncomfortable. He didn't want to meet my eyes, just a quick glance before he looked away, staring at the floor.

"Josh," his dad said, warningly.

Josh's head came up, but he still wasn't looking at me. He sighed, as if bored with the whole thing, and grudgingly said, "I'm sorry. I'm sorry I stole your car."

I waited a heartbeat longer than I needed to reply, "I'm sorry about your mother."

That got his attention, as well as his father's. Josh stared at me, shocked, while David sighed heavily, raising a hand to his face.

"You knew my mom?" Josh's stare was unblinking now. "Is that why your car was parked in front of our house?"

In front of his house? I shook my head, confused.

"I didn't know her well. We only met a couple of times." *And you don't need to know when.*

I looked at David, who nodded, saying nothing, as though he didn't quite trust his voice at the moment.

My heart went out to him. He was miserable, grieving, and forced to deal with a rebellious teenager when he least needed the hassle.

"Would it be possible for me to talk with your son alone, just for a minute? We can sit right over there." I indicated the hard plastic chairs in the lobby. "It won't take long."

"I'm not his son," Josh said rudely, shooting David a look. "He's my stepfather."

David straightened, visibly pulling himself together. "I'm the only father you've got," he said firmly, "and you'll show *me* and this young lady"—he pointed in my direction as he stared Josh down—"some respect."

The cop next to me gave a grunt of approval.

"Now go put your butt in that chair, and apologize for what you did."

I didn't wait to see if Josh did as his stepfather said, just walked toward the chairs as if I expected him to follow.

Thankfully, he did. The family drama seemed to be over, at least for the moment.

Taking a seat at the far end of the lobby, I looked at Josh. Red-rimmed eyes, wearing the same black clothes I'd seen him wearing in the E.R. three days ago. Bravado aside, he looked thin, hungry, and very, very unhappy.

"Look," he said abruptly, "I'm sorry I stole your car." A rebel to the end, he didn't sit, just planted himself in front of me, arms crossed. He had a small silver eyebrow ring on the right that I hadn't noticed before. "I'd just had a fight with my dad, and it was sitting right there in front of my house with the key in the ignition." He shrugged, shoving a lock of dirty black hair out of his eyes. "I wanted to get away. So I took it."

I had no time to wonder how my car could've possibly turned up in front of his house. This might be my only shot at getting this kid a message from his mom, and putting Angie Rayburn to rest was more important than I wanted to admit. I didn't want to keep looking over my shoulder for the Dark, and Angie shouldn't have to, either.

"You ran away," I said, stalling as I stated the obvious.

"I didn't do anything to it," he returned defensively. "Not a scratch. All your CDs are still there."

"Thanks for that. My name is Nicki, by the way."

His eyes flicked over me and away. "I know," he said. "I saw your registration in the glove box."

Little snoop.

"So I'm sorry, okay?" He was anxious to get away, and I didn't blame him.

"Listen," I said, raising a hand. "I need to tell you something really important."

He gave me a look I recognized as one I would've given at fourteen if a stranger'd said something like that to me.

I resisted the urge to sigh. "Your mom wants you to know that she loves you," I said quietly, "and that she's very sorry for what she did."

His face went pale, his look turning stony.

"She was overwhelmed with depression, it was nobody's fault." He said nothing, so I went out on a limb. "She loved you, Josh, and she loved your stepdad. She feels really bad about what she did, and doesn't want you two fighting, particularly now."

"What are you, some kind of *counselor* or something?" The scorn in the kid's voice surprised me; grief had turned to hostility in the blink of an eye. "I said I was sorry for stealing your car, so, like, *whatever* to the rest of it." He waved a dismissive hand in my direction as he turned away, striding toward the station house door.

"Joshua," called out David, behind us. "Joshua!"

Josh ignored him, walking through the glass door to the outside, where he stood near the flagpole, arms crossed, kicking his shoe in the dirt.

I heard a heavy sigh, then David came up beside me. "I apologize for my son, miss. We're going through a hard time right now."

"It's okay. My car is back, safe and sound, and so is your son." I tried to smile at him. "You must've been worried."

The poor guy looked haggard, strained to the breaking point. Did I dare try to tell him what I knew about Angie? It hadn't worked out well with Josh, so I was hesitant.

"You're very kind," he said, scrubbing a hand over his face. "Thank you." He stared out the glass door toward his stepson and gave a heavy sigh. "There's a memorial service for Angie"—his lower lips trembled, then steadied—"tomorrow at

St. Patrick the Divine, four o'clock, if you'd like to attend." He settled his gaze on me for a second. "How did you know her?"

"We met at a book club," I lied. "It was a long time ago. I ran into a mutual friend who told me what happened."

"Yes," he said, nodding faintly. "Angie always loved to read."

He turned and headed toward the door. Before I lost him for good, I offered, "She talked about you." He stopped, his back to me. "I remember. I could tell she loved you very much. If she . . ." I hesitated, uncertain what to say. ". . . if she was able, I'm sure she'd tell you she was very sorry."

His shoulders, already slumped, slumped a little bit more. Without turning around, he said again, hoarsely this time, "You're very kind. Thank you."

Then he walked outside to join a sullen and angry Josh, and our conversation was over.

I sighed, unsure what else I could do.

The universe wasn't being very helpful in pointing the way at the moment.

My car was filthy, coated in red clay dust from God knows how many Georgia back roads. The inside wasn't too bad, just some fast-food trash and empty cups, though it smelled like boy sweat.

My CDs were scattered all over the front seat and floor. It needed a good cleaning, inside and out, so I took it to the very first car wash I saw.

Fifteen minutes later, detrashed, straightened, and thoroughly vacuumed, my personal space had almost been restored. A good wipe-down and some solid spritzes of air freshener would have to wait until I got home, but I eased the car into the wash bay with a sigh of relief, feeling like things were almost back to normal again, or at least about to be.

"I'm so sorry about your car," came a woman's whisper, from the backseat.

"Holy sh—!" I'd nearly peed my pants. I craned my neck to see, though I had a feeling I already knew who it was. It had been a feminine voice, timid and hushed.

"Please don't be mad at Josh. He's a good boy. He made a mistake."

"Angie?" I couldn't see her. The dimness of the wash bay enveloped us, the swish of brushes, the sudden thrum of water on the roof.

"Don't say my name," she whispered frantically, from somewhere on my floorboards maybe. "It's still looking for me."

Great. I eyed the equipment surrounding my car, wondering if I'd damage any of it if I drove out in the middle of the wash. That bright patch of sunlight ahead of me at the end of the wash tunnel looked awfully good right now.

"It's all my fault," she said, talking fast. "I drove your car home, I left it on the street. I meant to give it back, I never meant to cause any trouble."

I tried to focus, though my heart was pounding. "*You* took my car?"

"I just needed to get home," she said. "I found myself at a gas station, thinking this was all just a horrible nightmare, and saw the keys in your ignition. I drove home, I had to get home. I never imagined Josh would take it—I can't believe he'd do such a thing."

Wow. I'd known that ghosts could manipulate objects, but drive a car? I had a sudden flash of those times when I'd arrived somewhere with no memory of the drive, and found it wasn't so hard to imagine a car driving itself, powered purely by thought or memory, on autopilot.

"Josh and David have been butting heads, but it's not always all Josh's fault. He's sensitive, and sometimes David is too hard on him." She sounded like a typical mom, having a typically hard time dealing with a typical teenager. How strange, under the circumstances. "It's my fault. It has to be. They used to be so close." She was still talking fast, as though there would never be enough time to say everything she wanted to say.

The car was moving slowly through the wash, cocooning us in water and sound, but I'd never asked to be anyone's confessor. *You need to learn to say no more often*, Evan had said, and he was right. While I sympathized with Angie's predicament, I'd done what little I could, and I wanted my life back.

"It's time to let go of all this and go into the Light, Angie." I figured a little bluntness couldn't hurt. "There's nothing more you can do to help Josh or David. Stop hiding, and look for the Light. Once you do, everything will be okay."

A wail of outraged grief startled me. "How can you say that," she cried, "when I've ruined *everything*!"

"Shhh . . ." I urged her, unable to help myself. As much as *she* didn't want the Dark to find her, I didn't want it to find *me*, either.

"You have to help me," she sobbed, and my heart sank. "You're the only one who can hear me, the only one who can help me fix it. Please. Please help me fix it."

The car wash jerked, and the equipment came to a standstill. A huge whooshing sound as the air-dry portion came to life, and a green light indicated I was free to drive on.

"I don't know how to fix it," I said, shaking my head. As tough as it was, I was going to have to be brutal. "You're dead, and I can't bring you back to life." There was silence from the backseat. "People make mistakes, and you made a big one—one you can't take back. The only thing you can do is move forward, and look for the Light."

"The Light doesn't want me," Angie whispered, as I drove out of the wash tunnel into the sun-drenched parking lot.

I pulled over a few seconds later so I could twist around in my seat and check the back, but there was no one there.

CHAPTER 11

"So when were you going to tell me that Butch saw a ghost at the store?"

Joe's question took me by surprise. I'd called him as soon as I'd gotten to Handbags and Gladrags and found the message Evan had scrawled on a sticky note, embellished with a giant heart, and stuck to the center of my computer screen. Subtlety had never been Evan's strong point, after all.

"Who . . ." I let the words trail off, because there was no doubt who'd told him about the woman in the mirror. In fact, it had probably been the first words out of Evan's mouth when Joe called. "I was going to tell you, babe, but we haven't exactly had a lot of time to talk lately, remember? I didn't even expect to hear from you until this afternoon." *Not that I minded.*

"Yeah, it's been a long shift," he said. "I just got off, and I'm beat, but I needed to talk to you."

"Aww." After my weird morning, a little attention from my boyfriend would not go amiss. "Seems like I haven't seen you in days, sweetie. You won't believe what happened to me today." I couldn't wait to tell him, feeling better just hearing his voice.

"You won't believe what happened to me, either," he said. "Selene Mathews came to see me again."

My budding warm fuzzies withered on the vine.

"She knows who you are, Nicki. She knows you can see the dead."

Alarm bells went off in my brain, followed by sirens, a helicopter, and 101 figurative dalmatians. "What? How does she know? *What* does she know?"

"Somebody in Little Five told her about that scene last year on the evening news." He was referring to the time I'd been caught on camera while possessed by a spirit, claiming to be a "channeler." "One of the other shop owners, I think."

Right.

"She came to ask me if the rumor was true. She thinks you might be able to help her."

I couldn't believe what I was hearing. For one brief, wild moment, I wondered if the steam rising from the top of my head was visible to the naked eye.

"She came to *you*?" *So that was the plan . . . oh, she was evil, this one.* I could see her now, slinking her way into Joe's office, the picture of distraught grief and helpless femininity. My imagination spared me nothing, from the way her flawless red lips trembled, to the diamondlike gleam of tears on her lashes. *Oh, help me, kind sir, please help me speak to my dear old mother one more time.*

"She came to you," I repeated, stunned at the audacity of her latest move, "instead of me."

"She, ah . . ." Joe cleared his throat through the phone. "She seems to think you don't like her."

"She's right about that," I retorted. "I've got her number now, and she obviously knows it. Kelly and I both did some research—we're pretty sure that she's one of the Moirae, also known as the Three Fates. I'm not exactly clear on what kind of game she's playing, but—"

"No offense, Nicki, but just because Kelly is willing to believe that Selene and her family are some kind of supernatural beings doesn't mean I am. I explained to you already that all Mary's tests proved before she died that she was very much human."

"That doesn't mean anything! We've seen some pretty strange things in the last year and a half—"

"Yes," he said tersely. "We have. But this situation isn't one of them."

It wasn't often I found myself speechless. What was going on? Why didn't he believe me?

I took a deep breath, and tried logic. "She's playing you, Joe. If Selene truly wanted my help, she knows perfectly well where to find me, so why did she come to you?"

"I explained that already. She came to me because she trusts me," he said tightly, while I struggled not to scream each time he said the word "she." "She said her mother's spirit came to her in a dream, that she's trying to get in contact with her."

"Are you *kidding* me?" My temper was rising by the second. "What a load of crap." The irony of the whole situation was not lost on me—her mother's spirit coming to her in a dream after they'd terrified me with one—puh-lease.

"I don't think it's crap, Nick."

Obviously not. I said nothing for a moment, not trusting myself to speak . . . but then the dam burst. "You know how I feel about inviting the spirits in—you know how I feel about not looking for trouble! Even if you don't believe she's one of the Moirae, why would you think I'd call up the spirit of a dead woman just because someone asked me to? What are you thinking?"

"Calm down," he said shortly. His voice had taken on an edge. "I told her you couldn't help her."

The breath left my lungs in a whoosh.

"What did she say to that?" I found it hard to believe she'd give up so easily.

"She didn't seem to want to believe me."

I know the feeling.

"When I called to tell you that you might be hearing from her anyway, Evan told me about what happened to Butch at the store. So now it doesn't matter what I told her."

My mind was busy thinking up ways to snatch Selene baldheaded, so I wasn't following him. "Why not?"

"I told her you couldn't help her because I knew you'd never deliberately call up a spirit. But now it doesn't matter, because Mary has shown up all on her own."

"Wait a minute." Joe never wanted me to "dabble"—never—even when I had no choice. "You actually expect me to help her?"

There was dead silence on the other end of the line. Finally Joe said, "I'm surprised at you, Nicki. This isn't like you."

"And this isn't like you," I returned heatedly. What the hell was going on? "I've told you I don't trust Selene, that I don't like Selene, that I don't want to be anywhere *near* Selene, whether she's supernatural or not." Okay, so maybe I was exaggerating what I'd said in the heat of the moment, but why hadn't he gotten the message yet?

"The woman's mother just died," he said quietly. "Why are you being so hard on her?"

I did the unthinkable. I hung up on him.

I expected him to call me back.

He didn't.

I waited about ten minutes, giving myself time to calm down. I was hurt, and I didn't understand; Joe was a smart guy, and I was baffled as to why he wasn't as suspicious of Selene as I was. I'd told him about the night visit, I'd told him my fears and suspicions. Could he actually be *choosing* not to believe me?

The thought gave me a sick feeling in the pit of my stomach.

Taking a deep breath, I called his cell phone.

"This is Joe Bascombe. Please leave me a message."

Undeterred, I hung up, then hit redial. Maybe he was just calling me at the same time. Yeah, that was it. The third time I got his voice mail, I knew the ugly truth; he'd turned off his phone and wasn't going to answer.

Evidently, Joe did not appreciate being hung up on.

"Oh, come *on*," I said loudly, to no one in particular. "Is *this* the way it's gonna be?"

"Are you going to stay holed up in the office all day?" Evan asked, sticking his head in the office door.

"Joe's not taking my calls," I said, angry all over again. "He actually wants me to help that horrible witch Selene speak to her dead mother. Can you believe it?"

Evan's eyes got big, either from what I was saying or how angry I was, I wasn't sure.

"I told him I don't like her, I told him I don't trust her—hell, I don't even think her mother is *dead*, much less even her *mother*!"

Evan's look turned to one of wary confusion, and I knew I was making little sense.

"Selene?" He came all the way into the office. "The hottie with the Furla?"

Snapping my phone shut and tossing it onto my desk, I sighed. "Yes." There was so much I hadn't told him. My head ached at the thought of how much I hadn't told him.

"The one whose mother collapsed on the sidewalk?"

"Yes," I said again, wearily.

"Her mother died?" Evan was like a dog with a bone. "You didn't tell me that!"

"Sorry." One-word answers seemed to be all I had in me at the moment. Why wasn't Joe answering his phone?

A look of horror came over his face. "Oh. My. God. Do you think the old woman Butch saw in the bathroom is Selene's mother?"

Oh, crap. I had a sinking feeling of *Titanic* proportions. "Maybe. Kinda." It was all so *complicated*. "Possibly."

"Then I agree with Joe," Evan said decisively. "You have to help Selene, because you have to get that old lady out of here."

"You don't understand—"

"What's to understand? I don't want some old lady looking over my shoulder every time I need to tinkle, and neither do you."

"We don't even know—"

"Oh yes, we know," he said, nodding his blond head energetically. "Don't you even *try* and pretend like we don't know. Butch saw her, and I've felt uncomfortable all day long, like someone was staring at me." He looked around, involuntarily, and it made me feel bad to see it. Leaning in, he whispered, "I want her out of here. Gone, for good."

Hoisted on my own petard. I had no idea what that

phrase even meant, but it leapt to mind. What little I'd told Evan of my suspicions had now come back to bite me, because he was now on Joe's side. And if I tried to explain that this situation was far more complicated than he ever dreamed, I'd only frighten him more.

With a sigh, I leaned forward, resting my weight on my elbows. "What happened to saying no to the spirits more often?"

He arched an eyebrow at me, obviously resolved. "Say it to someone else's spirit, and get this one out of our store."

Before I did something stupid like drive straight to Joe's apartment and pick another fight over Selene, I went out back where I had a little privacy, and leaned against my car while calling my sister. "Why is he even talking to her? Why is he taking her side in this?"

"Slow down," Kelly said. "I'm not sure I understand."

"It's like the nightmare just goes on and on," I said, *not* slowing down. "Every time I turn around, there's Selene, or something to do with Selene. Selene, Selene, Selene . . . it's all I hear. She's everywhere, particularly if there's a chance that Joe might be in the vicinity."

"Nicki," my sister said firmly, "calm down. You're starting to sound crazy."

With a sigh, I tried to regroup. "She's after him, Kelly. I've tried to tell him who she really is, but he doesn't see it! Now he's mad at me for not being 'sympathetic' enough toward her. Can you believe it?"

"Joe always sees the good in people," Kelly said quietly. "Even when they're not so good."

"Exactly." *Exactly.*

"She keeps throwing herself at him," I went on, "every chance she gets. She practically announced her intentions to steal him from me yesterday at the store when she just 'happened' to show up. The little girl is seriously creepy, by the way."

"You're talking about them like they're human," Kelly said. "Yesterday you thought they were the Moirae."

"They *are* human," I said impatiently, "or they might as well be. Just like Sammy could appear in the flesh—"

Sammy. Just like Sammy.

"Ah," Kelly breathed, at the same time I did. "Do you think he sent them?"

It certainly made sense, and it wasn't the first time I'd suspected it. "I thought he was gone," I said quietly.

"Grandma Bijou says he's never gone," Kelly answered, just as quietly.

If Sammy had sent them, then where was Sammy? It wasn't like him to miss out on the fun of tormenting me in person.

"I don't think so," I said thoughtfully. "I can't see his hand in it." I didn't want to, actually. If Sammy had sent his minions to bug me without showing up himself, that meant I'd moved down his list in the food chain. The teeny stab of loss I felt at the thought was surely proof of my twisted nature.

"Anyway, it doesn't matter. I just need to get Joe to understand how dangerous she is, and he won't even answer the phone!" I took refuge in the anger that prompted my call in the first place.

Kelly sighed. "What are you doing, Nicki?"

Baffled at her tone, I snipped, "I'm talking to you."

"You *need* to be talking to Joe," she said. "And when you do, you *need* to be nice to him. If he has to choose between a gorgeous damsel in distress and an angry girlfriend, which one do you think he'll pick? Don't give him a reason to pull away from you."

My jaw dropped. "Are you suggesting that I be nice to him on *purpose*, just so Selene doesn't win?" *Made sense, actually.* "I'm kind of pissed at him at the moment, if you hadn't noticed."

"Let me be blunt," she said bluntly. "I'm *suggesting* that you drive to Joe's house, get naked, and crawl into bed with him. It's called make-up sex. It'll work wonders."

Unable to believe I was hearing her correctly, I burst out laughing.

"It always works with Spider," she said cheerfully. "Sometimes I think we fight just so we can get to the good part."

"That is *way* too much information, sis."

"I think he's going to ask me to marry him, Nicki." Kelly's words changed the whole focus of the conversation. "I overheard him talking to Grandma Bijou about her favorite jeweler, and she's been beaming at me like she knows something I don't."

"She always knows something you don't," I said dryly. "She's a sensitive."

It wasn't exactly a shock, except for the suddenness of it. Kelly and Spider hadn't been together nearly as long as Joe and I, and here they were, already taking things to the next level. "What do you think? Are you going to say yes?"

"Of *course* I'm going to say yes," she said immediately. "I'm nuts about the guy. I can't wait to see what the ring looks like."

I laughed, happy for her. Spider was cool, tattoos and all, and Kelly was obviously on cloud nine.

True love. What more was there?

CHAPTER 12

Eight o'clock that evening found me pulling into the parking lot of Joe's apartment complex. His BMW was in its usual place, but there were no lights on in his apartment. Part of me felt guilty over what I was about to do, but a bigger part of me didn't.

He could sleep later, when I was done with him.

I was wearing my tightest jeans, my tightest sweater, and nothing at all underneath. I'd showered, smoothed and perfumed every inch of my skin, and unless Joe was made of stone—which he wasn't—I was about to follow my sister's advice to the letter.

I'd made up my mind. Selene wasn't going to drive a wedge between Joe and me. It was time to fight fire with fire, and I had more than a few sparks in my arsenal.

Instead of knocking on his door, I let myself in with my key. The apartment was dark, so I switched on the light in the foyer, took off my coat and shoes, and padded down the hall to his bedroom in my socks.

His bedroom door was open. I could hear him breathing, deep and even. I stood there in the doorway, listening, letting my eyes adjust. The light from the foyer barely reached here, but after a moment, I could make out his shape in the bed. That curve was his shoulder, that shadow his dark hair on the pillow.

Quietly, so I wouldn't wake him, I unzipped my jeans and pulled them off, along with my socks. It took only a second to draw the sweater over my head, and then I was naked, nipples immediately goose pebbling in the cool night air.

If he'd been awake, and wanted to, I'd have been willing to talk out our earlier disagreement until we were both satisfied, but right now I had satisfaction of a different sort in mind.

We'd have plenty of time to talk later.

The bed dipped as I got into it, but Joe didn't stir. I touched his shoulder and tucked my nose into his back, my belly to his bottom, and was rewarded by a warm "mmm" that told me I'd gotten his attention.

"Hey," I whispered, kissing the back of his neck as my palm wandered over the muscles of his bare arm and shoulder. Another murmur of sleepy pleasure from Joe as I savored the feel of his nakedness. The sheets smelled of him, and the bed was warm and familiar. I was nearly overcome with a wave of lust and love, and knew, in that instant, that I'd never felt this way about anyone before.

And never would again.

Smiling against Joe's bare shoulder, I let my hand slip down to his belly, then let it slip farther still.

He tried to roll onto his back, but I held him with the weight of my body, filling my palm with his maleness, soft with sleep, heavy with the weight of him.

Tenderness filled me, the heat from his body seeping into my skin everywhere we touched. I kissed his shoulder, cradling him in my palm, stroking and squeezing to my heart's content.

"Mmm," he moaned, louder now, and shifted so I had no choice but to let him onto his back. I settled myself in the curve of his shoulder without removing my hand, kissing the skin of his chest as it presented itself to me during the move.

"You're insatiable," he murmured sleepily, kissing the top of my head. "But I need a chance to recover."

My growing daze of pleasure was pierced by a brush of ice down my spine.

Joe stayed slack beneath my hand, his body boneless in relaxation as he nuzzled his nose in my hair. "So good, Selene," he mumbled. "That was so good."

I sat bolt upright, pushing off his groin and chest with a little more force than necessary.

"Hey!" he protested my rude handling, coming fully awake.

"Are you awake now? Good. Because my name is Nicki, *not* Selene!"

"What the—" Joe pulled himself up on his elbows, groggy with sleep. "What are you mad about *now*? What's the matter?"

What are you mad about now? The way he said it made it sound like I was mad all the time, which usually wasn't true. The only reason I'd been mad at him lately was because of Selene, and that was because she was out to get him however she could . . .

"Oh no," I gasped, in dawning horror.

"What the hell is going on?" Joe was wide-awake now, and obviously annoyed. "I was sleeping. What's the problem?"

He'd been sleeping. Just like he'd been sleeping when I found him in the living room, paying erotic homage to the moon. Just like I'd been sleeping when Selene first came to me, and first laid eyes on him.

"She got here first," I said stupidly, stricken.

He shifted himself higher in the bed. "What are you talking about?" He looked at the digital clock beside the bed. "You've been here over an hour. We just spent forty-five minutes—"

"No!" I shouted, startling us both. Scrabbling up off the bed, I headed toward my discarded clothes as my world came crashing down. I didn't want to hear what he'd been about to say. "*We* haven't been doing anything! It was her . . . it was Selene."

Joe's groan of frustration was almost as loud as my shout. Even in the dark I could see him raise both hands to his head. "*Why* are you doing this?" he asked angrily. "Why do you keep bringing her into everything?"

"Because she keeps putting herself into everything," I shot back, the tears having begun. "Tell me . . . tell me the truth, Joe . . . have you been dreaming of her?"

Silence answered me.

"She's the reason you were sleepwalking, wasn't she, the night I found you in the living room." I didn't expect him to confirm or deny anything at this point. My voice was shaky, and he had to know I was crying. "You dreamed of her tonight, too. You dreamed about sex with her."

"People can't help what they dream, Nicki," he said, in a low voice.

"She's not what she seems," I said, as calmly as I could, which wasn't very. I felt like I'd been cheated on, though Joe had done nothing wrong. Beneath the hurt she'd caused was a very real fear—*what did I have to do to get rid of her?* "She's not going to give up until she's in your bed for real."

Abruptly, he twitched aside the covers and stood up, striding to his dresser for a pair of boxers. He pulled them on in jerky, angry movements.

"I've had enough of this, Nicki," he said stiffly. "I'm tired, and I need some sleep. We can talk about this another time."

I stared at him in silence, knowing he couldn't see my tears in the dark.

"In fact, maybe you should sleep in your own bed tonight."

And then he turned and went into the bathroom.

I gathered up my things and left, closing the door very softly behind me.

Marley's Bar was a dump, but it was a fairly quiet dump, and that was just what I needed right now. At nine o'clock on a weeknight, the place was empty except for a fat old guy sitting at the bar, and the hard-faced woman who worked behind it. They were both watching some sports show on the TV, while background music was piped in low through the speakers. I headed toward a booth near the back, as far away from the bar as I could.

"What'll it be?" asked the fat guy, getting up from his stool as I walked past him.

"Jack and Coke," I said automatically. *Damn the red wine for my wimpy heart.* I needed something stronger tonight.

Sliding into the booth, my back to the couple at the bar, I closed my eyes and leaned my head against the seat. It smelled like old cigarettes and beer, but I didn't care. I let it ground me, help me stop the feeling that my world was spinning out of control.

What was happening? Joe and I had never been this far apart before. Every time I tried to make it better it got worse. I didn't know what to do.

He hadn't *actually* cheated on me, but it felt like he had. He'd also taken on the role of Selene's champion, which was troubling me even more than the dreams. The two things together, though . . . that was too much.

Every time I tried to say anything about Selene, he defended her. Anytime *he* tried to say anything about Selene, I got angry.

Selene. It was always about Selene.

She'd insinuated her way into everything, including Joe's dreams. *What if she won?*

"Here you go," said the fat guy, at my elbow. He slid a glass onto the table. "Wanna run a tab?"

I nodded, reaching for the drink. It was easy on the Coke, heavy on the Jack, so much so I coughed a little as it went down.

"You're welcome," said the fat man, heading back toward the bar. "Looked like you needed a stiff one."

Cautious now, I took another sip and put my head back again, closing my eyes to concentrate on the burn. I needed to feel something besides this ache in my heart and the prickling of my eyelids.

"It's man trouble, ain't it?"

The woman's voice made me jump. I opened my eyes to see the hard-faced woman from behind the bar sliding into the other side of my booth.

Appalled she'd be so pushy, I gave her a stony stare and didn't answer, figuring she'd take the hint.

She didn't. "I can spot man trouble a mile away," she said, nodding her head. "Pretty girl like you, coming into a dump like this all alone on a weeknight. Just had a fight with your boyfriend, didn't you?"

She had the raspy voice of a longtime smoker, and the wrinkles to match. Frizzy auburn hair, liberally streaked with gray.

"Take it from Maybelline, sweetheart," she said, the weathered creases around her eyes crinkling, "if you love him, figure out a way to work it out. If you don't, move on. Life's too short for anything else."

"I'm sorry," I said, refusing to be friendly, "but I came in here to be alone, so if you don't mind . . ." I tilted my head toward the bar, making my point clear.

"See that man over there?" she asked, eyeing the fat guy on the stool. "That there is Claude, the love of my life." She'd obviously decided to ignore my request to be left alone. "We was together twenty-eight years, Claude and me, before the cancer got me. Divorced twice, remarried once, living together 'til the day I died."

Oh, shit. I raised the glass in my hand and took a big swallow of Jack and Coke.

Why, oh why, did the dead tend to find me when I least needed finding? Selfishly enough, I wasn't in the mood to do anyone any favors right now.

Maybelline was smiling fondly at the fat guy, who was watching football, oblivious to us both. "He's not much of a talker, my Claude, but he's a good man. Two kids, a mortgage, and a business, but he always put food on the table. Solid, reliable—the kind of man you can count on."

She turned her head and looked me in the eye. "Not too bad in the sack, either, believe it or not. Your man like that?"

What was I gonna do, lie to a dead lady? "Yes," I answered, "He is."

Her smile broadened. She had a nice smile, though her teeth could've used some whitening. *Too late for that.*

"Can you do me a favor?"

Uh-oh. Here we go.

"Ask yourself the question, 'Am I better off with him, or without him?' If the answer is 'with him,' then you best make up your mind to go through some rough times, and fight for him. Promise me you'll do that."

I found myself confused, but it could've been the Jack. I took another sip, just to be certain. "That's the favor?" I asked, as it slid down easy. "Don't you want me to give Claude a message or something?"

Maybelline laughed, and I'd swear that Claude heard it, because he straightened on his stool and looked around for a second before going back to football highlights. "No," she said, shaking her head. "Thank you kindly."

Then she got up, giving the table between us a couple of taps with her fingers. "Take your time, sweetheart, and think about it. Me and Claude won't bother you none. Just let him know when you're ready for another drink."

She walked back to her spot behind the bar, leaning against the counter where she watched football highlights with her oblivious husband.

Unless he wasn't really oblivious, and knew, on some level, that Maybelline was still there.

With a sigh, I gave up trying to figure it out and leaned my head back against the seat once again. It was no business of mine if someone would rather hang out in a bar with her husband than cross over; if they were happy, I was happy.

True love. What more was there?

Bursting into quiet tears, I cried, alone in my booth, hoping that when the tears were over I'd feel better, and know what to do.

One hour and two damp, wadded napkins later, the only thing I knew to do was *not drive*. I hadn't set out to get tipsy, just relaxed, but two strong JCs had left my head spinning, so much so that I had to hold on to the booth to right myself when I stood up.

"G'night, Claude," I said to the fat guy on my way out. He barely acknowledged it until I added, "G'night, Maybelline." His head jerked in my direction while I cringed, mentally smacking myself for saying it out loud.

"You feel her, too?" he asked, not moving from his stool.

Maybelline smiled at me from behind the bar, not saying a word.

"Yeah," I answered him, nodding. "Yeah, I feel her, too."

He gave a grunt, and went back to watching sports, as I pushed my way out the glass door and into a nippy December night.

I had a plan after all, which was to walk the less than half block to Handbags and Gladrags, and sleep on the old leather sofa in the office. I'd done it many times before, back in my wild days, before my heart stopped. Before my wimpy, stupid, bruised, battered heart had started ruling my life. Before I'd opened my eyes and seen the love of my life bending over me, doing what he did best, which was helping people.

I was grateful for the streetlights, because Little Five's streets were mostly deserted. Most of the regular bums knew me, so I wasn't too worried, but I dug out a can of pepper spray just in case.

"He's just trying to be nice to her because that's what he does," I muttered, trying to convince myself of it as I walked. Turning up the collar of my coat, I wished I'd worn a heavier sweater instead of the thin black one I'd chosen for the evening. "And he can't help what he dreams."

The best thing I could do was to calm down, quit acting like a drama queen because my boyfriend had a wet dream about someone else, and figure out a way to get rid of Selene.

"Piece of cake," I mumbled, still talking to myself as I reached the front door of the store.

A shadow detached itself from the wall near the entrance and said, "Don't mind if I do."

I shrieked, aiming the pepper spray faster than you could blink.

"I love cake," Sammy said, stepping into the light. "Do you have any?"

CHAPTER 13

"Why, Nicki," Sammy said, cocking his blond head with a smile. "I do believe you're drunk."

His hair was longer this time, with a natural curl I hadn't noticed when it was short. It gave him a boyish, playful look. *No less sexy, damn him.*

"Get away from me," I said tightly, not lowering the pepper spray. His sudden appearance had scared me to death, and I was angry at myself for the relief I felt at the sight of him.

Relief, and a flutter of something suspiciously like happiness.

Which scared me even more.

"Come now," he said, keeping his hands in the pockets of his coat. It was the peacoat I'd sold him last year, the one we'd shopped for together before I knew he was the Devil. "You know I'm not going to hurt you."

Liar. It hurts me just to look at you.

I lowered the pepper spray, resigned. "What do you want?"

He frowned, rocking back on his heels. Tony Lama wingtip boots, well-worn and well-polished, beneath equally well-worn jeans. "Hardly the greeting I was hoping for. Here I was, under the impression that you'd missed me."

"Why would you think something like that?" I asked snippily, reaching for the door handle. I hadn't missed him. *I hadn't.*

"You defended me to your sister," he said softly, stepping closer. He took his hands from his pockets and spread them wide to show he was no threat. "When Kelly asked you if I was behind your latest bout of trouble"—he shrugged, close enough now for me to see the smile in his blue eyes—"you said no. You thought of me fondly, just for a moment."

I began to tremble, whether from his knowledge or his nearness, I couldn't tell. I took a step back, away from his open palms. "So you *are* behind it," I accused, choosing not to acknowledge his last statement. "I knew it."

The night air was cold, stinging my cheeks. The

ring of light at the base of the streetlamp felt like it contained the whole world. He was looking at me in a way that made my knees weak; the blond fallen angel with a weakness for the flesh, any woman's fantasy come to life.

"I knew better than to think of you, even for a moment," I said softly, finally admitting it to myself.

The words hung in the air between us. He held me pinned with those bright blue eyes, but there was no laughter in them just now. I got the feeling that I might as well have just announced that I was in love with him.

Which I wasn't, because I was in love with Joe.

Joe.

Sammy shook his head. "Oh, Nicki." He sighed heavily, slipping his hands back into his pockets. "You really don't know what's going on, do you?"

"No, I don't." Angry now, I didn't try to hide it, any more than I could hide that I was slightly tipsy. "Why don't you explain it to me, Mr. Scary Devil Man?" He grinned as I waved an unsteady hand in the general direction of the universe. "What have I ever done to you that you would pick on me like this? Why did you send those three troublemaking bi—" A hiccup kept me from the profanity. "—and what is the freakin' deal with Selene?"

"Is that what she's calling herself now?" he asked, surprising me.

A wave of dizziness had me leaning against the door.

Sammy reached out to steady me, and I let him, thinking it might be a good idea to sit down.

"Let me buy you some coffee," he said gently. "I'll explain everything."

The night was so quiet that I could literally hear the hum of the streetlight, and far away, the music from Vertigo's weeknight cover band. He smelled exactly as I remembered, like forbidden fruit and exotic spices, and for a second, just a second, I was tempted to lean my head against his chest. I felt his hand through the sleeve of my coat, and against whatever better judgment I thought I possessed, I nodded my head. "This had better be good."

Sammy smiled down at me as he led me away from the shop door. "How could it possibly hurt?" he asked lightly. "Two old friends, catching up over coffee." Before I knew it, he'd tucked my cold hand into the bend of his elbow, where I let it stay, only because I was freezing. "What could possibly be better?"

"I'm not drunk," I stated firmly. The guy at Marley's made a mean Jack and Coke, which I made a mental note to remember next time. "I just need something to eat, that's all."

"Two black coffees and a muffin," Sammy told the girl behind the counter at Moonbeans, who was smiling at him and ignoring me. "We'll be at the table in the corner."

Taking me by the elbow, he led me there, and I had to admit it felt good to sit down. Plus it was cold outside. In here it was warm and smelled like gingerbread.

He took a seat across from me, and suddenly there we were, face to face for the first time in months. His expression was hard to read; he was smiling at me, but his eyes were hooded. Honey gold hair, tipped with blond, nice tan—he looked like he'd been somewhere a lot warmer than Atlanta lately.

He did the same thing I did and examined me openly from tip to toe, or as much as he could see before the table cut him off, anyway. His smile got bigger.

"You're looking well," he said approvingly. "You've put on a few pounds."

"I have not!"

"You were too thin," he said, unbuttoning his coat. "Your trip to death's door obviously took its toll."

In more ways than one. My entire life had changed the day my heart stopped. I could see dead people, I'd met Joe, and now I had creatures like Sammy in my life. Incredibly sexy, hard-to-resist creatures . . .

"You said you'd tell me about Selene," I said bluntly.

"Patience," he said, looking up to greet the waitress, who'd arrived with our coffee, "is a virtue." He smiled at her as he said it, and I could literally see the flush of pleasure in her cheeks. She shot him a flirtatious glance as she slid a plate holding a muffin onto the table.

"Will there be anything else?"

I might as well have been invisible, but that was okay by me.

"Nothing, thank you," Sammy responded, not looking at the food. "It looks delicious."

She barely hid a little half smile as she walked away, back toward the counter.

"You can't help yourself, can you?" I asked him.

He shook his head, reaching for his coffee. "Why should I?"

I didn't have an answer for him, so I just picked up my coffee and took a careful sip. He sipped his as I broke off a piece of muffin and choked it down, not at all hungry but knowing I was going to need all the strength I could get.

"So trouble has found its way into paradise, I

see," he finally said, after I'd eaten two thirds of the muffin. "You and Prince Charming not seeing eye-to-eye these days?"

I was in no mood to be toyed with. "Enough with the bullshit. What are you doing here?"

He frowned. "Tsk, tsk. So unladylike."

"Why did you send the Moirae after me?"

A blond eyebrow arched. "Ah, so you're not entirely clueless, after all." He tapped the rim of his coffee cup with a finger. "Except the part about me sending them." Another frown, as he took another sip of coffee. "They came completely on their own."

I leaned back in my chair. "You expect me to believe that?"

He shrugged. "You'll believe what you like, you always do, but the fact remains that I'm innocent in this. You've stirred up a hornet's nest this time, Nicki, my love."

My love. "You're a liar."

"Yes, I am." He leaned back himself, resting an arm over the chair back beside him.

I had to give the big fat liar kudos for honesty.

Eyeing him mistrustfully, I said, "Okay, so you didn't send them. Call them off."

He laughed, with a flash of white teeth and a sardonic curl of the lip. "If only it were that easy."

"It *is* that easy," I insisted.

His peacoat had fallen open, revealing a pale blue cashmere sweater that matched his eyes, worn over a plain white tee. Simple, elegant, stylish. *Damn him.*

"They don't answer to me," he said, shaking his head. His eyes were drawn to my mouth, just for a moment. "I'm not all-powerful."

Finding that hard to believe, I just stared at him.

"*There are more things in heaven and earth, Horatio,*" he quoted, with a rueful grin, "*than are dreamt of in your philosophy.*"

"Hamlet," I responded, unimpressed. "I went to high school, you know."

"How fortunate for you," he said smoothly. "Lost your virginity at the prom, I assume?"

"I don't need your sarcasm," I said, getting angry. Of all the stupid things I'd done in my life, agreeing to coffee with Sammy was certainly right up there.

"No," he agreed, "but you need my help." Cocking his head, he let his eyes rove over my face. "If sarcasm is the price you pay, then so be it."

"You'll expect a much higher price than that, and we both know it." *I want to make love to you,* he'd once said. *I want to lick each of your secret places, taste your juices on my tongue.*

He gave me a rueful smile. "Not this time," he

said. "I have my own reasons for wanting the Moirae stopped."

I was silent for a minute, staring at him, challenging him to meet my eyes. "Why should I believe a word you say?"

He didn't flinch. His eyes were so blue, so beautiful. "You shouldn't," he said. "But I'm going to tell you the truth anyway."

A memory surfaced of the day I'd gone for a ride with him on a glorious spring afternoon; Stone Mountain Freeway, top down. He'd told me his side of the story of how he'd fallen from grace. This time—maybe it was just the warm quiet of the coffee shop that calmed my nerves, maybe it was the table between us—I wasn't as afraid to listen.

"Tell me."

CHAPTER 14

"When I was cast down," Sammy said, as though being thrown out of Heaven was an everyday occurrence, "I was not the only one punished." He looked away from me, out the window of Moonbeans into the dark streets outside. "Two of us sinned that day, after all. Lilith was cast from the garden with her miserable ape and his pitiful banana, sentenced to a life of pain and blood and death, destined to grow old before her time giving birth to a nation of savages. She deserved it, of course, far more than I did. It was her choice to sin, after all."

His bitterness was distracting. "Eve, right? You're talking about Eve."

"She has borne many names throughout the centuries," he said, still staring out the window. "Eve, Lilith, Naamah, Artemis, Hecate." He shot me a glance from the corner of his eye. "Including Selene, goddess of the moon."

The room seemed to swim. I grabbed the table with both hands and held on, feeling like one of the snowflakes in a Christmas water globe, shaken by a giant cosmic hand.

"Those first few years with Adam, she seemed fine," he went on with the story, heedless of my shock, "finding solace in our son, I suppose. A good-looking young man, not afraid of anything. I saw him a time or two. But then she had another son, with that miserable cretin she was married to. The two brothers never got along, apparently fighting all the time. When the elder son killed the younger, her husband cursed her, and Lilith realized she'd spawned more than just savages; she'd spawned evil, given birth to the concept of murder . . . brother against brother."

Horrified, I realized I was listening to Sammy's version of the Cain and Abel story.

"Adam, that idiot, tried to reverse the spread of evil by refusing to sleep with her. Claimed her womb was tainted, or some such nonsense. She had to trick him into fathering her third son, and then he hated her for it." Sammy shook his head, obviously contemptuous. "Wouldn't put her aside, but wouldn't have sex with her. Can you imagine the logic behind that move? A woman like that, created for pleasure, ripe with desire . . ."

"I get it," I said flatly, interrupting him. "She was hot."

He smiled, brought back to himself by my lack of appreciation for detail.

"Get to the point," I said, while my stomach churned. "What happened? What does this have to do with what's happening now?"

"She went mad," he said simply. "And then she came to me."

I swallowed, hard. "Sh-she came to you?"

"She took her own life," he said, then shrugged. "She was banned from Heaven, just as I was. It was inevitable that we'd run into each other."

Dumbfounded, I didn't know what to say.

"She was still young, still beautiful. She took a huge chance, banking on the hope that she could seduce me again." A short laugh. "She felt I *owed* her, because of her punishment," he sneered. "As if it were my fault that she'd corrupted my innocence, flaunted her bare breasts and belly before my eyes, stroked the damp crease between her thighs . . ."

"Enough!" I said, loudly enough that the girl behind the counter looked up from her paperback.

"Forgive me," Sammy said, not looking the least

bit in need of forgiveness. A small smile lurked at the corner of his mouth. "Some of those memories will never leave me."

"Lucky you," I said sourly.

"I let myself be swayed by her tears, I suppose," he said, picking up the story where he left off. His gaze slipped inward again as he took a sip of coffee. "I agreed to a division of power."

Confused, I just looked at him. "A division of power?"

"Don't frown so, Nicki," he said, "It's not that hard to understand."

"Explain it to me then."

"Even though Lilith—Selene, as she's calling herself now—deserved every earthly punishment she got, I took pity on her. I was immune to earthly punishment; my punishment was eternal. Selene felt I'd gotten the better of the deal. She wanted to share my fate." His lips compressed just the tiniest fraction. "She professed to love me, begging me not to leave her in the pit. Such pretty tears," he mused, "such a wanton waste of tears."

I was holding my breath at this point, hoping I wouldn't get lightheaded and pass out before he finished.

The shadows behind Sammy's eyes seemed to darken. "I hated her," he said starkly. "And so I granted her wish."

"You mean . . . you mean she's like *you*?" I still wasn't grasping what that meant.

"In a way. She's immortal, like me."

She's physically perfect, like you.

"I gave her what was given to me—an eternity to repeat the same mistakes over and over," he said. "And she uses it to corrupt and beguile the minds of men as she once corrupted mine. Endless sex, endless pleasure, but never, ever"—he shook his head ruefully—"any real satisfaction."

"Endless sex?" I repeated faintly.

"Have you never heard the term 'succubus,' Nicki?" He leaned back, looking at me curiously. "Between you and your sister, I would've thought one of you might." He smiled a wicked little smile, changing the subject abruptly. "How is Kelly these days? Still back at the family homestead, kneeling at the feet of your dear grandmama?"

"Leave my family out of this," I said coldly. My brain seemed to have frozen the moment he'd said "succubus," so it was easy to inject that ice into my voice.

I knew what a succubus was; the female equivalent of a psychic vampire, who came to men in their sleep and stole their essence.

Emphasis on the term "essence."

Sammy raised his hands in a defensive motion.

"Just making conversation," he said, obviously amusing himself at my expense.

"I—" Gathering my stunned wits, I had to stop and think. "Who are the other two? The old woman, Mary, and the little girl? We—Kelly and I—thought they were the Moirae."

"They are," he answered calmly. "She is. They are the three faces of Selene, and they are the three who have learned to weave evil into the webs of fate. Mara is the old woman Selene never lived to be, and Hecate, the girl, is the child she never was. Each of them reflects a different aspect of her personality, and together, all three of them make the whole."

Mara. *Mary.* Hecate. *Kate.*

My head was spinning again, but this time it was from the unreality of what I was hearing. What I was *doing.* I was sitting in a coffee shop with Satan himself, listening to an entirely new version of creation stories mixed with myth and legend, just as if we were talking about nothing.

"I told you she was mad," he said simply. "Her madness became manifest. She wreaks havoc in all three of her guises, confusing humans throughout the centuries, enticing them to follow her web of lies unto their doom. It's a game to her." His lip quirked as he added, mostly to himself, "Proving once and for all that the true root of all evil usually lies with women."

I wasn't going to argue. "What does she want with me?" My throat had gone dry. "Or Joe?"

"Ah." Sammy smiled, cocking his head. "Now it gets complicated."

"*Now* it gets complicated?" My voice rose, and the waitress looked our way again, letting her eyes linger on Sammy before going back to her book.

"She's a clever creature." Sammy drummed his fingers on the table. Nicely manicured, silver thumb ring on one hand. "Learned a few tricks over the years, developed some of her own skills. I've avoided her for eons, so I can't claim to know her mind, but I imagine you've ticked her off somehow, my darling."

"Don't call me darling," I snapped.

He threw back his head and laughed. "I've missed you, Nicki," he said, as if he meant it.

"Liar," I muttered, into my cup.

"Come," he said, pushing himself away from the table. "Let me take you home."

"You're not taking me home." Goose bumps rose on my arms at the very thought.

"Oh yes, I am," he said, buttoning up his peacoat. "Or you won't hear the rest of the story."

I gaped at him. "That's not fair!"

He smiled down at me, offering a hand to help me stand. "Whoever said life was fair?"

He was driving a small Mercedes coupe now, all black, inside and out. The leather seats were soft as butter, and heated. As we drove down Moreland I stared out the window at my store, Handbags and Gladrags, and saw it as others might see it: a funky little store with a color-changing Christmas tree in the window, looking cheerful but lonely on a chilly December night.

"I meant it when I said I missed you, you know." Sammy was watching the road, having made no threatening moves. He'd held the door open for me as I'd gotten in, but seemed careful not to touch me, which I appreciated. I felt trapped, manipulated, and extremely nervous—we were enclosed in a cocoon of silence and privacy, when I knew better than to be alone with him.

"I'm sure you've had plenty of other souls to torment," I said lightly, hoping bravado would get me through the few blocks to my house. He hadn't asked for directions, I'd noticed, making a right turn without my prompting.

"Torment." He laughed. "What do you know of torment, Nicki?"

I didn't answer.

"Torment is wanting something very badly, yet

knowing you can't have it," he said. "Torment is loving someone, knowing you can never be together."

"Love," I countered. "What do you know of love, Sammy?"

He shot me a sideways grin. "Your tongue gets no less sharp when you're tipsy and overwhelmed. What does it take to be licked with it instead of flayed with it?"

His attempt to shock me failed, except for a tiny little tingle in my nether regions that no one needed to know about. "Don't start with me," I said, reaching for my purse. "I've still got my pepper spray."

Even in the dark I could see him smiling. "Why on *earth* do you keep threatening me with pepper spray? We both know you're not going to use it, and even if you did, it wouldn't hurt me. I come from a very hot climate, remember?"

A weak joke, but one that made me smile a little in the dark.

"I love peppers, in fact. The hotter the better. I know a great Mexican place in midtown. May I take you there sometime?"

Stunned, I just looked at him. "Did you . . . did you just ask me on a date?"

I couldn't read his expression—he was concentrating on the road—but his shrug spoke volumes. "What if I did?" he asked.

"I can't go out with you!" To my relief, he'd just turned onto my street. I could see the streetlight in front of my house, and there was my house itself, front porch light gleaming. Dad set it up on a timer years ago, just for nights like these.

As if there ever were any nights like these.

"Why not?" He'd reached the driveway and pulled in, putting the car in park. Shifting so he faced me in the seat, he asked me directly, "Is it because you want me as much as I want you? Because you burn for me like I burn for you?"

Shocked, I had a hard time formulating an answer beyond an automatic "No!"

"Who's the liar now," he whispered. He reached a hand toward my face, slowly, while I sat frozen, a mouse hypnotized by a cobra. "You're afraid that if I touched you, just once, the way I want to touch you, you'd burst into flame." His fingers came close, so close to my cheek, but he held back.

"Don't," I whispered, completely unnecessarily. His scent was familiar to me now: pomegranates, chocolate, rumpled sheets made of silk.

"Admit it," he murmured, holding my eye. The porch light gleamed in his short blond curls. "Just admit it. That's all I ask."

"Yes," I whispered, shakily. *Admitting it was not the same as acting on it.* "But you'd burn me to a cinder, and laugh while you did it."

His face drew nearer, while my heart beat a crazy tattoo. "You know all my secrets," he murmured, "all my limitations. You know I can't make you do anything you don't want to do."

His breath smelled of cloves, and I couldn't help but remember that kiss . . . that one kiss he'd claimed as a forfeit when last I saw him. I'd tried for months not to think of it, but the moment came rushing back—the breathless, expectant swoop of a roller coaster, the faintest brush of his tongue against mine.

"You want me," he said, low in his throat. His blue eyes gleamed in the darkness, and his presence filled the car: potently male, simmering with juices and brimming with heat. "I know you do." A sexy curl of a lip as he drew closer. "I can smell it. You smell so sweet, little Nicki . . . so very, very sweet . . ."

A sharp rapping on the window behind me made me jerk as if stung. Sammy pulled back as we both heard an angry male voice say, "Open the door, Nicki. What the hell is going on?"

It was Joe, who'd evidently been waiting at my house for God knows how long.

It didn't take a brain surgeon to figure out that I was in deep shit.

CHAPTER 15

"You were supposed to be asleep," I said stupidly as I got out of the car.

"Nice to know," Joe said tersely, hand on the car door. "Felt safe to party, did you?"

I'd never seen him so angry. He grabbed the sleeve of my coat and dragged me away from the Mercedes, slamming the door, hard.

"It's not what you think—"

"What is it, then?" He released my arm as if he couldn't bear to touch it any longer, and took a step back. "I've been waiting for you for over an hour, and you pull up with *him*." He gestured toward Sammy, who was just getting out of the car. "Sorry to interrupt your little make-out session."

"We weren't making out," I protested, but I didn't get very far.

"I'm not blind!" he spat. "I was sitting right there on the front porch! If you hadn't been so wrapped up in him, you would've seen me, and if I hadn't tapped on your window, you'd be all over him by now!"

Stung, as much by the accusation as by the truth that was in it, I took refuge in my own anger. This was all his fault, after all. "At least he knows my name!"

I knew as soon as I said it that it was the wrong thing to say—his eyes narrowed at my spiteful reminder of what had happened between us earlier in the evening.

"Oh, he knows your name," he said grimly. "He knows your name, your number, and your every weakness, one of which is *him*." He glared at me, absolutely furious. "And I know it, too."

"Now, now," Sammy said mildly, from the other side of the car. "Nothing happened. No need for all this drama, surely?"

Joe lunged, and so did I, grabbing his arm with both hands and holding on despite his attempt to wrench himself free.

"Don't," I yelled, petrified at the thought of what Sammy might do to him—I'd seen a bare fraction of what he was capable of, and knew he could be merciless. "Joe, stop!"

He dragged me around the front of the car before I got him slowed. "Please," I said, in what I tried to make a normal tone. "There's no need for this. Please."

Sammy didn't retreat, resting an arm on the top of his open car door, one foot propped on the car frame.

I shot him a furious look, wishing I had a free hand to slap the smirk right off his face.

"Let's go inside," I murmured urgently to Joe. "Let's talk this out inside."

His arm felt like stone beneath my hands. He shook me off with a sharp, sudden wrench that left me feeling completely alone. "No need," he said harshly, not taking his eyes off Sammy. "I can see you're busy."

"I merely brought the girl home," Sammy said. "She'd had one too many." He ignored my glare. Waving a red flag before the bull, he added, "Poor thing needed a shoulder to cry on because you've evidently become interested in someone else."

"Get out of here," I spat, before Joe could respond. Taking a step forward, I said it again. "Get out of here and don't come back."

Sammy shrugged, preparing to get in the car. "I was leaving anyway," he said with a grin.

The slam of his car door was one of the best things I'd heard in a long time. I backed away, toward the house, not taking my eyes off him until he'd backed out onto the road and put the Mercedes in drive. His taillights were still in view when Joe turned and started walking toward his own car.

"Joe."

He ignored me.

"Joe!" I went after him. He was parked on the street, which is why I hadn't noticed his car earlier. At least that's what I told myself. "Where are you going?"

He turned on me, and unleashed a torrent of words I'd never heard him say before, shocking me to silence. When he was finished, he went straight into "I can't believe you've been hard-timing me all week about another woman, and yet I find you with *him*!" The sentence ended in a shout, and set the neighbor's dog barking.

"It wasn't like that," I protested. "We just had coffee—"

"You had coffee? Then what's with him driving you home because you'd had too much to drink?" He clearly thought I was lying about the coffee.

"That was before—"

"Great," he shouted. "Just great! You got drunk, you had coffee, he brought you home. Sounds like a lovely evening." His sarcasm, combined with the noise volume, made me lose my temper.

"I didn't go on a date with him," I shouted back, rousing another dog, down the block. "You're being a jerk."

"*I'm* being—" He shook his head, disbelieving. Then he stared at the ground for a minute, while neither of us said a word, the sound of barking filling the night. "You claim to be terrified of him, but you're not afraid to get in his car. Looked pretty damn cozy in there together, in fact. You told him about our argument earlier, didn't you?"

"No," I said sharply, but he cut me off, pouncing as if he'd caught me in yet another lie.

"Then how did he know about Selene?"

I stared at him, trying desperately to get my temper under control and not helped by the mention of her name. "You wouldn't believe me if I told you," I said huskily, knowing it was true. Right now, Joe wouldn't believe anything I said.

Biblical stories brought to life, blended with myth and legend to explain a creature like Selene the succubus were better left until everyone's head was clear.

"Tonight was not what you think," I stammered, trying to find the words to explain. "It wasn't planned, it wasn't a date. He showed up out of nowhere—I was just trying to get information from him, that's all."

He gave a short laugh. "Yeah. Sure you were."

Stung by the sarcasm, I glared at him. "You're just going to have to trust me on this one, Joe."

"Like you trust me?" His voice was hard. "You've been in a jealous snit all week about another woman, and yet the second my back is turned I find you with another man. A man—or whatever the hell he is—who's already tried to come between us on more than one occasion." He paused for a second. "Have you been seeing him behind my back?"

I was shocked he'd even ask. "You know it's not like that," I said, a sinking feeling growing in the pit of my stomach.

"How is it, then?"

I was afraid to answer, afraid I'd say the wrong thing and mess things up even more than they already were.

"I've tried very hard to be with you, Nicki," he finally said, in a low voice. "I've tried to accept who you are and what happens in your life."

My heart stuttered as though it had just been kicked down a set of stairs, tumbling and falling, leaving smears of red to mark its passing as it fell to the ground. *Tried?*

"I don't think this is working anymore."

The world went red as my heart splattered and burst like a water balloon in the dirt beneath my feet.

"How can you say that?" I barely managed to whisper, tears choking my throat.

He tucked both hands into his jacket pockets in a self-contained gesture. Only two feet away, yet it might as well have been two miles.

"Things feel different between us these days." His eyes looked black in the moonlight. "Too much tension, too much anger. Now this." He looked away, toward the empty street, dotted by streetlights and porch lights. "To see you drive up with him . . . I feel like I don't know who you are anymore."

The dogs were quiet now. I could see my breath steaming in the night air as my lungs went on pumping, my blood kept on flowing, and I wondered how it was possible. "Joe," I said, hearing my voice tremble, "we can work this out. It's not that bad—"

"Yes, it is," he said quietly, turning to leave.

"Joe," I said pleadingly, not too proud to beg. Tears crested, overflowed, streaming down my cheeks, but I didn't care.

"I'm going home now," he said, in a flat, unemotional tone that hurt as much as his anger. "I need some time to think."

And so I stood there alone, choking back sobs as he got in his car and left.

The worst part was, he didn't look at me as he left. Not once.

* * *

Once inside my house, the dam of my emotions broke.

I cried, I stormed, I raged. I threw myself on the sofa and pounded the cushions with my fists. I kicked a wicker snowman across the room on purpose. I picked up every single cinnamon-scented pine cone I could find and threw them all into the fireplace, then lit them in a huge whoosh of flame that nearly singed my eyebrows.

"Burn, you stupid bastards," I yelled at them, as if the oil-soaked husks were responsible for the death of my dreams. I turned on every light in the house while I stormed through it, tossing my jacket on the bed and ripping off my too-tight sweater and my too-tight jeans while I sobbed and cried. Pulling on my ugliest flannel pajamas and a thick pair of socks, I wrapped myself in my rattiest old robe and wished for a cat, just so I could pull its tail and hear it yowl. A noise like that would express how I *really* felt.

How could he do this? I fell to my knees beside the bed, wracked by a fresh wave of sobs.

Time? He needed time? *How could this happen?*

I sat there, indulging myself in tears as long as I could without tissues. When the sleeves of my robe started to get too damp, I hauled myself to my feet and forced myself to find some. In the

end, a roll of toilet paper seemed the perfect solution, and I took it into the living room with me.

We were supposed to be together forever.

Temporarily cried out, I blew my nose, picked
up the phone, and curled up with it on the couch,
calling the one person in the world who *had* been
there forever, and always would be.

"Evan?" He'd answered on the second ring.
"Can you come over?"

"What's happened? What's the matter?" He'd
heard the tears in my voice immediately, just as I
could hear the worry in his.

"Joe broke up with me," I squeaked, through a
throat gone suddenly tight. I could hardly believe
I was saying the words out loud. I had to hold a
wad of tissue to my mouth to keep from bursting
into tears again.

"No," Evan breathed. "I don't believe it."

My silent head bobbing was enough to convince
him, however, even though he couldn't see it.

"Oh, honey," he said lovingly, in a voice filled
with regret. "I'll be right there."

And ten minutes later he was at my door, letting
himself in with the key he'd had since junior high
school. He had his coat off and his arms around
me less than a minute after that. We sat on the
couch, and I tried to tell him what happened, not
shielding myself from blame. I told him about our

disagreements over Selene, how Joe had called me by her name in his sleep. My visit to Marley's, having Sammy show up outside the store. How we'd gone for coffee, and he'd brought me home. How Joe had been waiting, presumably to make up from our earlier fight, only to find me with Sammy.

I stuck with the basics—I didn't see any reason to go into how Selene was somehow the reincarnation of Eve, complete with a split personality and a sex addiction, and the reason I was spending time with Sammy to begin with. Strangely enough, it seemed kind of irrelevant at this point, and Evan was already trying so hard to be brave—I saw no reason to freak him out when all I wanted to do was talk about Joe.

"Okay." He sighed. "He had a right to be mad at you about Sammy." Thankfully, he didn't belabor the point, moving on to Selene. "But him calling you by her name, even if he was sleepy . . . you were right. She's bad news." He shook his head, nearly as downcast as I was. "Joe never struck me as the type to have his head turned by a pretty girl."

"Hey," I protested faintly.

"Except you," he amended, putting an arm around my shoulder and giving me a comforting squeeze. "He was lucky to have you. I can't be-lieve he'd do this."

"I can't, either," I said numbly, still in shock.

"It's just not like him," Evan repeated. "You don't think he's actually *seeing* her, do you? That would explain why he's so eager to break up."

"What?" The thought hadn't even occurred to me. I sat up straight, not wanting to even consider the possibility that Joe'd done more than dream about Selene's charms.

"That's what men do," Evan said, gazing inward with a sigh. "Something hotter and sweeter ap-pears on the scene, and *poof*"—he gave a flick of the wrist—"they've moved on. Always better if they can make you think it's your fault, too. Re-member Allen? That guy with the hairy chest?"

I whapped him with the back of my hand with-out looking at him. "It's about me right now, thank you. I can't believe Joe would do that. He can't be seeing her—we just made love a couple of days ago."

Evan said nothing. When I glanced at him, he was struggling to keep his expression neutral, but I knew what he was thinking.

"He's been working," I said defensively. "Double shifts the last two days."

"Uh-huh," was all he said.

I didn't believe that. I didn't *want* to believe that.

A part of me recognized a kernel of truth, though, hidden deep inside everything. Whether or not Joe and Selene had physically shared a bed, he *had* been sleeping with her, at least in his mind.

Even if we found our way back together, could I ever truly forgive him for that?

"Of course he's not seeing her behind your back," Evan changed tack, obviously trying to cheer me up. "He'll probably call you tomorrow and say he's an idiot and that he's sorry, and you can tell him that you're an idiot and you're sorry, and you two will be all made up."

"I don't think so," I said quietly. "Something's different this time."

Unrolling another wad of toilet paper, I leaned my head against Evan's shoulder and watched the last of the cinnamon pine cones burn to ash.

"Will you stay the night?" I asked Evan softly, a long time later.

"Of course. My pajamas are in the car."

CHAPTER 16

I woke up the next morning in a fog. I was emotionally drained from all drama and all the tears—I hadn't cried like that since my parents died—and I had a killer headache.

"You look like hell," Evan said, for the third time. He was buttering a piece of toast at the kitchen counter, about to head out the door. "Stay home today. Get some sleep."

"I've taken too much time off lately," I repeated stubbornly, "and I don't want to leave you alone at the store again until I know it's safe." He'd been nervous there alone, despite his efforts to be brave, and I didn't blame him. Selene's "Old Hag" routine was pretty creepy.

"Nothing happened all day yesterday," he said, making an effort to sound positive. "Nothing's happened since you and Kelly said your little charm to repel the spirits, or whatever it is. Kelly e-mailed me a copy of it, you know. I'm going to read it out loud every time I get nervous. Maybe it's working . . . maybe she's gone." I knew he was trying to convince himself as well as me, so I wasn't going to argue with him.

"Fridays are always slow—I won't really need you until tomorrow. I'd rather have you all bright-eyed and bushy-tailed on Saturday than looking like death warmed over today."

"Gee, thanks," I said sourly, sipping my second cup of coffee. The first one had done no good, and I'd been sitting here staring at the sun catchers on the kitchen windowsill for a good half hour.

"What if . . ." I didn't really want to conjure Mary's image in my mind by saying her name. "What if something spooky happens?"

"I'll put on my big girl panties and deal with it," he said placidly, surprising me. "Now eat this toast," he urged, putting it in front of me. "And take a shower. You look like a death metal groupie the morning after an Ozzy Osbourne concert."

Only someone you loved could say things like that to you and get away with it.

"Love you, too." I saluted him with my coffee

cup, and decided to let him be brave. "Promise to call me if anything happens?"

"I will." He snatched up his keys and headed for the door, then hesitated. "I was thinking, Nick."

"Oh, Lord," I groaned, only half joking.

"You should call Joe."

I went still.

"Don't wait for him to call you. Those things I said about him were all true—I can't believe he'd be cheating on you. There has to be a way to patch this up."

I just looked at him, letting him talk.

"If he did cheat on you"—Evan looked pained, but resolute—"then you deserve to know, not just wonder. And if he hasn't, then I think you need to find a way to fix this before the evil hottie gets her hooks into him for real. Joe's too good to let get away."

I nodded, acknowledging the truth of what he said.

"And while you're at it," he added, "you need to ask yourself what you were doing last night in a car, alone with . . ." He didn't finish, knowing he didn't have to.

There was a silence between us as I thought about what he'd said.

"Who *are* you?" I finally said, with a reluctant half smile. "Oprah Winfrey's long-lost sister?"

He responded cheerfully to my teasing. "She should be so lucky." And then he turned and left, leaving me alone with my thoughts.

Which were still pretty bleak.

A shower seemed like a good idea, so I took a long, hot one. I turned on some music when I got out, knowing from long experience how music influenced my moods. Today it was Radiohead, and I turned it up loud, letting it fill the house with sound as I dried my hair. Dreamy, thought-provoking, neither upbeat nor depressing. I pulled on sweats and an old Bowie T-shirt, dragged a blanket off the bed, and headed for the couch, where I seemed to be spending a lot of my time lately.

I lay there a long time, listening to music and thinking about my life. I hadn't *asked* to be a beacon to the dead or a temptation to the Devil. I never *wanted* to get involved in the lives of strangers and their lost loved ones, and yet it happened, time after time. "Do unto others," the Voice inside the Light had said, and I wasn't foolish enough to ignore it; I wanted to hear it again. I wanted the brilliance of the Light to be the last thing I saw when I left this earth, wanted to hear again the music that colored the air with emotions, all of them loving, accepting, and good.

But right now I had to settle for Radiohead, and

the warm, safe cocoon of my own house. Which wasn't so bad, really.

Was it fair to expect Joe to accept me the way I was—ghosts, Devil, evil spirits, and all? Was it fair to expect him to never set a foot wrong when my life turned to chaos, as it so frequently did?

The answer was a resounding no.

So why didn't I feel better? Why didn't I just pick up the phone, call Joe, and beg him to talk this out with me? We could start again, work together to solve this latest problem, just like we always did.

I lay there, being honest with myself, and eventually the answer became clear. I was jealous of Selene, yes. Angry at the thought of Joe being turned on by her, angry that he'd ever be so aroused by someone else, asleep or awake. Calling me by her name had felt like a knife to the heart.

But there was yet another reason I didn't call Joe, one that left me very troubled; I'd nearly kissed Sammy again, and the truth of the matter was that I'd really wanted to.

Really wanted to. *Still* wanted to.

For all my squawking about Selene, how committed to Joe was *I* if I could feel like that about another man?

Throughout the morning I dozed, thought, and dozed some more. I finally got my butt off the couch for a very practical reason—the piece of toast Evan fed me had been just about the last scrap of food in the house.

There was no ice cream. There were no chips, there was no comfort food.

It was almost noon, and Joe hadn't called. I hadn't called him, either, but I'd been the one left crying in the front yard, after all. After working double shifts for two days, he was probably still sleeping, but it hurt that he hadn't called. Junk food was the only solution, so a trip to the grocery store was a necessity.

Reluctantly, I got up and got ready. Knowing there was no way I was going to feel like a million bucks today no matter what I did, I didn't bother with makeup, dragging on a light denim jacket over my T-shirt and sweats. A pair of tennis shoes, a pair of sunglasses, and I was good to go.

I had a five-block walk ahead of me to get my car, which I'd left parked near Marley's Bar, but I didn't mind. I liked walking, particularly in my neighborhood, and the fresh air felt good. Ansley Park was peaceful, shaded houses and leaf-splattered sidewalks, lots of hedges. The streets were deserted except for an occasional cat, lying in the weak winter sun. I reached my car in Little Five Points in no time flat.

I was tempted to go check on Evan at the store,

but I didn't. The only place I wanted to be today was on my couch.

With a quart of mint chocolate chip ice cream, and maybe a movie.

Fifteen minutes later, I was having a hard time choosing between mint chocolate chip or cookie dough. My cart was half full of the regular staples; bread, milk, wine, along with a big bag of chips and a box of fudge-covered cookies. I'd thrown in a bunch of bananas to make myself feel like I was getting some nutrition.

"Someone looks hungry," a woman said.

I turned my head, and there she was. My worst nightmare. Selene, smiling at me over the handle of her grocery cart.

"Oh, are you ill, Nicki?" Her fake concern was obvious. "You look awful."

She, on the other hand, looked perfect. Dark hair in a sleek ponytail, ivory coat with just the right earrings, skinny jeans, and boots.

I stood there, frozen. In the freezer section, no less. Shoving both ice cream cartons onto the nearest shelf, I faced her down.

"I know who you are," I said flatly. Part of me wanted to go for her throat, and another part of me wanted to run like hell. "Lilith."

"Ah." She didn't bother to deny it. "Clever girl." Her lips curled in a little smirk.

Red lips, dark hair, porcelain skin. *Evil incarnate.*

"Where are your friends," I dared ask, furious enough to risk a taunt. "Mara and Hecate?"

She dismissed them with a negligent wave of a hand, not bothering to deny their existence. "I only let them out when I have a use for them, and their usefulness is done, at least for the time being. Mary drew his attention and Kate drew his sympathy; I can easily do the rest."

The callousness of her reply left no doubt who, of the three, was in charge, and no doubt of her intent when it came to Joe.

"You haven't won yet," I said, though I wasn't sure of that at all. "Why are you doing this, anyway? What have I ever done to you?"

Instead of answering my questions, she asked one of her own. "Do you remember the night we met?" she asked, almost idly. "It amused Kate to let you remember."

Those words had pretty much the same effect she wanted them to have. They brought back the dream, in all its nightmarish glory, and for a moment, I was terrified.

This creature was ancient, with powers beyond my imagining. The gloves were off, but was I ready for this particular fight?

"I could've killed you then, let Mary smother you into oblivion, and stared into your eyes while you died," she said, as if cold-blooded murder was nothing. "But I was curious to see what you'd do. I wanted to watch you for a while."

I swallowed hard, unable to think of a thing to say.

"You're bold, I'll give you that," she mused, "but you're impulsive, foolish. And arrogant—oh, so arrogant. You think you know the answer to everything, just because you once had a glimpse of eternity."

My near-death experience. I shook my head, unthinking. *She knows my story.*

"Tell me," she said, in a near whisper, though there was no one else around. "When you saw the web of fate, spreading its glory across the universe, did you see the little spider, lurking over in the corner?"

Goose bumps rose all over my body.

"That was me." Her smile was one of cruelty, and her eyes, old as time, were filled with madness.

I took a step back—I couldn't help it. My fingers grazed the cold glass of the freezer to my right, and I jumped as though bitten.

"What do you want from me?" I asked again, but she just laughed.

"I've spent many years working the patterns," she murmured, still smiling. "A stitch here, a tear there, too small to be noticed on their own, all part of a much grander design. I won't allow you to unravel them."

"I have no idea what you're talking about," I said tightly.

"It's simple. If you help the boy, I'm going to strip you of everything you love, starting with Joe Bascombe," she said calmly.

I couldn't believe my ears. What a cold-blooded, calculating *bitch* she was. "The boy? What boy?" Pissed as I was, I still had no idea what she was talking about.

"The mother is mine, too, you know. You can't keep her from the Dark forever—it will find her. It is her fate."

Angie Rayburn. The boy . . .

"Josh Rayburn? You want Josh Rayburn?"

Selene cocked her head, playfully. "I've already measured him for his trench coat," she said lightly. "He'll go out in a blaze of glory, just as he desires."

A guy with a baby in his cart was wending his way down the aisle in our direction. An older man with a ball cap was eyeing the frozen pizzas a few feet away. The whole scene seemed surreal—a parody of normalcy, underlaid with horror.

"I've already talked to Josh," I said stiffly, my mind recoiling from the image she'd painted. "He wasn't interested in anything I had to say."

She looked at me and stated, "He will be."

I had no idea what that meant, but she seemed pretty sure of herself.

"Did Sammy send you? Is he behind this?" *It had to be.* The whole scheme was too diabolical.

She laughed, drawing the admiring eye of every red-blooded male in the vicinity. "As if I'd do the bidding of a weakling such as he," she murmured, so only I could hear. "Prince of Darkness, my ass."

My veins seemed suddenly filled with ice water. I mentally floundered, searching for an anchor, and found it in Joe.

"Whatever happened between you and Sammy has nothing to do with me," I said, trying my best to act brave. "Joe is mine. Whatever you're up to, it isn't going to work." *When in doubt, bluff.*

"Oh, I think it's working quite well," she replied.

I tried to suppress a rising sense of panic.

"I'm not going to let you use my boyfriend to force me into anything. Don't you think I'm going to tell him everything you just said?"

She held my eye for the space of a few heartbeats.

"Oh, do tell him," she said, smiling. "Tell away. Just don't expect him to believe you."

And then she turned and left the store, leaving her empty shopping cart behind to block the aisle.

CHAPTER 17

"This is Joe Bascombe. Leave me a message."

I was sick of Joe's cell phone message, and I wasn't going to leave yet another request for him to call me. If he couldn't be bothered to talk to me, then screw him.

I threw the phone down onto the passenger seat as I drove, thinking furiously. Should I drive to his apartment? What was I going to say, anyway? What if he didn't answer the door? He said he needed time. Did I dare let myself in with my key?

I drove to his apartment. His car wasn't in its assigned spot, and my heart sank, but I decided to go up anyway. I called him one more time before

I got out of the car, this time on his home phone, but his answering machine picked up. "This is Joe Bascombe . . ."

Abandoning the phone as useless, I stuck it back in my purse and went slowly up the stairs to his apartment, unsure what I was going to say if he *was* there—*Listen, Joe, I know you're mad at me right now, but Selene is a succubus, a sex-starved demon who comes to men in their sleep. And oh, by the way, she's Sammy's ex-girlfriend. They go a lonnng way back . . .*

Luckily, or unluckily, I had no need to worry, because Joe wasn't there. He didn't answer my knock, and since his car wasn't there, I didn't feel right going in, even though I had a key. I stood there, fingering it, wondering just for moment if I shouldn't leave it. Slide it under the mat and leave Joe a message that I'd done it.

How would he react to that? Would he call me *then*?

In the end, I couldn't bring myself to do it. I took my keys and my explanations and headed back down the stairs.

"Hey, Nicki!" A silver-blue Lincoln Town Car pulled up in the parking lot of the apartment complex, window down. Inside was Lee, from the garage, waving and smiling as the car came to a stop.

Not in the mood to chat, I gave him a weak wave and kept walking.

"What are you doing here?" he called out the window, putting it in park. "Looking for me?"

I shook my head, having had no idea Lee lived around here. "Just visiting someone," I said, as he opened the door of the Lincoln and got out.

"Any word on your car?"

It would've been rude to keep walking away at that point, as he obviously wanted to talk. "Yes, I got it back. They found it in Fayetteville."

Lee was smiling broadly as he walked toward me, and I could see his relief. "I feel so bad about the whole thing, girl, I really do. I wish you'd let me make it up to you."

I shook my head. "No need. All's well that ends well."

"C'mon," he said cajolingly. "Let me take you out, buy you dinner." He wasn't dressed for the garage today, wearing jeans and a basketball shirt. I was struck again by what a good-looking guy he was—tall, almond-eyed, and toffee-skinned—but the fact remained, he was not the guy for me.

"No thanks." I smiled to lessen the blow, but turned to go. "I've got groceries melting in the trunk."

"You're breakin' my heart here," he said, with a self-conscious laugh. "You're not mad at me, are you?" He'd gotten closer, and I got a whiff of weed. He probably kept a joint in his ashtray.

I shook my head, wanting only to go home and get my thoughts in order. "No. Seriously, I've got to go."

He didn't seem to want to take the hint. "How about I come over, get them out of the trunk for you? Today's my day off, and I got no plans . . . you?"

With a sigh, I shook my head again. "Lee, I have a boyfriend, remember?"

"Hey," he replied, raising his hands in a defensive way, "I ain't talking about getting *married* or nothing." His pupils were dilated, and his eyes were bloodshot. *Stoned.* Definitely stoned. "I'm just talking about a little hookup."

I knew exactly what he was talking about, and I wasn't interested. "Look, you're a nice guy and I'm flattered, but no." I had to go before things got awkward; I didn't want to have to find a new garage or a new car mechanic. "I'll see you around, okay?"

His face fell, and I almost felt bad, until I remembered that all his reactions were exaggerated right now.

"No hard feelings?" he pressed, giving me a doubtful look.

"No hard feelings."

When he opened his arms for a hug, I hesitated, but he lurched forward anyway. Before I knew it, my cheek was against his chest and his arms were banded around me like a python.

I tried the old "friendly pat on the back" thing to get him to release me, but he didn't.

"Mmm," he murmured, "you smell good."

It's the scent of desperation and panic, I almost said, but saved my strength for extricating myself. "Okay," I said firmly, trying to get my hands on his biceps. "That's enough."

"C'mon, baby," he murmured. "Don't be like that."

I could smell the weed on his breath, and felt a sudden surge against my right hip where his groin was pressing. Drastic measures were in order.

"Lee." I said his name as coldly as I could, turning to stone in his arms. "Let go of me right now, or you are going to be singing soprano for a long time."

He paused, his face and body far too close to mine.

"I mean it." And I did, too. A quick knee to the nuts was not outside the realm of possibility.

"Ah-aight," he said grudgingly, letting me go. He stepped back and I met his eye, glaring.

"I didn't mean nothing," he said, shaking his head. "I apologize. I got carried away."

"Yeah," I said, "you did."

I turned away, and the second I did, I saw Joe, whose car had evidently been sitting in the parking lot for quite some time. I hadn't seen him pull up, but then again, I'd been distracted.

He was idling the BMW, watching us. I couldn't see his eyes, as they were hidden behind sunglasses, but his mouth was set in a grim line. When he realized I'd seen him, his lips turned downward.

"Joe!" I raised a hand, signaling him I wanted to talk.

Instead, to my complete shock, he backed out of his parking space and drove away.

"That your boyfriend?" Lee asked, sounding genuinely curious, as if he hadn't just made a bad state of affairs infinitely worse.

I turned and gave him a look that finally got through; he gave me a sheepish wave and backed off, heading toward his car.

Knowing now that Joe's cell phone was turned off on purpose, I knew better than to start calling. With a discouraged sigh and a troubled heart, I drove home. I had ice cream melting in my trunk and that deserved saving, particularly after what I'd gone through to get it.

A part of me was extremely pissed. Surely he'd seen me push Lee away . . . how could he have just driven away like that?

I wasn't going to try and track him down at the hospital, if that's where he'd gone. I'd give him another hour, and if I didn't hear from him by then, I'd try calling him again.

Nagging doubts kept me company on the drive home.

What if he wouldn't talk to me? What if he really didn't care anymore? Had he meant it when he said it wasn't working? Were we *truly* over?

I'd dated a lot of guys before Joe, but never let any of those relationships get too serious. I'd honestly thought I'd never get married; if I couldn't have what my parents had, I didn't want it, and I was having way too much fun being young, single, and financially independent. Joe was the first man I'd allowed myself to think about a future with.

"Stupid," I muttered to myself, refusing to cry, though my eyelids prickled. "Stupid, stupid, stupid."

I'd known better than to get involved, known better than to let my guard down. *That's what men did*, Evan had said, and he was right—it was exactly what my high-school boyfriend had done with Cindy the cheerleader. They'd gotten their just deserts, though, having been miserably married ever since. *Hah! Take that, Erik!*

I'd dodged a bullet with Erik Mitchell, and I'd probably just dodged another one with Joe.

But my heart, the stupid wimp that it was, didn't believe that.

I pulled into my driveway, and my wimpy heart gave a leap—there was someone on my front porch. He was sitting on the steps, actually, and rose to his feet at the sound of my car.

It was, unfortunately, the person I *least* wanted to see: a fourteen-year-old kid named Josh Rayburn.

Caught completely off guard, I wasn't sure what to do—get out, stay in the car, call the police. The fate Selene had in store for this kid fit his angry misfit image, and, let's face it, he was a thief. He'd stolen my car.

He was wearing the exact same clothes I'd seen him in twice before, and he looked thin, apprehensive, ready to bolt at a moment's notice.

Taking a deep breath, I consoled myself with the thought that if I really had to, I could probably kick his ass. I was a healthy twenty-nine-year-old woman, and he was a scrawny fourteen-year-old kid.

"Please don't call the police." Josh held up his hands and stayed way back, but I could hear him through the car window. "I'm not here to cause trouble, I promise."

"Why *are* you here?" I frowned at him from the front seat, making a point to not sound too friendly. He'd been pretty rude to me at the police station, and helping him would most likely bring an avalanche of trouble down on my head. "What do you want?"

"I . . ." He hesitated. "I'm hungry. I haven't eaten in two days."

My heart sank. Trust the kid to pick the one thing that would make it the hardest to turn him away. He did look hungry. Starving, in fact.

"I'm sorry I stole your car, I really am," Josh said, through the window. "I've never done anything like that before. I was upset. Listen, I don't even have to come in. If you could just give me a jar of peanut butter or something . . ."

With a sigh, I leaned my head against the steering wheel.

"I'll be gone in five minutes, I swear," he said, lying his skinny little ass off, because I knew, as hungry as he was, he wasn't here for peanut butter.

He was here because of his mom.

And because no matter how much I wanted to avoid who I was, fate always managed to find me.

I should call the police. I should get this kid out of my yard, and out of my life. Maybe then Selene would let me have Joe back, and life would go back to normal.

And then evil would win, and I'd have to live with the consequences.

Shit.

I opened the car door and got out, watching him warily.

He wrapped bony arms around himself and stepped back, making no threatening moves.

Face to face, I could see what I hadn't seen before: he was pale and exhausted, the dark rings beneath his eyes darker than they were the day before. I realized instantly that he'd probably run again as soon as his stepdad brought him home, and had probably been out all night in the cold.

"There are groceries in the trunk," I said gruffly. "Bring them in, and if you touch me, you die." I held up my pepper spray to show I meant business.

The kid's eyes got big, just for a second, and I was satisfied that he took me seriously, because I meant it. I was sick and tired of having to protect myself from men these days—I almost welcomed a chance to use the spray.

Five minutes later he was sitting at my kitchen table having his second peanut butter sandwich and his second glass of milk. "Got any Red Bull?" he asked, his mouth full.

"Yes, but you can't have it," I answered calmly, no longer seriously worried he was going to do anything stupid. Josh was far more interested in food than in proving himself a tough guy. He was scrawny, pale, and had a habitual hunch—probably spent *way* too much time playing video games. "Now tell me what you're doing here. How did you know where I lived?"

Josh looked away, chewing, as he answered. "Your registration. In the glove box."

Of course.

"Why are you here? Does your dad know where you are?" I needn't have bothered with the second question, since I already knew the answer, so I repeated the first one. "Why are you here?"

"You said you knew my mom." He put down his sandwich, staring at this plate. "You talked about her like—"

Like she was alive. He couldn't bring himself to say it, but I knew that's what he was thinking.

"You said you had something important to tell me, something my mom wanted me to know."

Juvenile delinquent in training or not, I couldn't help but feel sorry for him. Beneath the drama, the dyed hair, and the eyebrow ring, he was just a kid who missed his mom.

Since I understood the feeling all too well, my heart went out to him. But, having once been a juvenile delinquent in training myself, I knew sympathy was not the only thing Josh needed right now. A solid dose of honesty over his mother's death might help him cope, and it didn't look like he had anyone else to talk to—he and his stepdad obviously had some communication issues.

I had to admit, I was afraid. Did I really want to get involved? Whatever relationship I had with Joe was hanging by a thread, and Selene had made it clear that she held a very sharp pair of scissors.

If Joe'd had a chance to avoid another Columbine, would he take it, no matter what it cost him personally?

He would, because that's what heroes do.

It truly sucked to be me right now.

"You're going to have a hard time believing what I'm about to tell you," I said, rising from the table to pour him another glass of milk. I wasn't going to tell him all of it, of course—there was no need for him to know about the Darkness or how his mother hid from it. That story wasn't over yet, and I didn't know its ending.

"Sometimes I see the spirits of the dead," I said bluntly. "Sometimes they talk to me." I snagged him a banana from the counter on my way back to the table with the milk, and put both in front of him.

The look he was giving me was skeptical, but I could see a faint glimmer of hope in it. "So, you're what . . . like a psychic or something?"

Since my fondest hope was to *never* be taken as a backroom Madame Zelda, I answered flatly, "No. I just sometimes see the dead. Take it or leave it. Oh, and whatever I tell you doesn't leave this room. Don't you dare go back to school and tell your World of Warcraft buddies who I am, no matter how cool it might make you sound."

He was silent, eyeing me as carefully as I eyed him. He nodded, and I went on.

"I was at the hospital the morning your mom died," I said, deliberately trying to be as matter-of-fact as possible, though I knew it had to be hard for him to hear it. For Angie to accept her own death, Josh needed to accept it, and to quit running away from it. I knew that instinctively, having run wild for a time myself after my parents died. "I saw her in the corridor. She was very, very sorry about what she'd done."

Josh's face screwed up with grief, mask of teenage coolness slipping, but I kept going. "She wanted you to know how much she loved you, and that she was sorry."

"Why'd she do it, then?" His voice was strained. The look he gave me was desperate. "Why?"

My heart ached for him. "Depression is an illness," I said softly. "It can be overwhelming."

He cracked, bursting into noisy sobs, shoving aside his plate and burying his face into his crossed arms. His elbows were thin and dirty, and the sight of them made me blink back tears of my own.

"She didn't used to be like that," he sobbed, without lifting his head. "She used to be happy." More sobbing, then he muttered, low beneath his breath, "It was my fault. She did it because of me."

I went cold, hearing him blame himself that way. "What happened to your mother was not your fault," I said firmly. "Don't think that for a minute. She wouldn't want you to think that." *No mother would.* "She told me she wasn't taking her medicine. It wasn't your fault," I repeated.

"You're right," he said, lifting his tear-streaked face to mine. "It's not my fault, it's *his* fault! They were always fighting!" The switch from grief to anger had been quick; Josh was glaring at me defiantly, as if waiting for me to argue.

I shook my head, wishing my old therapist, Ivy Jacobson, was here. "Your mom loved both of you, Josh," was all I could say.

He didn't answer me, putting his head back down on his arms so I couldn't see his face.

"Your mom made a mistake," I said, daring to touch him on the shoulder. His hair was dirty, and he smelled ripe—he'd been on the run for at least four days. "Everybody makes mistakes. You have to forgive her. In order for her to rest in peace, you have to forgive her."

I sat with him for a while, saying nothing. When

he got his emotions under control, he sat up, dragging a sleeve over his eyes.

I handed him a paper towel. "We should call your dad," I said, hoping the worst was over.

"No." Josh shook his head. "I'll just go."

I stood, ready to look for my car keys. "Okay. I'll take you home."

"I'm not going home."

"What do you mean, you're not going home? You have to go home."

"No, I don't."

I began to understand how quickly a stubborn teenager could try your patience.

"Your dad must be worried sick."

"He's not my dad." That stony look I'd seen in the police station was back on his face. "And I hope he *is* worried sick."

I found myself frowning. "Shame on you," I scolded, sounding for all the world like my own mom would've if she'd been there. "He loved your mother, too, you know, and he probably has plenty of his own guilt to deal with. Give the man a break."

Josh shrugged, choosing to look away and play it cool again.

"What about your mom?"

I wasn't above playing dirty to get him in the car and out of my house.

"Her service is today, at four o'clock at St. Patrick the Divine. Are you going to miss your mom's funeral just because you're mad at your stepfather?"

His face, already pale, went white. For a second, I thought he was going to be sick.

"Will you go with me?" he whispered, catching me off guard for the second time that day.

I sighed, giving him a look. *Doomed, I was doomed.* "Only if you shower first. Shampoo and towels are in the bathroom down the hall, second door on the right."

So much for a quiet afternoon on the couch.

He swallowed, trying to regain his cool. "You won't call my dad while I'm in there?"

I noticed his slip, and wanted to smile, but didn't. "No, I won't call your dad."

CHAPTER 18

St. Patrick the Divine was a huge, vaulted cathedral on the outskirts of Atlanta's midtown district. I'd never been inside, but I knew where it was. It was an institution, and if you were unfortunate enough to need a funeral, this was a pretty impressive place to have it.

Angie Rayburn must have been loved, because a steady stream of people were going inside.

I'd loaned Josh a plain black T-shirt—I had plenty of those—and the tuxedo jacket Evan had left in the hall closet last New Year's Eve. It was a little big on him, but nobody would notice, and he looked far better in it than whatever suit his dad might've picked out, I'm sure. His jeans were his own, and none too clean, but they'd have to do. At least his carefully sleeked black hair was clean. He was still pale, but I liked to believe that he looked stronger than he'd been when he'd first shown up on my doorstep.

He looked older, too. With his hair slicked back and his face clean, I could see the young man emerging from the bones of his face.

I hoped, despite what Selene said, that he'd be a good man.

In fitting with the occasion, I was also wearing black, from my velvet jacket to my suede scrunchy boots, with a flowy black gypsy skirt and a long sweater. Beneath the skirt I wore a pair of warm, black tights. It made me feel better to know that if I needed to, at any time during the service, I could strip off the skirt and run like hell without exposing my assets.

Nervously getting out of the car near the cathedral, I looked around for Selene, wondering if she was going to show up and interfere, or if, having delivered her warning, she'd leave me to my fate.

I'd made up my mind, you see; I really had no choice. I had to do the right thing by Josh. I couldn't, and wouldn't, abandon a scared kid on the day of his mom's funeral.

Thoughts and worries over Joe kept intruding, though. Now, more than ever, I was *sure* that I loved him, despite an occasional twinge of weakness over someone else. I was only human, after all, which was a big part of the problem. As soon as the funeral was over, I was going to do my very best to find Joe and talk to him. I'd tell him the truth about everything, I'd make him listen, no secrets, no interruptions, no fighting.

And if we were meant to be, he'd hear me, and we'd get past this.

If he didn't, then we weren't meant to be.

But I didn't have any more time to think about it just then, because we'd arrived at Angie Rayburn's funeral, the cathedral steps looming ahead.

Josh's dad was standing in front of the open doors of the church, looking worried and sad and stretched to the breaking point. I saw his face in the instant he saw Josh, and knew the relief and caring there was genuine. He obviously loved his stepson, despite their differences.

"Josh." He left off shaking someone's hand to rush toward us, but we were still coming up the steps, and a woman in a large hat cut him off.

Beside me, Josh stiffened. "Be nice," I hissed. "He needs you."

The sidelong look I got for that statement was surprising—it seemed a bizarre concept to the boy. "No, he doesn't," he muttered.

"Yes, he does," I whispered. "You're still a family, even without your mom."

"Josh." David reached us, hand outstretched, but stopped short of actually touching his son. "Where have you been?" His glaze flicked to me, confusion clear. "I've been worried sick."

"He showed up on my doorstep earlier today, Mr. Rayburn," I said quietly, not wanting any of Angie's mourners to overhear. "He's fine. Everything's fine."

Liar, I called myself, quaking inside. The more I helped this kid, the worse Selene was going to make it for me, but what else could I do?

"Call me David," he said to me, not taking his eyes from Josh. "Have you eaten? You look thin . . . are you all right?"

Giving reluctant nods to both of those questions, Josh offered a grudging "I'm fine. I'm sorry. Let's just get through this, okay?"

David's eyes filled with moisture, which he blinked back. He reached out and took Josh by the shoulder, firmly now, like a man. "We have to stick together," he said softly, looking deep into his stepson's eyes. "It's what Mom would've wanted."

Throat suddenly tight, I looked away and let them have their moment, hoping it would be enough to start the process of rebuilding some bridges.

"Joshua—oh, Josh, sweetheart, are you all right?" A woman rushed up, taking Josh by the shoulders, worry written all over her perfectly perfect face.

Of course. I struggled not to faint.

"I'm fine, Selene," Josh said. "Don't make a fuss."

"Don't make a fuss?" Selene exclaimed, drawing Josh into a hug that made it clear she knew him quite well. "Where have you been? We've been worried sick."

I couldn't miss her use of the word "we." Spots appeared before my eyes, but I closed them briefly, warding off weakness.

David spoke up. "He's fine, Selene, the boy is fine."

"And who is this?" Selene turned an arched eyebrow in my direction, acting as if we'd never met before.

Josh said nothing. A quick glance revealed him scowling down at the ground, Selene's perfectly manicured hand still on his shoulder.

"This is the nice lady who helped Josh," David said, a bit awkwardly. "I'm sorry, but I don't know your name."

"Nicki," I murmured, still reeling.

"Nicki, this is—was—a friend of Angie's, Selene Mathews."

With friends like you, who needs enemies? I couldn't help but wonder if Angie's depression had begun before or after she'd met Selene. Either way, the cruelty involved made me sick.

She wore a black suit that hugged her curves in all the right places, yet still managed to be sedate. Her dark hair was pulled in a ponytail, low on her neck, and the only color on her was her lips, a muted shade of red.

I found her respect for the dead truly touching. *Not.*

An older man came up to David and touched his arm, murmuring something in his ear.

"It's time," David said, taking a deep breath. He looked at Josh, who'd gone very quiet. "Thank you for bringing Josh home," he said to me. "I can't tell you how worried I was."

"You're welcome," I said, "but I think you should tell him. He needs to hear it."

Josh shot me an uncertain look, but I laid it on the line, despite Selene being *right there*, listening to every word I said. "Your dad loves you," I said, "whether you think so or not. Your mom wouldn't want you to blame anyone for her death—let the anger go, Josh."

David swallowed and nodded, sliding an arm around Josh's shoulder. "Thank you," he said again, and turned his son toward the church.

"Thanks for everything," Josh said to me, over his dad's shoulder. His eyes met mine, apprehensive but bright, and I knew I'd done the right thing. I gave him a nod and watched as, together, he and his dad went toward the cathedral doors.

Selene lingered, Josh and David still in earshot. "Coming in, Miss Styx?"

"You go on ahead," I said. "I'll find my own way."

And I would, too.

She gave me a "suit yourself" shrug and victorious little smirk. "You'll find it alone," she whispered, in a voice that sounded like the slither of a snake in the garden, "because Joe now belongs to me." And then she walked away, letting herself be swallowed up by the group of people heading into the church.

I stood there until I was the only one left outside. And then I turned, looking toward my car, parked in the church's lot. Sure enough, there was the telltale blond head; a man, leaning against my fender. He saw me looking and smiled, for all the world as if I'd been expecting him.

In a way he was right, because I wasn't surprised.

He'd never finished his story, after all.

"What the hell is going on?" I marched right up to Sammy and demanded answers, tired of playing games. "What does Selene want with the Rayburns? Why is she *in my face* every freakin' time I turn around?"

He watched me come, leaning against my car with his hands in his pockets of his coat, à la James Dean, if James Dean were the Devil. Unruffled by my approach, he waited a moment before answering.

"Love the jacket, but that baggy skirt and sweater hardly go with the sexy sprite look. You're hiding your best assets."

"Thanks for the fashion advice," I replied, refusing to be sidetracked, "but nobody asked you. What is Selene doing here? Why is Josh so important to her?"

I didn't want to think about what she'd said about Joe. I *couldn't* think about what she'd said about Joe . . .

Sammy sighed, shaking his head as he eyed my long skirt with regret. "My guess is that the boy is not the least bit important to her—she just wants you to *think* he is."

My brain seemed stuck. "What? Why?"

"Think, my darling."

"Don't call me darling," I snapped.

"Selene could corrupt anyone she wanted," he said patiently. "Boy, man, anything male on two legs would find it impossible to resist her." His warning carried a personal note. "She's a creature of great power who routinely bends men to her will, and she knows what she's doing. The real question is, why would she want this particular boy?"

"She told me she was going to make him into the next Columbine kid or something—"

"Oooh," Sammy interrupted, "nice touch."

I gave him a glare for his insensitivity.

"Maybe she wants the boy, or maybe she just wants to torment you further while she dallies with your boyfriend. Your precious doctor has cheated our side out of a few souls himself, you know. It gives her pleasure to use 'good' to accomplish 'evil.'"

My blood ran cold at that one.

"Misdirection, misinformation, smoke and mirrors . . . I have to hand it to her, she's learned a great many tricks through the ages," he said admiringly. "If you'd just minded your own business that day at the hospital . . ." Sammy made a *tsk*ing noise. "She already had you in her sights, of course, but you gave her the perfect excuse to go after you, which is exactly what she was waiting for."

"You know about that?" I mentally cringed, having hoped it would never come up. I didn't want to think about that black mass of boiling evil

I'd seen in the corridor—I had enough problems right now.

"Of course I know about that—the Darkness was quite hungry that day, and you denied it. Got the imps and the ethereals all aflutter, so they were happy to let her teach you a much-needed lesson. It cleared the way for her to do what she wanted, with no repercussions from the Dark side. Come, let me buy you dinner and I'll tell you all about it."

"Are you joking?" I stared at him like he was from another planet, which, as he had just reminded me, he technically was. "After last night?" I took a deep breath, last night's fiasco fresh in my mind. "How could you possibly think I'd *ever* go anywhere with you again?"

Imps and ethereals? No, thank you.

He smiled, blue eyes twinkling in the winter sun. "It was worth a shot."

"Tell me what is going on with Selene," I demanded. "No more 'maybes.' You know what's going on, I know you do."

"It's simple, darling."

I gave him a fulminating look, which anybody else would've heeded.

"You've pissed off the Dark side royally over the way you've played me for a fool," he said lightly. "I'm willing to take my lumps like a man and deal with it—it isn't over yet, after all. But there are others who don't feel the same."

"Others?" I asked faintly, still trying to absorb how anyone could *possibly* think I'd played Sammy Divine for a fool. That word wasn't in his vocabulary. Hell, it wasn't even in his universe.

"It appears my reputation as the Great and Mighty Satan has been tarnished," he said, with a rueful smile, "by my attraction to a certain mortal woman with a penchant for do-gooding."

"Right." I wasn't buying it. "What a load of crap."

"It's true, like it or not." He gave me a bland look that almost—*almost*—had me believing he was telling the truth. "I should've dealt more harshly with you, I know that. Softness can so easily lead to a downfall . . . I'm proof enough of that."

I stared at him, feeling very vulnerable all of a sudden. I'd begun to take for granted that he'd never hurt me, based purely on the fact that he never had.

"I—" Unsure how to respond, I blurted, "Thank you for . . . for not being harsh," and left it at that.

He smiled, faintly. The silence between us was filled with something I couldn't name—something sad, something wistful and fragile—there, then gone.

"I'm about to prove my critics right." He sighed. "By telling you things I shouldn't."

"Tell me." I didn't care about his critics; I just wanted to be rid of Selene.

"The point here is that *I'm* the one being tested, not you," Sammy said, stunning me into silence. "Selene is here to make your life a living hell, simply because I didn't. I now have to choose whether to intervene, or to let you suffer the consequences of your actions. She knew I would learn of what she was doing. She wants to see how much power you have over me. Who will I choose to aid: you, or her?"

"Flabbergasted" is a word my mom used to use, and in that moment, I finally understood what it meant.

I stared down at the toes of my scrunchy boots, not seeing them. I focused instead on the pavement beneath them, gray and unyielding. After a moment, I raised my head and asked him shakily, "And when will you decide?"

"I don't know." Leaning back on my fender, he cocked his head and shrugged. "The way I look at it, I'm damned if I do, and damned if I don't, so I see no need to hurry."

CHAPTER 19

"So this is all your fault?" I was furious all of a sudden, fear taking a backseat to anger. "I'm some sort of a *test* among the inhabitants of Hell to find out how evil you are?"

He shrugged, beginning to smile as he always did when I got angry. "Enlightenment dawns."

"The hell with enlightenment! You really expect me to believe that"—I waved a hand toward the cathedral, spluttering—"that *creature* in there is stronger than you?"

"I explained last night about the division of power," he said calmly, reminding me of what he'd said in the coffee shop. "She is her own crea-

ture. I didn't send her, she came of her own voli-
tion." Another slow smile, lazy and self-satisfied.
"I do, however, have the power to stop her, so I
suggest you stop yelling at me. I suggest, in fact,
that you become very, very nice to me."

"Get your ass off my car," I snapped, pushed to
the breaking point by the implied threat. I'd never
bargained with my body, and I wasn't about to
start now.

His eyes gleamed. The silence between us was
very different this time, taut, knife-edged with
tension.

I was trembling, a combination of fear and anger
that left me feeling wild and reckless. "You're
never going to have me," I said, voice low, "and
blackmail is a piss-poor seduction technique."
Once started, I had a hard time shutting up. "But
what else should I expect from the Great and
Mighty Satan?"

How close I came to incineration I'll never know,
but I do know that if looks could cause a person to
burst into flame, I was millimeters from it.

I bit my lip, holding his eye as long as I could,
but I was the one who looked away first.

Sammy stood, rising from the hood of my car
with careless grace. He turned up the collar of
his peacoat, shoved his hands in his pockets, and

walked away, the silence he left in his wake more frightening than any words.

I watched him go, knowing that if I called him back I was doomed.

I was doomed any way you looked at it.

And since doom was right around the corner, and time short, I got in my car and did what my heart and mind had been urging me to do all day, and drove to Joe's apartment.

This time, his car was there.

I parked mine close by, nervous suddenly. What if he was still mad? What if he wouldn't talk to me?

Taking a second, I checked my makeup in the mirror on the back of the visor, and fluffed my hair a little. Then, because I was desperate and because I knew it couldn't hurt, I wiggled my way out of the gypsy skirt and tossed it into the backseat. My sweater came to midthigh and my boots to the knee, so I was covered. Then I took a deep breath and got out of the car, going straight to the stairs that led to his apartment.

It seemed like forever before he answered the door, though it was probably wasn't that long. He'd been sleeping, obviously. His dark hair, always unruly, was mussed, and he was wearing nothing but a pair of scrub pants and the maroon robe I'd bought him for his birthday. He wasn't smiling.

He wasn't frowning, either. His face was a blank, leaving me uncertain.

"I—I was hoping we could talk," I said.

"I'm tired, Nicki. I'm not up for a scene."

He looked tired. A couple of days' worth of stubble and a couple of dark circles beneath his eyes.

"Neither am I," I answered, hurt.

There was a pause, then he stood back, holding the door for me to enter.

Hardly a great show of enthusiasm, but I took it. As soon as the door closed behind him, I turned. "Joe, listen . . . I'm sorry for my part in all this, I really am."

He brushed past me on his way to the living room, where he sat wearily on the couch.

"I know I shouldn't have gotten in that car with Sammy. It was stupid and I was wrong, but nothing happened! I love *you*, and I want to work this out."

He sighed, rubbing his eyes.

Not exactly the reaction I'd hoped for.

"I swear I'll never do it again." And I meant it. "Like I said, it was stupid . . . but I found out some things you need to know, Joe, about Selene."

"Here we go again," he muttered, but I refused to be discouraged. "This has nothing to do with Selene."

I ignored him, because it had *everything* to do with Selene.

"She's not at all what she appears—she's a demon, a female demon called a succubus."

He stopped rubbing his eyes and looked at me, giving me his full attention.

Encouraged, I went on. "She comes to men in their sleep and—"

"I know what a succubus is," he interrupted, voice level.

"She's mad at Sammy for something that happened a long time ago, in their past, and she's taking it out on me!" I wasn't going to go into the Garden of Eden story just now; it was too much. "She's using you to get to me—that's why you keep dreaming about her."

He leaned forward, resting his elbows on his knees. I'd known that maroon robe would look great on him, and was glad he never used the belt. My fingers itched to smooth his hair—an errant strand stood up crazily over one ear.

"Is that what the golden boy told you?" he asked, peering at me intently.

Uh-oh.

I nodded, knowing I deserved the sarcasm.

Another sigh, and then Joe leaned back, resting both arms on the back of the couch. I had a great view of his chest and abs, but the view didn't do me a bit of good right now.

"So the guy you claim to be the Devil has told you that the woman you hate is some sort of soul-sucking man-eater. How convenient."

I blinked at his choice of words. "I don't *claim* he's the Devil. He *is* the Devil."

"I used to believe that," Joe said flatly, "until I realized that you would never trust him the way you do if that were the case."

"I don't trust him!" I protested, my voice rising. "He's a lying bas—" *Double uh-oh.*

"You don't trust him?" He leaned forward again, skepticism apparent. "And yet you stand here telling me some cock-and-bull story he told *you* about Selene Mathews being a succubus, and expect me to lap it up like cream." He wasn't angry, which was the worst part. "I think you've been playing me, Nicki. I think Sammy is just a guy from your past who refuses to go away, and I think you *like* it that he refuses to go away. All this bullshit about him being the Devil is just that . . . bullshit."

Stunned, I actually *felt* my heart shrivel into

a tiny ball, leaving nothing but emptiness in its place.

"Where is this coming from?" I couldn't believe what he was accusing me of. All the fury I should've felt, that I'd felt earlier in the parking lot with Sammy, seemed burned out of me, leaving me cold as ice.

"I thought about it all night," Joe said. "It finally became clear about three in the morning."

Three in the morning.

"Even more clear when I saw how cozy you were with my new neighbor—that guy's had a string of girls coming and going since he moved in. I thought you had better taste than that."

My jaw dropped. "Lee is my *mechanic*," I protested, feeling unfairly put upon.

"Right," he said flatly. "Everybody hugs their mechanics."

"You think I'm lying to you?"

"I think you've been lying to me all along. Did you meet Sammy during our trip to Savannah, or before that? Never mind"—he shook his head—"I don't need to know. When he showed up causing trouble earlier this year, I backed off, gave him his space because you claimed he was the Great and Mighty Satan—"

A definite chill went down my spine at his choice of words, since I'd heard the phrase twice already today.

"—but now I think that was just your way of keeping us apart so you could play us both." Shaking his head, he laughed a little as he stared down at the carpet. "I'm guessing you broke it off with him back then, but now he's back for seconds. When I think about how I stood there in Divinyls, and watched you kiss him good-bye . . ."

I honestly couldn't believe what I was hearing. "You—you're kidding, right?"

He raised his head, no longer laughing, and said nothing. Joe, who was usually an open book, seemed completely shut off.

"You think I made it all up, so I could—" I couldn't even finish the sentence.

"Date two guys at once?" He gave me a direct stare. "You going to tell me you've never done that before?"

He knew I couldn't deny it. I'd told him everything about my past by now, and he knew I'd done it once or twice, never for very long and never with any level of seriousness. "I never loved them," I answered, stricken. "I love you."

Abruptly he stood, and walked past me toward the door.

"I don't believe you anymore. You need to go."

In a state of stunned disbelief, I saw him open it. It was a stranger I saw, standing there in Joe's robe. Same heartbreakingly green eyes, same look of wholesome goodness that had sucked me in over my head.

"Good-bye, Nicki," the stranger said, and the drowning began.

CHAPTER 20

"Cheer up, buttercup," Evan said to Butch, in the front seat of the Volvo, two days later. "All the money raised from the bazaar goes to Toys for Tots. It's all for a good cause."

"Are you sure we really need to go shopping today?" Butch asked, glancing toward me in the backseat. "Nicki doesn't look too excited."

I stared out the window, not bothering to confirm or deny his comment. It would be a long time before I ever got excited over *anything*, ever again.

"Nicki needs to cheer up," Evan said firmly, eyeing me in the rearview mirror. "And shopping is the perfect way to do it. Life goes on, and the store is running low on inventory. Time to clean up on designer duds from the good people of Buckhead who wouldn't be caught dead wearing last year's fashions. The Buckhead Bazaar is an annual tradition," he said to Butch. "Whatever we don't sell in the store, we sell on eBay." He waited a heartbeat or two for me to chime in, but I didn't. "Right, Nicki?"

Faced with a direct question, I nodded, but I didn't stop staring out the window. "Right."

He made a noise of frustration. "C'mon, Nick. You really don't sound like your heart's in it."

What a stupid thing to say. Of course my heart wasn't in it. My heart was lying on the floor of Joe's apartment, where I'd left it two days ago.

Two long, incredibly miserable days.

Evan had dragged me out of the house today, spoiling what otherwise promised to be a perfectly gloomy Sunday afternoon. "We're going to stop by on the way home and get you a Christmas tree," he said decisively. "You need some Christmas spirit."

I almost smiled at the unintended irony, but couldn't. The last thing I needed this Christmas was anything to *do* with spirits.

"I don't want a tree this year," I said, watching some beautiful Buckhead homes slide by my window without really seeing them. "I already told you that."

Evan made a rude noise this time. "Christmas isn't Christmas unless we watch a black-and-white movie at your house on Christmas Eve—it's going to be Dickens's *A Christmas Carol* this year, by the way—then have mimosas and cinnamon rolls under the tree in *your* living room the next morning, which means you're getting a tree."

"We could do it at your apartment this year." I didn't really care, either way, even though Evan was right—we always had Christmas at my house.

"I do Thanksgiving, you do Christmas," Evan said firmly, not letting me off the hook. "You're getting a tree."

I gave up, not willing to argue. I never wanted to argue with anybody, ever again. Let Evan get me a tree. Let Evan decorate the tree. Let Evan have his imaginary perfect Christmas under the tree at my house with Butch, the love of his life.

Who cared?

I wasn't going to cry anymore. I wasn't. I'd had no word from Joe—no calls, no e-mails—and didn't expect any. I'd bagged up his navy sweater and his medical magazines and his shaving stuff and put them in the back of the closet. He could have them if he wanted them, but I had a feeling he wasn't going to ask. Not a lot to show for the past year and half of my life, but all I had.

She'd won, and I'd lost. I knew who'd poured poison in his ears. She'd warned me—I knew the cost of helping Josh, and I'd done it anyway. Losing Joe was the price I paid.

I glanced at my hand, nails chewed, polish chipped. I was still wearing the antique marcasite ring he'd given me for Halloween, simply because I couldn't bring myself to take it off. I would, someday, but I wasn't ready to yet—it seemed too final.

Maybe someday, when I was old and gray, someone at the morgue would pry it off my cold, dead hand, and sell it on eBay, where it would end up in a vintage shop just like Handbags and Gladrags.

I found myself strangely comforted at the thought.

Evan roused me from my morbid wanderings the easiest way possible. "Hey, Morticia! Look alive, we're at the bazaar!"

The Buckhead Bazaar was held annually at the King of Peace Episcopalian Church, and hosted by the Buckhead Women's Auxiliary. Each year, the philanthropic housewives of upscale Atlanta outdid themselves in cleaning out their closets and garages, and selling everything in one big garage sale, with the proceeds going to charity. It was well-advertised and always packed, and

today was no different. The church's indoor basketball court had been transformed into a giant
retail space, organized neatly into sections: small
furniture, appliances, clothing, jewelry. Buckhead
ladies were nothing if not organized.

"Let's start with the jewelry," Evan suggested,
surveying the room with a practiced eye. "It's
crowded over there, but if we wait too long we'll
miss the best pieces."

"You go ahead," I said, having thought enough
about jewelry today. "I'm just going to look
around."

He gave me a frown. "Nicki . . ."

"I'll scope out the room and come back. We've
both got our cell phones . . . I'll find you."

"Let her go, Ev," Butch said, touching his arm.
"Let's go look at jewelry."

I shot him a grateful look, and he smiled before
leading Evan away. "Tell me again what we're
looking for," I heard him say to Evan. "How can
you tell whether it's designer or not?"

"Look for a hallmark," Evan answered, a familiar note of excitement in his voice, "usually on the
clasp . . ."

I turned, heading in the opposite direction
on general principle. My best bud meant well,
but there was only so much nagging and forced
cheerfulness I could take at one time. I'd nearly

exceeded my limit in the car, and needed some time alone.

A chair in the corner sounded nice, but it was a big room, and there were a lot of people—I didn't see any chairs except the ones for sale. An old rocker caught my eye, and I had to go over and give it a closer look. It would look great on my front porch, and we could use it in the spring window display. The paint was chipped and the armrests were worn—it was definitely in the "well-used" category, which was why it hadn't sold yet. A little sandpaper and some spray paint would give it new life—it was technically a steal at twenty-five bucks. Not yet motivated to buy, I made a mental note to look at it again when I'd finished my circuit of the floor, and turned away.

"You like the chair?" someone asked, at my elbow. It was one of the auxiliary ladies, easily recognizable by the matching Christmas aprons they wore during the bazaar. She was elderly and plump, with carefully coiffed gray hair and a double chin.

I nodded vaguely, not wanting to commit myself. "Maybe. I'm going to look around a little."

"You should buy it," she said. "I think you need it."

Shaking my head, I turned and walked away.

"Seriously," the woman said, behind me. "I want you to buy this chair. Please."

Something in her voice made me stop, and turn around.

"You're going to need this chair one day," she said, "to rock your grandchildren." The woman reached out a hand and touched the chair lovingly, starting it rocking. "You'll have three of them, two boys and a girl. One of the boys will remind you of your husband, and the girl will be like you—a bit wild but with a good heart."

My throat became tight. Talk about a raw nerve; I couldn't have responded if I wanted to.

"Your daughter, the mother of these children, will have dark hair and a quick laugh." The woman, a total stranger, spoke with the assurance of someone who knew things I didn't. "She will love you dearly, as you will her."

I stared at her, forcing myself to swallow. "Who—who are you?"

"The web of fate is woven by many," the woman answered, with a gentle smile. "There are those who wish to warp it, and those who wish to mend it. Let not your heart be troubled, Nicki. Buy the chair."

For a moment I wondered if I was hallucinating. The whole exchange had an "otherworld" feel to it.

"Was it"—I gestured toward the rocker—"was it yours?"

She nodded, smiling, and crossed plump hands

in front of her apron. "And now it's yours. When you sit in it, remember that while there is evil in the world, there is good, too." She leaned in a little and gave me a wink. "And we do-gooders tend to stick together. Evil wins when good does nothing. You're not alone, dear. We're watching."

And then she faded away, right before my eyes. One second I was standing there talking to an elderly woman in a Christmas apron, and the next I was talking to myself.

"Wow." *Evil wins when good does nothing.*

I felt better suddenly, as if everything the woman had said were true. I had a future, and it sounded pretty nice, even if I did have a hard time envisioning myself as a grandmother. I'd be the coolest grandma ever, I promised myself.

More importantly, I'd just learned that I wasn't alone. Just as Sammy had opened my eyes to the fact that there were other creatures on his side of the veil, the woman had pointed out that there was balance on the good side, too.

I'd never believed in angels, but from here on out I'd be picturing them as elderly, plump, and wearing Christmas aprons, arranging garage sales to raise money for kids.

Then, with a laugh, I realized that I also thought of them as sweet little girls who loved babies, and grizzled red-haired barflies named Maybelline, who offered advice to the lovelorn when they most needed it.

The three phases of womanhood—maiden, mother, crone—reflected in goodness to balance Selene's madness. Maybe that was the way the universe meant for it to be, all along.

CHAPTER 21

"Could you put the rocker in the backyard, Butch? I'm going to sand it down and clean it up a little."

"Are you going to repaint it?" He hauled it out of the back of the Volvo like it was a child's toy. "I kind of like it like this, all battered and peeling." The chair had been painted white, long ago.

I smiled at him, glad he had the good taste to recognize buried treasure when he saw it. "The look is called distressed," I told him, reinforcing Evan's teachings. "I'm just going to scrub it down, and sand off the loose paint. It'll be the same, only better."

"Good," he said, satisfied, and hoisted the chair high over his head as he carried it toward the back of the house. A baldheaded gentle giant, who knew how to handle with care.

"Did you see the Florenza pieces?" Evan proudly showed me his two favorite finds of the day, a woman's bronze trinket box and matching mirror. They were all that was left of an ornate woman's vanity set from the 1950s. "Too bad the brush is missing. Still, the velvet inside the trinket box has a great nap."

"Beautiful," I agreed. "We got some great deals."

"You're feeling better, aren't you?"

I gave him a rueful smile, knowing I was about to get an "I told you so," but not really minding.

"I knew it. I can tell. I told you this would make you feel better, now didn't I?" He grinned smugly, and offered me his cheek to kiss, hands full of treasure.

I obliged, giving him an appreciative smack. I did feel better, but not necessarily for the reasons Evan expected. No harm in letting him think so, though. "Thank you," I said. "It was a good day."

"You're welcome. I'll sort through the clothes and see what needs what," he went on. Nobody could sew a hem or a button better than Evan, and if we ever needed anything major sewn, we knew a great seamstress down in Little Five who always gave us a deal. "You want to tackle the handbags and the shoes?"

We'd found three fabulous bags this trip: a Judith Leiber coin purse with only a few missing rhinestones, and a couple of satin clutches with the original Coro clasps, all in need of cleaning. The shoes weren't going to need much work; some gorgeous designer pumps and sandals that had been worn once, maybe twice, if ever. The wealthy ladies of Buckhead could afford fabulous shoes, and were always replacing them with new ones.

"Sure, I'll get them cleaned up," I said, looking forward to it. I needed something to do the rest of the afternoon anyway. Working on the chair and the bags would keep me from moping over Joe.

"We can unload the rest of this stuff at my apartment," he said, "and then we'll go pick out the tree."

I made a groaning noise, having forgotten about getting a Christmas tree, and not really up for it.

"What?" Evan gave me an exasperated look.

"Why don't we do it tomorrow?" I suggested quickly. "It's Monday, the shop's closed, and Butch will still be around. We'll make a day of it, do it tomorrow afternoon."

He frowned at me, knowing weaseling when he saw it. "Monday afternoon *early*," he stressed, willing to compromise. "No excuses."

"No excuses," I said, glad to be off the hook today. I did feel better, but I wasn't quite in the Christmas mood just yet.

"Butchie's making vegetable lasagna tonight," Evan said hopefully. "Why don't you dump these things in the house and come have some with us?"

"Yeah, Nicki." Butch had come back, and was rearranging the trunk. He found the box with the purses and pulled it out. "Come on over and have a glass of wine with us while I put it together."

"Thanks, guys, but no." I shook my head, knowing I'd reached the limit of my desire to socialize at the moment, and not wanting to take up their evening. "You've done enough babysitting today. Go home and relax."

Evan gave me a worried look and Butch gave me a sheepish one.

"I'm fine," I insisted. "Really." I took the box from Butch, and standing on my tiptoes, gave him a kiss on the cheek, too. "You're sweet. I love you both. Go home."

I waved them good-bye from the front porch as I let myself in. The high-pitched whine of the alarm, the gleaming hardwood floors, the ensuing quiet—all so familiar. I loved my house, even if it was a bit messy at the moment. I'd been in such a funk that I hadn't done the dishes, and my blanket and pillow were still on the couch. Empty glasses and cereal bowls littered the coffee table.

With a shrug, I ignored the mess. I wasn't ready to clean it up, and besides, who was going to see it? Instead I took the box of bags and shoes to the dining room table, where I laid them out, one by one. What we'd bought for under three hundred dollars could easily be sold for double that, if we were patient. The coin purse alone was worth three times what we'd paid for it.

That done, what I really wanted to do was get to work on the rocker. I'd changed my mind about putting it on the porch, and was thinking it might look great in front of the fireplace—I could use all the good karma vibes I could get *inside* the house.

So I went outside and down the back porch steps. Butch had left the rocker on the concrete patio just outside the garden shed, which was right where I wanted it.

I had everything I needed inside the shed; sandpaper and a small hand sander, rubber gloves, and a hard bristle brush.

As soon as I stepped inside, though, I knew something was wrong. The air in the shed felt different somehow, far colder than the outside, where it was only slightly chilly. Darker, too, with only one small window to let in the late afternoon light.

"Shut the door"—said a panicky voice from the corner, as I nearly jumped out of my skin—"before it finds me."

Angie Rayburn was crouched on the floor behind an upturned wheelbarrow and a bunch of old boxes. Her frightened face peered at me from behind the wheelbarrow, then disappeared as she ducked. "Please," she urged in a loud whisper, "please shut the door."

"Oh, Angie." I sighed. "What are you doing here?"

I'd hoped beyond hope that Josh's safe return and her very big funeral at St. Patrick the Divine had put her to rest. My focus had been on Joe the last few days, and there'd been no weird occurrences, until today.

"I'm begging you," she whimpered, still cowering, "please shut the door."

So I did, knowing I'd come to regret it.

Evil wins when good does nothing.

Why, oh why, was it always up to me to do *something*?

"Angie, listen to me." I crouched down on the floor of the shed, right where I was. "You need to stop this. You need to stop hiding and go into the Light."

"I can't," she keened softly. "I'm damned. I'm damned to Hell for what I did."

"No, you're not." This whole notion of being damned for being mentally ill at the time of your death made no sense to me. "It didn't take you, did it?"

It being the Dark, of course.

"It wants me," she whispered urgently. "It didn't take me, but it wants me . . . I can feel it out there, waiting."

The hair rose on the back of my neck. I knew exactly what she was talking about, and turned up my collar to drive away the image of that evil black mass, patiently waiting . . .

"Then beat it to the punch," I said firmly, "and go into the Light—it can't follow you there. Look for the Light, Angie. Look up, look past what you see around you."

The sound of crying came from the corner.

"Stop it," I said sharply. There'd been enough crying around here lately. "Stop feeling sorry for yourself. You did what you did, and now you have to live with the consequences." Well, not really *live* with the consequences . . . "Josh is home safe, David will take care of him, and everything is going to be all right." *I hoped.*

"Josh is safe?" I could barely see the outline of her head in the dimness of the shed. "How do you know?"

"He was here, just the other day." Didn't she know that? "I took him to your funeral service myself."

"My funeral service?" She seemed honestly shocked. "That can't be possible."

I was beginning to get annoyed. My legs were cramping, the shed was cold, and I was losing daylight while I argued with a ghost.

"St. Patrick the Divine," I offered, by way of proof, "two days ago. Lots of people came—"

"But the church doesn't sanction suicide," she interrupted.

I shook my head, though she probably couldn't see it. "I'm telling you that you had a funeral service at the cathedral two days ago. The sign out front said something about the Mass of Christian Burial. There were tons of people there."

She started crying again, while I crouched on the floor, feeling helpless.

"I didn't think—I didn't expect that," she quavered. "David would've had to get a special dispensation from the diocese."

A lightbulb went off. "So you thought you were damned because you couldn't have a service in the church?"

"Of course," she said, sniffling.

I wasn't Catholic, so it made no sense to me, but whatever.

"But you *did* have a service"—deliberately making my voice more upbeat—"so you're not damned." I started to smile. "You don't have to hide anymore."

And that's when it began. The room became

very dark all of a sudden. I glanced toward the window to see if dusk had fallen, and saw instead a rising shadow that nearly froze my heart with terror.

My cramped knees gave out, and I landed hard on my butt. I heard a moaning sound, and realized it was coming from my own throat.

The Dark loomed, slowly growing until it filled one side of the shed. My dad's gardening tools— his rake, his shovel, the lawn mower—all became gradually obscured by the deepening darkness. Scrabbling backward on my hands and ass, I came up hard against the door, and realized I could go no further.

"It's here," Angie whispered, in a voice filled with horror. "Do you see it?"

Wishing desperately for a wheelbarrow of my own to hide behind, all I could do was nod.

"It still wants me," she said. "The Mass did no good."

"*Nicki.*" I heard a voice, inside my head. "*You already know the secret, my love. It has only as much power as you give it.*"

It was Sammy, calling me "my love" and offering advice. If I wasn't already on the verge of a heart attack, I would've passed out.

Holy crap on a freakin' cracker. Should I trust him?

The atmosphere in the shed turned heavy, pervasive, as the last of the light from the window faded, leaving nothing but shadows and shades of gray.

"It'll never leave me alone," Angie said despondently, from the corner. "Who was I fooling? I committed the ultimate sin. I abandoned my son, I abandoned my husband." She was no longer crying. "I'm worthless. I deserve to go to Hell."

"No, you don't!" I felt a surge of energy, and was afraid to ask myself where it came from. "It *wants* you to think that!" Gathering my feet beneath me again, I prepared to stand. "That's where it gets its power."

Doomed, either way I was doomed.

"Don't look at it, Angie," I urged her. "Think about how David got that special dispensation so you could have a Mass. Think about all those people who came, because they loved you. Think about Josh, who loves you, even though he didn't understand at first why you did it."

"Josh," she murmured. "I'm so sorry I did this to him."

"He knows," I said hurriedly, one eye on the Dark. "I told him." And then I played my trump card. "Don't you want to see him again? If you let the Dark have you, you never will."

For that's how it worked. I understood it now.

The Dark didn't take you, you *let* it take you. It didn't come roaring out of closet or under the bed and swallow you whole; it was far more insidious than that. It waited, it lingered, it hypnotized, it mesmerized—and only the strong could resist it.

"Don't let it win, Angie." I said, rising to stand on my own two feet. "Ignore it, and look for the Light. I promise it will be there. Do it for Josh."

"I—I'll try," she answered, voice wavering. "For Josh." I heard a quick intake of breath from behind the wheelbarrow. "Oh, my God," she murmured, awestruck. "I see it. I see the Light." And then there was silence.

I wished *I* could see it. I stared in the direction of the wheelbarrow but caught just a tiny flicker, like a flashlight had been turned on, then off.

Leaving me alone in the darkness.

With *it*.

"Angie?" I whispered, knowing I wasn't going to get an answer. I'd done my job too well, it seemed, and my timing sucked.

"Get away from me," I said to the growing Darkness, scrabbling behind me for the door handle. I found it, but it wouldn't turn. I risked trying it with both hands, which meant I had to momentarily turn my back on the Dark, but I kept an eye on it over my shoulder. It was definitely getting bigger.

"Dammit." The doorknob wouldn't turn. I spun around again, resting my back against the door. The only window was behind the . . . the *thing* . . . and it was completely obscured. I had nowhere to go.

The Dark began to boil, right before my eyes. Black billows of soot, shifting and roiling in a constantly changing pattern. Horrified, I watched it, aware as I did it that I shouldn't, but unable to help myself. It was like staring into a fire and seeing faces in the flames, only these faces were far more frightening. I thought I was imagining them, until one of the faces rose out of the darkness on a billow of black smoke, coming far too close to me for comfort. Slitted eyes, pointed ears; it hovered there, at eye level, and gave me a good, solid wink.

I couldn't help it—I shrieked, loud and long, just before everything went black.

CHAPTER 22

I woke up on the floor of the shed sometime later, unsure of how long I'd lain there. It was still daylight, sun coming high in the window to make an angled patch on the floor. The shed was empty except for me.

Getting to my feet, I took stock; nothing bleeding, nothing broken, nothing hurt. I could hardly believe my good luck. Wasting no time, I grabbed the doorknob, which turned easily in my hand, and I was *outta* there.

The rocker was sitting on the patio, right in front of me, and for a split second I was sure I saw someone sitting in it. I blinked, and there was nothing, but I felt oddly comforted, nonetheless, as though I hadn't been alone during my ordeal in the shed.

My brief sense of peace vanished, however, as I heard a loud crash, followed by a woman's angry voice. Both noises came from inside the house—*my* house.

"You lying bastard," I heard her shriek, and then another crash. Without conscious thought, I ran up the back steps and into the house, knowing that whatever what being broken was *mine*.

"I knew it!" Another shriek, another particularly loud crash. "You helped her! You chose her over me and you helped her!"

I came into the living room to find an enraged Selene and a smirking Sammy, facing each other from opposite sides of the room. The mess I'd left the living room in earlier was nothing to the mess it was in now; the coffee table had been overturned, cereal bowls and empty glasses broken on the floor. My snowman collection had been decimated, it appeared, by the sweep of an angry hand; eighty percent of them lay scattered all over the floor.

Speechless, I could only stand there, and try to keep a grip on my sanity.

"Come now," Sammy said smoothly to Selene, ignoring my entrance. "You didn't expect me to do otherwise, did you? When have you ever known me to give in to blackmail?"

"The rest of the ethereals will hear of this," Selene shouted, plucking up my favorite snow globe off the mantel and pitching it at his head.

He ducked, smiling, and I couldn't keep silent anymore.

"Hey!"

Neither one of them looked at me. Selene kicked a wicker snowman out of her way, glaring at Sammy.

"Cut it out!" I shouted.

I might as well have been invisible.

If looks could kill, he'd be dead, but Sammy was unconcerned. "Calm down, Lil. Why must you always be such a drama queen?"

Selene's shriek of rage made me want to cover my ears. She went for him with her bare hands, but he danced out of her reach, ducking behind the couch and keeping it between them.

It would've been funny, if she had been anyone else. The Prince of Darkness, trying to avoid getting his ass kicked by an angry woman.

"Hello?" I said, risking getting hit by a lightning bolt. The way the sparks were flying, I wouldn't be surprised. "Could you two take this someplace else, please?"

There was a silence. Sammy and Selene stared at each other over the couch, seemingly at a stalemate. Then Selene turned her head and looked at me, and instantly I knew I was in trouble.

"This is all your fault," she hissed, in a voice filled with venom. "I don't see it, personally. You're not nearly as clever as I expected. You're not even very pretty."

I'm fairly sure my jaw dropped.

Her contemptuous gaze flicked to Sammy. "No accounting for taste, I suppose."

Sammy, who'd given every indication of being amused by Selene's anger up to this point, was no longer smiling. I watched him straighten, moving slowly, as though any sudden move might set her off again.

"Give me one good reason why I don't smother her in her sleep tonight," she said to him, a cruel light gleaming in her eye.

I could sense his tension, see it in the set of his shoulders, and wondered if she could see it, too. "Because you know I'd never forgive you," he said gently. "Never. In all eternity."

My mouth was so dry I could barely swallow. He wasn't looking at me, but I could feel him willing me to stay quiet, to stay calm.

"Can you live with that?" he asked her softly. "To know that you've given me reason—yet again—to hate you?"

The light in Selene's eyes began to fade.

"You already hate me," she said, tonelessly, "so what does it matter?"

And that's when it clicked.

Selene was in love with Sammy. Had obviously *been* in love with him for some time, probably from the beginning.

The two original fallen, doomed to be together forever, yet forever apart.

Oh, Sammy was far more diabolical than I ever imagined. I shuddered at the cruelty of it.

I hated her, and so I granted her wish, he'd said, though I hadn't understood what he'd meant at the time.

"You've grown weak," she spat, getting ugly again. "Over a puny little mortal."

"Much as I did with you," Sammy shot back. "You didn't seem it to mind at the time."

Holy shit.

She gave him a look that scared the crap out of me, but he was undaunted. "All this trouble just to get my attention." He sighed. "Really, darling, you could've just waved a fig leaf, like you did the first time. I'd have come running."

Darling?

Selene's tension seemed to ease, just a tiny bit. "So you *do* remember," she said, watching him closely.

"How could I forget?" he said smoothly. "I've dreamed of it for eons."

She eyed him warily. "You've never said."

"Ah, well," he answered, spreading his hands. "You've never seemed wanting for male companionship." He smiled at her ruefully, turning on the charm. "Understandably so."

And damned if it didn't work.

She tossed her head, giving him a small smile beneath her lashes. "Yours was the only companionship I ever wanted, darling, you know that."

"Oh, I know," he said with a wicked grin. Pressing his advantage, he went on, "I suppose I should be flattered that you'd go this far to get my attention."

"Yes," she said, seizing on to his words. "That's exactly it! I was only trying to open your eyes, darling." Shooting me a venomous glance, she added, "She's not worthy of your magnificence."

I opened my mouth to speak, but Sammy swung around, pinning me in place with blue eyes made of ice. "No," he said dismissively. "She's not."

Shut up, be quiet, and let me save your life, those eyes said, and I decided to listen.

On the other side of the couch, Selene relaxed, going so far as to rest a hip against it, trailing her fingers along the velvet fabric. "What's to be done about her, then? Her boyfriend is entirely my creature, though I can't say I've gotten much enjoyment from him yet."

"I'm not surprised," Sammy said, with a little

grin meant just for me. It gave him secret pleasure to hear Joe maligned in the sack, I'm sure. "It was your tears, I presume?"

She laughed, anger all but forgotten. "Yes. It began when he gave poor Mary mouth-to-mouth, of course; she made sure to get some of her own breath into his lungs, and Katie made sure to cry pitifully against the skin of his neck, paving the way for me. Mary's so-called death gave me the perfect excuse I needed to weep my heart out all over his shirt. He was no match for me after that."

My brain went numb. *Mary's breath? Katie's tears?*

Sammy turned away, so I couldn't ask him, but I felt as if I'd been given a gift. A reason why Joe had turned from me so suddenly.

"You are clever," he told her. "Perhaps I should've tried that with this one"—meaning me—"and saved myself a good deal of trouble."

Selene eyed me speculatively, as though as I were an object she considered buying, and said, "It's not outside the realm of possibility." Looking him in the eye, she gave him a slow, sexy smile. "Give me a few moments, and I can get her to do anything you like . . . how does a threesome sound?"

My breath caught as Sammy made an appreciative noise, deep in his throat.

The bastard was truly enjoying this.

"It sounds too delicious for words," he said, in a voice that made my knees weak. "Some other time. Right now I'm only interested in one woman." He moved toward her, reaching out a hand, and she slid hers into it, eyes gleaming with pleasure at his nearness. "And that would be you."

She glided into his arms with a satisfied smile. He pulled her close, holding her loosely at the waist.

"How could I have forgotten how beautiful you are?" he murmured, and she melted. In two seconds she was draped all over him, and he gave every appearance of enjoying it. His hands were everywhere, squeezing and smoothing. "It's been far too long."

I stood there and watched, speechless, as he lowered his head and kissed her, passionately, right in front of me, while she moaned and wiggled and pressed closer in his arms.

Blechh.

Convinced the roiling in my gut was nausea and not jealousy, I looked away, wondering if I dared make a break for it. I could run back out the way I'd come, out the back door and through the neighbor's yard.

And go where?

It didn't matter. Anything was better than

standing here and listening to the noises Selene was beginning to make, noises that told me Sammy was touching her in places better left private.

I turned to go, but Sammy's voice stopped me.

"Let's go somewhere more comfortable, darling," he said huskily to Selene. "I know a lovely rooftop garden in Istanbul. The moon should be full to bursting tonight."

"Mmmm," she purred, "sounds just like old times."

He laughed, low and husky, and I couldn't help but look at him again, my eyes drawn to his blond head, the masculine lines of his face, taut with desire. He'd turned Selene so her back was to me, pressing her against the couch, lean hips hard against the vee of her thighs.

My breath caught in my throat as he looked up over her shoulder, blue eyes burning, to see me watching. "I've learned my lesson," he said, nuzzling her neck, while never taking his eyes off me. "I should never have neglected you for so long. Why settle for hamburger when you can have caviar, mm?"

I didn't dare make a sound, but my eyes widened. *Had I just been compared to hamburger?*

Smoothing Selene's dark hair away from her

neck with one hand, he curled his lip in amusement at my reaction, and I knew the cut had been deliberate.

"Oh, darling," she breathed, tilting her head back to allow him greater access to her neck, "I knew you'd come to see things my way."

"Some things are inevitable," he murmured, grazing her skin with his lips as he spoke. His eyes were still locked on mine, and I knew he was sending me a message. "It's never over until it's over, is it?"

"No," she said, gasping. She had her hands twisted in his shirt, ready to rip it off him at any moment.

"And the girl?" He finally drew her attention back to me, stroking the line of her neck with one finger.

She shuddered at his touch, eyes half closed as she shot me a careless look. "What about her?"

"You'll leave her alone?" He watched her now, trailing his finger over her lips. "No more fits of jealous rage?" he murmured, leaning in to brush his cheek against hers. "No more attempting to force my hand?"

"Only here, my darling," she whispered, rubbing herself against him shamelessly. He held himself still, and let her, but said nothing.

"All right," she gasped, grasping frantically at his shoulders, which remained unmoving. "Whatever you want, just—"

I never heard the rest of that sentence. There was a loud pop, like a fuse being blown, and both Sammy and Selene disappeared. A sizzle, and a noxious smell, like burned hair, lingered.

I hope it singed her eyebrows.

Stunned, shaken, and more than a little confused, I stood there in my living room, looking around at the destruction.

Hell hath no fury like a woman scorned, indeed.

CHAPTER 23

By seven o'clock that evening I'd reclaimed my house and set everything to rights. I'd lost several porcelain snowmen to Selene's spite, but most were intact. There was a dent in the wall where she'd thrown the snow globe, and a new scratch on the coffee table. I'd thrown an afghan over the back of the couch where she'd touched it, until I could have the fabric cleaned. It was one of my favorite pieces of furniture, and I wasn't going to let the image of her leaning against it force me to get rid of it.

Two of a kind. I should've known—they deserved each other.

The room was cleaner than it had been all week, and I was still full of energy. I needed something else to clean, so I started on the rest of the house.

I didn't want to think about where Sammy might be or what he might be doing. I didn't want to think about Joe, and where he was, and wonder if Selene's poisonous crocodile tears would ever wear off. I didn't want to think about Angie, and whether she'd gone into the Light, and I didn't want to think about the face that had leered at me from within the Darkness in the shed.

So I just kept polishing what I could polish, and scrubbing what I could scrub, until hunger made me call for a pizza delivery around eight.

That's what I was expecting when the doorbell rang at eight-thirty. But when I looked through the peephole, there stood Joe.

I wasn't ready yet. Oh God, I wasn't ready.

And yet I could no more stop myself from opening that door than I could stop earth from spinning on its axis.

He looked drawn, and tired. So tired. Joe always stood tall, like a hero, but tonight he was slump-shouldered and weary.

It was all I could do not to open my heart as quickly as I'd opened my door, but I didn't. "Hey," I said stiffly, leaving explanations up to him.

Poison or no poison, I'd been hurt, and the wound was deep. And still fresh.

"Can I come in?" he asked, and I almost didn't let him. I almost said no and closed the door, because in a way it would be better. It would be better if I just said good-bye to Joe right now, and finished working my way through the pain, because he was a great guy who didn't deserve someone like me. He didn't deserve to be hounded by evil spirits, no matter how gorgeous they were, and he didn't need to be put through the emotional wringer every time he turned around. Most of all, he didn't deserve a girl who lusted for someone else, even if only in her heart.

So I almost said no, but I didn't.

"Come in." I stepped back and let him in, nervous suddenly. What if he'd just come over to get his stuff? The bag was still in the closet . . .

"What's happened to us, Nicki?" He hadn't taken more than a few steps before turning to face me. "Are you seeing another guy? Tell me the truth."

Surprise nearly made me laugh, but I didn't. I'd expected an apology, confusion, disorientation maybe. *He* was the one who'd been under a spell, not me, and I'd assumed we were about to go from there.

Instead he was demanding an explanation, as if I'd done something wrong.

Which I had. I should never have let Sammy get close enough to even *think* of kissing me that night in the car. For everything else, I had no regret, because I'd needed Sammy to fix things. Joe would never be free of Selene if Sammy hadn't gotten involved—he wouldn't be here right now, in fact.

"No, I'm not seeing anyone," I answered honestly. "I never was. Lee is my mechanic, and everything I've ever told you about Sammy is true." *And then some.*

"I want to believe you," he said, looking into my eyes. "But I know there's something between you two, something you're not telling me."

I could see the pain in his gaze. I tried to meet it, but failed, and was the first to look away.

"You have feelings for him, even though you know he's bad news. It's in the air, every time you're near him."

"I—" I couldn't bring myself to confirm or deny it, unable to choose between "sick and twisted," or "liar."

He swept a hand over his eyes, making a noise of frustration. "I've tried to ignore it, tried to tell myself that I was imagining things." He turned and strode into the living room, hands on his hips. "I thought that I could prove to you, over time, that I would always be there for you, that you could trust me, that *I* was the better choice."

Tears prickled, but I blinked them back. "Joe—"

"You've been so angry with me lately, so jealous and quick to accuse," he went on, raking a hand through his hair. "Were you trying to drive me away so you could be with him?"

I realized that Joe's version of recent events, while entirely different from my own, had some validity. I'd been in a jealous snit over Selene since the moment she appeared on the scene.

"No, it wasn't like that. I told you I was only with him to get some information out of him, and that's the truth."

"And yet you claim he's the Devil himself."

"He is."

"Must've been some pretty important information."

I held his gaze this time. "It was."

"Do you love him?"

This question, I could answer honestly. "No," I said. Whatever I felt for Sammy, it was not love.

I could see the relief in his eyes. His face grew earnest, intent. "I'm glad. Because if you did, it would kill me."

There was a silence, in which I realized I was

trembling. I wasn't sure how much more I could take today.

"I can't eat," Joe murmured, staring at my face. "I can't sleep." His eyes roved over my hair. "I can't work." He took a step closer. "I do nothing but lie on the couch and think of you, and I am utterly, totally miserable."

Tears blurred my vision.

"Please come back to me, Nicki," he said softly. "I'm sorry. I miss you so much."

The pain of the last few days was still there, throbbing and aching between my breasts.

"You broke my heart," I said, voice cracking.

"I know I did," he whispered, taking another step. "I'm so sorry. I think . . ." He hesitated. ". . . I think I was afraid you were about to break mine."

Clever, clever Selene. Work on someone's worst fear and turn it to your advantage.

I was crying now, openly, because that was exactly what she'd done to me. "What if . . . what if it happens again?" I held out a hand to ward him off, but he took it instead, wrapping his warm fingers over mine.

There was bound to be more spiritual mayhem in my life, and Joe would always be an obvious target. Could I survive losing him the next time, or the time after that?

"Trust me," he murmured, tugging me gently in his direction. "I won't mess things up again. You're special and you're wonderful and you're a huge pain in the ass." A smile lurked at the corner of his lips when he said it. "The most beautiful pain in the ass I've ever seen," he added. He had me by both hands now, making me face him. "You're as vital as the air I breathe." Cupping my face in his hands, he drew me closer. "I can't go back, Nicki. I can't go back to the man I was when you met me."

"Dr. Joe was a very dull boy," I said faintly, through my tears.

"He was, wasn't he?" He pulled me closer, sliding his arms around my waist.

Mine came up to circle his neck, as if they had a mind of their own.

"Never a dull moment when I'm with you," he said low, beneath his breath, and then he kissed me, and nothing else mattered in the world except the feel of his lips, the way he smelled, the way he *felt* in my arms.

And now that he was there, back where he belonged, I held on to him, tight, scared to death he'd break my heart again someday—or I'd break his—but knowing that either way, it was worth the risk.

* * *

The moon shone full over a rooftop garden. A man stood there, looking out over a city awash in moonlight. He was naked, shadows moving across his shoulders and back as the night breeze moved the potted palms that lined the roof.

"Yes, it's a dream," he said to me, without turning his head. "It seems to be the only way we can communicate these days."

"You saved me," I said softly, staying well away from him. I could smell exotic spices, the faint perfume of flowers. A tub of roses sat near my feet, but the blooms held no color, everything washed in the silver-gray of moonlight. "Why?"

Sammy turned, leaning against the balustrade. His bare chest was beautiful, smooth and hairless, sculpted muscle caressed by shadow. "I have no idea."

"Liar."

He laughed softly, cocking his head to watch me, where I stood among the flowers. "Does it matter, little Nicki? A whim, an impulse . . ." He shrugged. "Perhaps I just have a weakness for strong-willed women."

"You didn't want to go with her." I had no idea where my words were coming from, but I was certain of the truth of them. "You still hate her for what she did to you." The Fall. The loss of his innocence. The loss of grace.

"There's a very thin line between love and hate," he murmured. "Haven't you figured that out yet?"

I said nothing, feeling the loneliness he carried reach out to me across the space that separated us. It was his burden to bear, not mine, but I found myself wishing I could ease it, just a little bit.

A breeze rose, setting the potted palms rustling, one brushing my arm with the lightest of touches. I looked down, and to my surprise, I was nude also. With the realization came acceptance—I felt no shame, being here on this quiet rooftop with him.

I thought of Joe, and knew that on some level of my consciousness, he lay beside me, warm and alive. He'd be waiting there for me when I woke up, to offer me a cup of coffee and a loving touch. I hoped he would be there always, until the day one of us died.

But right now I was here, adrift in a world all its own, made of shadows and palms and moonlight. I should feel guilty, terrible for the pleasure I took in it, but I didn't.

That confused me for a moment, until he said, "No need for confusion." He came toward me, hand outstretched. "And no need for guilt." His body, half hidden by shadows, revealed itself as he came closer. He was perfect, and beautiful, an angel cast in God's own image, then cast down to suffer, with sinners like myself.

"People can't help what they dream," he murmured, taking my hand. "And this is my dream, not yours."

CHAPTER 24

"Nicki, wake up."

Something soft went around my shoulders, enveloping me in warmth, though until that moment, I hadn't realized I was cold.

"Wake up, baby," Joe said gently, the weight of his arm settling around my shoulders as well, pulling me back into the real world.

I swayed, blinking in confusion as I opened my eyes to find myself in the living room. In front of me was the window, moonlight slanting through the blinds. "What the—?" My tongue felt thick, my brain like mush. "What's going on?"

I looked around, searching for the plants and flowers I'd been surrounded by a moment ago, but there was nothing except the fake poinsettias I'd set out when I'd rearranged my snowman collection.

"You were dreaming," Joe murmured, not letting go of my shoulders. The warmth I'd felt was an afghan, the one I'd draped over the back of the couch earlier.

I clutched at it, dragging it around me as the cool air in the room touched the bare skin of my stomach and thighs.

I was naked.

"Come sit down." Joe led me to the couch, steadying me as I nearly stumbled, still dazed.

"I'm sorry, I—"

"Shh," he said, settling himself next to me. "It's okay."

We sat there in silence for a moment, as my brain caught up with the reality of the situation. I'd been dreaming, and the things I'd been doing in my dream made my cheeks heat. The hall light was on, but the living room was mostly dark, so I was hoping Joe couldn't see my face.

"Here," he murmured, wrapping me more securely in the afghan and tucking the ends around me. "You're shaking. I'll start a fire."

I didn't answer, finding it hard to look at him. He got up and busied himself by opening the fireplace screen and tossing a few logs in from the basket I kept beside the hearth. There was kindling there, too, and a lighter. I heard the flick as he set the kindling alight, blowing gently as it caught. The growing flames illuminated the planes of his face, but I saw only his profile; his eyes were still in shadow. He closed the screen, and coming back to the couch, wrapped both arms around me and pulled me close.

"You'll be warm in a minute."

I buried my face against his chest. He smelled like sleepy male and clean cotton, his T-shirt soft against my cheek, muscles hard beneath the fabric.

With a sigh, he rested his chin on the top of my head, holding me tight. The fire crackled, burning higher, but other than that, the house was quiet.

"You said his name," he finally said, "and more. That's what woke me."

I stiffened, tried to sit up, but he tightened his hold. "No," he murmured. "Stay here."

There was no reason to ask whose name, or whatever else he'd heard. Horrified with myself, I tried to apologize. "Joe, I—"

"Shh," he said again. "Let me talk."

Raising a shaking hand to my face, I subsided.

"I owe you an apology," he murmured, surprising me. "I never realized how hard it must've been for you, knowing I was dreaming of someone else."

I went still. We hadn't delved too deeply into the topic of what had happened between Selene and him yet, though I'd told him all about Josh Rayburn and Selene's role in Angie's death. I hadn't wanted to talk about the things she'd done to him, or with him, in the dark of night, but with a sigh of my own, I realized that now was as good a time as any.

"I told myself that dreams were only dreams, and that they meant nothing in the big scheme of things," he went on. "I blamed you for making me feel guilty about it, when secretly I didn't want the dreams to end."

"It wasn't your fault," I said, still tense. "She had you under a spell. Mary's breath, her tears . . . you were a victim, a pawn in something much bigger than either of us ever imagined."

He shook his head, denying my words. "You tried to tell me, more than once, that there was something supernatural at work, and I wouldn't listen. I was a *willing* victim—I know that now. There was . . ." He hesitated. "There was a part of me that knew, all along, but I didn't care."

My breath caught. I stared into the flames, and let it out slowly.

"So now you know," he murmured against my hair. "My own dark, dirty little secret."

This time, when I pulled away enough to sit up,

he let me. "Why are you telling me this?" To be honest, I wished he hadn't told me; it was a lot easier to believe otherwise.

"Because I don't want any more secrets between us, Nicki. We've been through too much together, and I love you too much to lie to you, even in my heart."

I could see his face clearly now. His beautiful, beloved face, wearing an expression of guilt and worry that I never wanted to see there again. Blinking back tears, I whispered, "You're a much better person than I am."

He made a noise of disgust. "Hardly. You were willing to risk everything, including our relationship, to help a troubled kid through a very tough time, while I was thinking only of myself."

"You didn't know," I said again, but he wasn't having it.

"I *should've* known. I *would've* known if I'd just paid attention." He looked away, into the fire. "I let myself be seduced, thinking I was somehow special because she'd chosen me over all the other men in the world." Giving a short laugh, he shook his head. "It wasn't until I heard you say his name tonight, and knew you were with him in your dream, that I truly understood how hard it is to resist that teeny, tiny voice inside our minds that says, *No one will ever know.* I never realized, until now, that we all have a piece of our soul where darkness hides, sometimes even from ourselves."

I was silent for a moment. "I'm so sorry about tonight, Joe." Here he was, confessing his secrets, while I'd so far been unable to confess mine. "I know what you mean about feeling special because you've been singled out, even when it's for something you didn't think you ever wanted." Uncomfortable, I stared into the flames along with him, finding it easier to admit my own guilt if I didn't look at him. "I love you, not Sammy, but whenever he's around it's as though my body has a mind of its own. He's made it clear that he wants me, and I guess there's a secret part of me that was flattered by his attention. I've always resisted him, always, but tonight . . . this dream . . . I feel like I've been unfaithful to you."

Joe sighed, rubbing my shoulder. "No more than I, baby."

"What are we going to do?"

He looked at me, and pulled me close again, lips against my hair. "We're going to do what we've always done, and work through it. Right now, though, we're going to sit here a few more minutes and enjoy the fire, and then we're going to go into the bedroom and light an entirely different one."

I smiled, snuggling against his chest with an overwhelming sense of relief.

"And if I ever see that guy again, I'm going to punch first, and ask questions later," he said firmly. "Prince of Darkness, my ass."

"Does that mean I'm allowed to scratch Selene's eyes out if she shows up again?"

He didn't hesitate. "Only if I get to watch. Every man in America enjoys a good catfight."

"Rowrr," I murmured, contentedly.

CHAPTER 25

"No fair," protested Evan, "it's my turn to open a present!"

"What a baby," I said good-naturedly. "Butch has his already, so you'll just have to wait."

Butch held up the box in his hand and shook it, deliberately prolonging the moment. "Hmm," he said, "what could it be?"

"Open it," Evan cried, never one for patience. "Rip it open!"

"Bloodthirsty, isn't he?" Joe laughed, leaning back on the couch next to me, and putting his stockinged feet up on the coffee table. Not that there was much room between the torn wrapping paper, bits of ribbon, cinnamon rolls, and coffee cups that littered it. "It's like watching my sister's two-year-old at Christmas." He looked happy and relaxed in his sweats and T-shirt, wearing the brand-new blue robe I'd gotten him. The maroon one held bad memories for me now, and it would find a great home at the homeless shelter.

"I think it's a book," Butch teased, knowing full well that it was too big to be a book.

Evan, knowing he was being tormented, tossed his head and took another sip of his mimosa. He was wearing flannel pajamas and a silk robe, with fur-lined slippers. "Why must we take turns, anyway?" he asked. "We should all just open everything at one time."

"He says that every year," I murmured sotto voce to Joe, knowing Evan could hear me perfectly well. And then I said to him, "Because this way is much more fun, and you know it. Lasts longer, too."

"Well." Evan sniffed, taking another sip and reaching for another cinnamon roll. "I'm all for anything that lasts longer."

"Hey!" Butch swatted at him and Evan pretended to flinch, smiling. "That's what you get," he said sweetly. "Now open the present!"

Butch's "book" revealed itself to be a pair of slippers, the perfect match to Evan's own, only bigger. I'd gotten a pair, too, although mine were black with teeny pink skulls on them.

"Okay, your turn," I said, after Butch had put on his slippers and pronounced them fabulous. I tossed Evan his gift from me, and we all watched as he gleefully put aside his breakfast to make short work of it. "A cashmere sweater!" he exclaimed, as if the idea had never occurred to him. "Just the right color, too."

"Amethyst," I said dryly. "I hear jewel tones are in this year."

"It's Joe's turn to be Santa," Evan cried gaily. "Let him hand out the next round of presents." He leaned back in his seat, stroking his new sweater like a pet as he and Butch exchanged a smiling glance.

"Okay," Joe said, readily enough. He got up to rummage beneath the tree, which was on my side of the couch. "Let's see, Butch just opened one, Evan opened one, that means it's Nicki's turn . . ."

Right then the phone rang. Since it was sitting on the coffee table right in front of me, I could see from the caller ID that it was Kelly's cell phone.

"Wait just a second," I said to Joe. "Let me tell Kelly and Grandma Bijou Merry Christmas."

"Merry Christmas to you, too," Kelly said, when I answered. She was cheerful, buoyant. "I have some great news!"

"Yeah?"

I was watching Evan, wondering why he and

Joe were looking at each other so strangely, when she said, "Spider proposed! We're engaged!"

"Kelly and Spider are engaged," I announced excitedly to the guys. "That's wonderful!" I said to Kelly, and meant it. "You two are meant for each other." Besides, it was what she wanted. "What's the ring look like?"

Both Evan's and Butch's expressions went slack, which surprised me. I would've thought they'd have been happier for her.

"A round solitaire in a gold band," she said, with a sigh. "Simple. Perfect."

I smiled at the image of Kelly standing there, admiring her ring, and vaguely wondered why Joe, Evan, and Butch were so quiet.

"Grandma Bijou wants to talk to you, and you have to say hello to Odessa—"

"No, I don't," I said automatically, though I would. Odessa was more than just Grandma Bijou's housekeeper, and for all her gruffness, I knew there was a softie underneath. Somewhere. Buried under mountains of soul food and mournful disapproval.

"Spider wants to ask you about getting him a vintage tux for the ceremony."

"A vintage tux? I knew the man had great taste," I said, laughing. "I'll put Evan right on it!"

Evan, however, didn't look too thrilled at the

assignment. He and Butch exchanged another look, and I could no longer ignore that something was up.

"Listen," I said to Kelly, "let me call you back, okay? I've, ah, I've got to get the turkey in the oven or it won't be ready on time." Which was a total lie because it was already *in* the oven. Evan had helped me with it before we sat down to open presents. "It'll just be a few minutes."

"Okay," she said cheerfully. "When you call back I'll tell you all the details," she went on, obviously still excited. "Spider got down on one knee right in front of the Christmas tree, while Bijou and Odessa were watching. They knew all about it beforehand, of course . . . it was so romantic!"

"I want to hear all about it," I said. "Talk to you in a few minutes." As soon as I broke the connection, I looked around the room at three of the most unhappy faces I'd seen in a long time. "What's the problem here?" I asked. "What's going on?"

Joe cleared his throat, and I looked at him— really looked at him. He was on one knee, right in front of the Christmas tree, next to where I sat. He was holding a small red box.

"It appears that Spider has stolen my thunder," he said softly, "but Nicki Styx"—he opened the box and held it toward me, offering it, along with his heart—"will you marry me?"

Evan made a faint noise of suppressed excitement, but I was barely aware of it.

I got the faint impression of sparkles—lots of sparkles—but I was looking at something far more important. All I saw were those deep green eyes, and that dark hair that would one day belong to our children—even if we only had one child, a girl with a quick laugh who would, in turn, give us three grandchildren.

"Yes," I said, without hesitation. "I will."

"Yay," squealed Evan, as I fell into Joe's arms and kissed him, right there on the floor, nearly knocking him over.

"The ring," Evan urged, once the kiss was over, nearly beside himself with impatience, "look at the ring!" He was beaming from ear to ear, as were Joe and I.

He didn't need to say it a second time. Joe still had the box, and he held it toward me, one more time.

It was vintage, I could tell at a glance. Square-cut diamond, framed by smaller diamonds, in an ornate silver setting. Edwardian, maybe.

Not simple, nothing like Kelly's.

Perfect.

I reached for it, fascinated, but he pulled it back.

"Uh-uh," he said, grinning at me. He took it

from the velvet himself, and reached for my hand. "Let me."

It slid onto the third finger of my left hand like it had been made for me.

"Oh my God," I breathed. Joe leaned in and kissed me again, while I, for some reason, just couldn't stop smiling.

"Wow," breathed Butch, leaning back in his chair. He took a sip of his mimosa and then clinked glasses with a bouncy, jubilant Evan. "That was intense."

"It was, wasn't it?" Evan beamed. "Like a fairy tale. A Christmas fairy tale."

"A Christmas carol," Butch corrected him happily, "where everyone lives happily ever after." He raised his glass, and offered a toast to the room at large. "This has been the best Christmas ever," he said, holding his glass high, "and here's to happily ever after."

Joe and I picked up our mimosas, and we all four clinked on it.

"Now," said Evan, ever the busy little busybody. "How soon do we get some babies in this house? I saw the most adorable little blue T-shirts the other day that said, 'Spit Happens.'"

I shook my head, laughing. "Pink, Uncle Evan. You're going to need to buy pink."

Joe arched an eyebrow at me. "You sound pretty

sure of that, babe. Is there something you're not telling me?"

She will have dark hair and a quick laugh, and she will love you dearly, as you will her, the woman at the Christmas bazaar had said.

Reaching out to ruffle his dark hair with the fingers of one hand, I looked into his eyes, smiling. "Some things are just meant to be, my love. After all, who are we to question the ways of fate?"

WELCOME TO THE WORLD OF NICKI STYX. . .

Whoever said "dead men tell no tales" obviously wasn't listening very hard.

Unfortunately for me, I've always had a very good ear. And dead men *love* to talk. A lot.

But dead women are the worst.

My name is Nicki Styx, and I'm a dead chick magnet. A psychic magnet, if you will. One near-death experience and my life was changed forever. Now restless spirits seem to sense a kindred one in me, and they all want to tell me their stories.

DEAD GIRLS ARE EASY

"My name is Nicki Styx and I thought I had the world all figured out. Then I regained consciousness. . ."

There's something about almost dying that makes a girl rethink her priorities. Take Nicki Styx—she was strictly goth and vintage until a brush with the afterlife left her with the ability to see dead people.

But before you can say boo, Atlanta's ghosts are knocking at Nicki's door. Now her days consist of reluctantly cleaning up messes left by the dearly departed, leading ghouls to the Light . . . and one-on-one anatomy lessons with Dr. Joe Bascombe, the dreamy surgeon who saved her life. All this catering to the deceased is a real drag, especially for a girl who'd rather be playing hanky-panky with her hot new boyfriend . . . who's beginning to think she's totally nuts.

But things get even more complicated when a friend foolishly sells her soul to the devil, and Nicki's new gift lands her in some deep voodoo.

As it turns out for Nicki Styx, death was just the beginning.

"She's coding. Give me another round of epi, stat."

"Doctor—"

"Keep bagging her, nurse. I'm not letting her go yet. Charge it to 360."

Had I left the TV on? I'd never cared much for medical dramas. Too much intensity, too much crying, too many doctors undergoing personal crises of faith—I'd rather believe they were professionals who knew what they were doing and leave it at that.

The body on the table jerked at least a foot in the air when the paddles touched its chest. A hand flopped to the side, revealing red fingernails and a silver thumb ring. A woman.

A high-pitched whining from one of the machines was getting on my nerves, but I had to give the director credit. The urgency on the faces of the people clustered around the gurney looked pretty real.

"Again." That doc just wasn't gonna give up, was he? Maybe he was hoping for a daytime Emmy—wasn't that what they gave for bad soap operas? The heartburn that made me lie down on the couch was finally gone, but it seemed too much trouble to look for the remote, so I just watched.

The camera angle shifted so that now I was above the action, looking down from a high corner of the room. There was a blond nurse standing at the head of the table, squeezing a bulb-like thing over the patient's face.

The body flopped again at another jolt of electricity while I winced in sympathy. She wasn't a car battery, for goodness sake.

"Check her pupils." The nurse holding the bulb stepped back while another one leaned in with a little flashlight and pried the woman's eyelid open with a thumb.

"No reaction, Doctor. Nothing on the EKG, either."

The guy holding the paddles let his shoulders slump, while the two nurses gave each other significant glances. It was then I got a good look at the woman on the bed. Dark hair, cropped short like a boy's, with a telltale streak of pink.

She was me.

No sooner had the realization hit when a pulling sensation jerked me up and out of the deathbed scene. Suddenly I was in a dark tunnel, rushing along like I was on the subway, only there were no seats, no drunks, and no rhythmic rattle of rails. There was just me, and a light that grew steadily brighter the faster I went.

I was weightless, and somehow a *part* of the light, becoming more so the closer I got. It radiated and shimmered like coiled lightning, pulsing white with a golden center, and it drew me like a lodestone. I couldn't wait to see what lay beyond it.

Silence gave way to music, but it wasn't like any I'd ever heard before. It seemed to be coming from the light itself, yet it was all around—true music of the soul. There were others there, though I couldn't see them clearly, bright shapes pulsing and flowing.

My forward progress slowed, then stopped. I heard a voice.

"It's not your time, Nicki."

"I'm dreaming, right?"

"You've awakened unto Life, but the dream is not yet over."

I can't explain what perfect sense that statement made, any more than I could explain how so many things that had troubled me in the past suddenly made sense. Like why my mother gave me up for adoption before the cord that bound us had even been cut, or why really bad things happen to really good people. For a few precious moments I actually saw the fabled "grand design" stretched out before me like an infinite spiderweb. I barely had time to grasp it before it was snatched away.

"Go back, Nicki, but don't forget—do unto others as you would have them do unto you."

My body felt strange, heavy. It was an effort to open my eyes, and when I did, I wished I hadn't. The glare of a fluorescent bar surrounded by stained ceiling tiles was not the light I longed for.

"Hey." I felt a hand touch my hair. Evan's face came into view, a very uncharacteristic look of concern in his blue eyes. "How you feeling, girlie?" he asked.

My chest felt like there was an elephant sitting on it and my mouth was dry as sand, but I managed to croak out a reply.

"Like shit."

That brought back the lopsided grin I knew so well, and made me feel a little better. My best friend since childhood, Evan wasn't the type to play nursemaid unless there was a handsome guy around who wanted to play doctor. We'd shared backyards, homework, and confidences while we were growing up, so it had come as no big surprise in junior high when we shared a crush on the same football player.

"What happened?" Talking was an effort.

"You faked a heart attack and almost gave me one in the process." Evan's joking still carried overtones of worry. "Good thing I decided to come check on you when you didn't answer the phone. I knew you didn't have a date, and I couldn't believe you'd go out for Chinese without me."

I licked dry lips, not entirely sure I was awake. "A heart attack?"

"Mitral valve prolapse."

I slid my eyes toward the unfamiliar voice. There was a dark-haired man at the foot of the bed, studying my chart. He wore green surgical scrubs and the typical stethoscope around the neck, and when he glanced up, I recognized him. He was the soap opera guy who tried so hard to save the woman on the gurney.

Me.

"A small heart defect, normally benign, but in your case nearly fatal."

He moved to stand across the bed from Evan. "We thought we'd lost you, Miss . . ." He consulted the chart again. ". . . Styx, is it?"

A MATCH MADE IN HELL

Ghosts, spirits, phantoms, spooks. Call them what you like, but don't call them too loudly—they might hear you.

A brush with death left Nicki Styx able to see and hear spirits, and, boy, do they want to be heard! Luckily her new boyfriend, sexy doc Joe Bascombe, is there to help, especially when Nicki faces her latest ghost, a woman in pink sequins who holds the key to some family secrets.

Unfortunately for Nicki, it turns out that there are more skeletons in the family closet than she thought, including a twin sister and a mysterious house full of spirits and surprises. Things go from bad to worse when the devil shows up determined to lure Nicki from Joe's side. Will she give in to temptation and sell her soul (or someone else's) for one incredible night?

Demons may be a ghoul's best friend, but with this particular hottie, it could be a match made in hell!

The place was jumping, all loud music and moving bodies. Constantly shifting purple and orange lights streamed from a giant disco ball; spotlights cast shadows of witches, black cats, and skulls over the crowd. Spiders and spiderwebs dripped from the ceiling, while skeletons and ghosts dangled from the rafters. The music was so loud it made the walls tremble. It was crazy and deafening, and I loved it. We made a beeline for the bar, easing our way through a seething mass of humanity.

I'd no sooner been handed my Black Magic when I felt a hand on my ass.

I whirled, pointed my whip at a man in a gorilla

suit and threatened, "Watch it, buddy. Don't make me send my flying monkeys after you!"

Gorilla Man raised his hands and shook his head, backing off. I wasn't sure if he was claiming no responsibility or apologizing, but it didn't matter either way.

"What are you drinking?" Joe was right beside me, but he wasn't having much luck getting the bartender's attention.

"Vodka and Kahlua, with a twist of lemon." I took a greedy sip, savoring the rich flavor of Kahlua. I was restricting my mixed drinks for special occasions now—hard liquor isn't as good for the heart as red wine. "Want a sip?"

He shook his head. "I'll stick with beer, if I ever get one."

"There's another bar in that corner." I pointed. "The bartender's a woman. Go flash those dimples at her."

He laughed. "There you go, treating me like a sex object again."

I reached around and smacked him on the butt. "You love it."

Joe leaned over and spoke directly in my ear. "You're right—I do." He bit my earlobe, and my knees went weak. "Stay here, Little Miss Wicked. I'll be right back."

I watched him walk away, admiring the view, then took a sip of my drink.

"Hello, gorgeous."

The voice was unfamiliar.

I turned, and met the eyes of one of the hunkiest guys I'd ever seen in my life. Spiky blond hair, cheekbones a fashion model would kill for, and a wicked grin. He was wearing a sleeveless black leather vest, no shirt, and tight jeans with the cuffs laced into combat boots—the perfect "bad boy."

He winked at me like we were old friends, raising his glass. "Looks like we're kindred spirits," he said. "I can't get enough of that old Black Magic either."

Old habits die hard, I guess. *Besides, a little flirting never hurt anybody.* I tilted my head and touched the tip of my whip to my chin.

"Let me guess . . . Spike, from Buffy the Vampire Slayer."

He shook his head, still grinning. A silver earring glinted from one ear.

I guessed again. "Billy Idol?" *God, I loved a man in black eyeliner.*

"That old punk?" He laughed, pretending to be insulted. "Way overrated."

"Who are you, then?"

"I'm the man of your dreams, baby."

I'd heard that one before, so why did it sound so different when *he* said it? I watched as he took a sip of his drink, blue eyes never leaving me.

"How original. Is that the best you can do?" Despite the lousy come-on, I found myself intrigued, and more than just a little attracted. His eyes were an unusual shade of blue—very pale, and very striking. Warning bells should've been going off, but I felt wrapped in silk. Smooth, slippery silk.

He took a step closer. "Talk is cheap. Let me prove it to you." He smelled like cloves, a spicy scent that made my mouth water. I didn't pull away when he leaned in close to whisper in my ear. "I'll bet I know just how you like it: you on top, and me inside you. Hard, hot, and eager to please."

His breath was tickling my neck, and my belly fluttered at the mental image that popped into my brain. Up close, I could see that the silver earring was actually a small skull and crossbones.

Walk away, Styx. Walk away.

I wanted to, but my body seemed to have a mind of its own. One lean, muscular shoulder was right in front of me, and I wanted to lick it—just once—to see if he tasted as good as he smelled.

"Nicki? Yoo-hoo, Nicki!" Evan's voice broke the spell.

I jerked back, avoiding eye contact with Mr. Eye Candy.

Evan was at my elbow, looking garishly feminine in his wig and fake eyelashes. The look he was giving me was laced with warning.

"The costume contest is about to start." The look turned more pointed. "Where's Joe?"

"Joe?" I was flustered, off-balance. *What'd they put in this drink, anyway?*

"Joe." Evan was beginning to get that tone in his voice. "Your boyfriend—remember?" Someone jostled my elbow, and I glanced over to find Butch standing on my other side, giving my new friend an expressionless stare. I sighed, recognizing the drill. I was in the middle of an overly protective "Minelli" sandwich.

"He's right over there." I pointed toward the corner bar, and saw Joe watching me across the room. The crowd shifted, and I lost sight of him, but I'd seen enough to tell that he wasn't smiling anymore.

My Billy Idol look-alike glanced that way, then turned back to me. He ignored my gay security squad and raised his drink in an admiring salute. " 'Abashed the Devil stood, and felt how awful goodness is, and saw Virtue in her own shape how lovely; saw and pined his loss.' "

My jaw dropped. It was weird enough to hear

some guy spouting quotes in a bar, but his choice of quotes . . .

"Milton. *Paradise Lost*," he added, with another wicked grin. His pale blue gaze flicked over Evan and Butch. "And apparently it is." He winked at me. "For now, anyway. See you around, Nicki Styx."

Then he walked away, his blond head quickly lost in the throng of people on the dance floor.

"Who the hell was that?" Evan didn't mince words.

"I don't know." And I wasn't sure I wanted to. "Just some guy, that's all."

I'd never told him my name.

YOU'RE THE ONE THAT I HAUNT

The Devil went down to Georgia . . .

Nicki Styx has always known that the devil's in the details—but does he have to move in next door, too? Worse, he won't take no for an answer. Nicki would never leave her beloved boyfriend, ER doc Joe Bascombe, but hell hath no fury like a devil scorned. He's determined to make Nicki's life a living hell—even if it means exposing Nicki as an unwilling ghoulfriend to the dead.

Now, just when she was getting used to being able to see and hear—and help—spirits, Nicki's got a whole new set of problems. With ghosts descending from all sides, the bereaved knocking down her door, and Joe trying to take things to the next level, Nicki may finally be in over her head. It would be so easy to dance with the devil . . . but if Nicki crosses over to the dark side, she may never leave.

"Nicki!"

Speaking of studs.

Joe's shout caught me by surprise, very pleasantly so. We'd talked on the phone last night, but I hadn't been expecting to see him until the weekend. He was smiling as he sprinted toward me on the sidewalk, narrowly evading a collision with a fat tourist couple in matching socks and sandals. Dark hair brushed his collar—he needed a haircut, but he looked so sexy. His surgical scrubs were wrinkled . . . he either needed a nap or had just woken from one.

"Hey, baby." I couldn't hug him properly holding two cups of coffee, but I stood on my tiptoes for a quick kiss. "What are you doing here?"

"I missed you," he said simply, and my heart did that little flippy thing it does. The sensation used to scare me, but now it feels like an old friend.

After all, if I didn't have a wonky heart valve, I would never have met Joe.

I kissed him again, a quick smack, which he enthusiastically returned. He smelled like antibacterial soap and male sweat. Running an emergency room was a tough job, one I could never do in a million years. Yet his green eyes were smiling, and his mood was upbeat. He looked terribly happy to see me.

"You look good enough to eat." Joe held me at the waist, checking out the black camisole, the hot pink tee. The jeans were my new favorites—indigo denim flares worn with a pair of thick-soled Louis Vuitton boots, circa 1980.

I gave him a naughty grin, glad he was still hungry. "Later, baby, we'll eat later." I wasn't talking about food, and the gleam in Joe's eye showed he wasn't either.

We'd been dating almost six months now—definitely a record for me. A failed engagement in my late teens had left me a "commitment phobe" for the last decade, until Joe.

"How about a Mocha Latte for now?" I handed one over without a qualm; I'd get Evan another one.

Joe lifted the lid on the coffee cup and inhaled blissfully before taking a sip. "Ah. Just what the doctor ordered." He tilted his head toward an empty sidewalk table. "Come sit with me."

I glanced involuntarily toward Handbags and Gladrags, knowing Evan was waiting to tell me his boyfriend troubles. But I couldn't resist the chance to spend a few minutes with my own boyfriend, so I slid into a chair.

As I did, I noticed a girl watching us. Early twenties, blond hair to her shoulders, very thin. Too thin, in fact—her shoulder blades jutted like clothes hangers beneath her T-shirt, low-cut jeans skimming prominent pelvic bones. She was staring right at us, and she looked pissed.

"What a night," Joe said, bringing my attention back to him, where it belonged. "Gang fight over in Riverdale, and we got the overflow. Forget the gunshot wounds—it's unbelievable what knives and baseball bats can do to people."

"Ugh." I wrinkled my nose, not really caring for the visual images that statement conjured up. "How you handle all that blood and pain on a daily basis is beyond me."

Joe cocked his head, smiling as he reached across

the table to take my hand. "It's like a battle," he said, "between me and death." It seemed an odd thing to say, yet it made sense. "Sometimes death wins, and sometimes I do." His thumb smoothed over the skin of my knuckles. "And it's all worth it. All I need to do is look at you to remind myself why I do this."

I smiled at him, squeezing his fingers. "I'm glad you were in the E.R. that night. You brought me back to life." I leaned in over the table, letting my voice go all throaty. "In more ways than one."

"How sweet," came a syrupy voice.

I looked over Joe's shoulder to see the blond girl, now standing right behind him. A nasty sneer curled one corner of her lip, a bony elbow jutted sharply from a hip.

"Excuse me?"

"True, I do know how to make you tingle," Joe said. "Electric shocks, kissing the back of your knees . . ." He gave me an intimate grin, then took another sip of coffee, oblivious.

A chill ran down my spine. I looked at his face, then back at the blonde.

Crap. Not again.

"What's the matter, Nicki?" He lowered his cup. "You look like you've seen a gho . . ." His voice trailed off.

"Isn't he the clever one," the girl said. "Too bad he wasn't that clever last night."

Little Miss Nasty was beginning to tick me off.

"Who are you?" If she wasn't going to bother with the niceties, neither was I. "What do you want?"

Joe swiveled in his chair to see who I was talking to, and of course, saw no one. "Um, Nicki?"

Poor guy. He'd gotten a lot more than he bargained for when he started dating me—a girlfriend who talked to dead people was hardly every guy's dream.

More like a nightmare.

The blonde looked at Joe, her expression getting uglier by the minute. "I'm Crystal," she said. "Ask him if he remembers me."

I didn't take orders well, and I really didn't like her tone. Dead or alive, she was *not* my boss."Why should I?"

She lifted her eyes from Joe's face. They were filled with hate.

"Because he killed me," she snarled. "And I want him to remember."